This book is dedicated to young adults who were raised in the Christian Church but lost their faith in their creator for various reasons, including the failure of church leaders to:

(1) Model God's love for all his children;

(2) Reach out aggressively to those who have fallen away from the faith with the most powerful communication tools available;

(3) Join forces together with leaders from other Christian faiths to spread the basic Gospel message as widely as possible; and

(4) Present the Christian narrative in a way that is consistent with logic, scientific understanding of our universe, and just plain common sense.

April 2019

A Chance to Regain
Paradise

Erin,

With best wishes,

Mike McCleary

A Chance to Regain Paradise: What Preceded the Big Bang
© 2017 Michael C. McCarey

Published by J-ALM Publishing
3403 Miller Heights Road
Oakton, VA 22124

ISBN: 978-0-9885929-2-6

Library of Congress Control Number: 2017916952

Book design by Mark Cugini
http://cugini.party
Cover Image Credit: NASA

For information about discounts for bulk purchases of ten or more books, contact J-ALM Publishing at j-almpub@att.net.

For additional information about *Chance* and the author, visit http://www.chancetoregainparadise.com

The photo on the front cover is a composite image of the Crab Nebula, a supernova remnant. NASA advises that this image was "assembled by combining data from five telescopes spanning nearly the entire breadth of the electromagnetic spectrum: The Very Large Array, the Spitzer Space Telescope, the Hubble Space Telescope, the XMM-Newton Observatory, and the Chandra X-ray Observatory." NASA, ESA, NRAO/AUI/NSF and G. Dubner (University of Buenos Aires) participated in the creation of this image.

A CHANCE TO REGAIN PARADISE

WHAT PRECEDED THE BIG BANG

MIKE McCAREY

J-ALM PUBLISHING, 2018

Acknowledgements

Several folks were kind enough to read and comment on the *Chance* manuscript. While not endorsing every opinion expressed in this work, they nonetheless provided constructive criticisms, helpful editorial suggestions, and encouragement to press ahead with this project to publication. This list of contributors includes Matthew Becker, Peter F. Corro, E. David Doane, Brian Eckenrode, Carl T. Johnson, David McCarey, Eleanor Nelson, Terry O'Rourke, and Donna Taylor.

Bruce Chadwick was enormously helpful in making *Chance* a more polished literary work. His careful review of the manuscript identified several inconsistencies in the storyline and grammar glitches in its presentation. Many of his suggested language changes found their way into the final version of *Chance*.

My chief editor and life partner of 53 years, my wife Willi, suggested revisions to the manuscript that I initially rejected but eventually adopted when I recognized the richness they would add to the storyline.

I am deeply indebted to these kind and generous individuals. Without their assistance and encouragement, I would not have completed this project.

Preface

Why do we humans exist surrounded by a spectacularly beautiful universe? There are only two realistic possibilities: We are either the result of the random interaction of the universe's natural forces, or we are the handiwork of an intelligent creator.

If we are accidents of nature, there is no transcendental significance to human existence.We are simply the life form that occupies the top of the food chain. We are not endowed by a creator with certain unalienable rights, among which are life, liberty, and the pursuit of happiness. There are no unalienable rights. There is no higher moral law handed down to us from above. We are ruled by man-made laws which are little more than exercises in political expediency, and the only moral philosophy that makes sense is: Eat, drink, and be merry (or do whatever else makes you happy), for tomorrow you may die, and for you, existence will be over.

If we are the handiwork of a creator, there may be a great deal of significance to human existence. The values of our creator would constitute a higher law that supersedes whatever legal codes humans may enact. And where we spend eternity, if there is life after human existence, may depend on whether the values and loyalties we demonstrate during our earthly lives are consistent with those of our creator.

Accidents of nature or the handiwork of a creator, which is more likely? The available empirical evidence tells us that about 13.8 billion years ago, there was a moment of creation. A tiny amount of matter expanded (possibly exploded), filling the universe with what eventually became enough matter to form at least a trillion stars and probably several trillion planets, moons, and other celestial bodies. This expanded universe seems to have been carefully designed. It contained exactly the right forces and components needed to remain stable for billions of years. It also included what in time became the elements needed for life and at least one planet with an environment capable of sustaining life. The idea that all this might have happened through a random process stretches credulity and raises a fundamental question: Can you have a finely-tuned universe without an intelligent being doing the fine-tuning?

If there is a creator, what can we say about her? First, we know she is extremely powerful. Any being capable of creating enough matter to form a trillion suns is powerful beyond what human minds can comprehend. Second, we can assume that creating a universe that would remain stable for 13.8 billion years and laying the groundwork for life required a major effort. But why did she go to all that trouble?

Through the medium of fiction, I have tried to show that there might be a logical answer to that question. The answer set forth in *Chance* may not be **the** answer. But that is beside the point. *Chance* sets forth one possible scenario in which a religious explanation for existence would make a great deal of sense. Of course, there may be other scenarios that do as well.

I wrote *Chance* from the Christian perspective. But I did not write it to convince readers to become Christians. My goal was to invite readers to resolve life's most fundamental question —why do we exist—on the basis of whatever evidence seems persuasive to them. A second goal was to point out that many of the reasons offered to dismiss the existence of God in our secular society defy logic: God has never appeared to me; therefore, there can't be a God. Bad things happen to good people; therefore, there can't be a God. Church leaders have done evil things; therefore, there can't be a God. *Chance* is a plea not to answer existence's most basic question with a non-sequitur.

Over the past two millennia, Christian church leaders have missed many opportunities to grow the Christian church. One of their most recent failures is ignoring how the scientific evidence describing the beginning of the universe and the beginning of life point to a creator. In its early years, the Catholic Church strongly supported scientific research and inquiry. Church leaders believed the more we understood creation, the more we would understand the creator. As a result, many of our earliest scientific discoveries were made by monks and scientists supported by the Catholic Church. But when Galileo, Darwin, and others began to describe a material world that differed from what church leaders had imagined based on their interpretations of scripture, this movement slowed. And for some Protestant faiths, these different scientific explanations for existence became an intellectual call to arms to rebut what was viewed as heresy.

Approximately sixteen hundred years ago, St. Augustine warned Christians that mindlessly rejecting scientific evidence would make them look foolish to their contemporaries and undercut the faith. Many of today's young, sophisticated thinkers are turning away from the church and its rejection of empirical evidence, proving once again that Augustine was one of the great intellects of the ages.

I hope you enjoy reading *Chance*. And I hope it leads you to think about, if not prayerfully consider, the meaning of your own existence.

Mike McCarey

Prologue

"...all things were created by him and for him."
Colossians 1:16, Bible, King James Version

"So God created man in his own image..."
Genesis 1:27, Bible, King James Version

The Primary Universe, from which all other universes were created, exists in another dimension that is unknown to us. Eons past, before our universe was formed, there was an epic struggle over who would control the Primary Universe. The outcome of that struggle determined the future course of existence, down to the present day. This is the story of that struggle and its aftermath.

1.

On a bluff high above the Great Mensa Sea, an old brick warehouse stood guard over the churning surf below like a silent sentry watching for seaborne raiders. Judging by outward appearances—weather-stained bricks and wood trim badly in need of paint—this guardian was long past its prime. But that was artful artifice. The warehouse was home to Sensing Station 29, and it was filled with highly trained technicians and state-of-the-art sensing equipment. SS-29 was part of a network that monitored the levels of positive and negative energy throughout the Primary Universe. This mission was crucial, because it identified which of two competing kingdoms was in control of existence every millisecond of every day in the Primary Universe's infinite expanse of time and space.

The third watch at SS-29 began routinely on day 357^9 ZMC-6487-42-89. At exactly 27:00 hours, Ran-tom, the youthful watch commander dressed in a light gray uniform that accentuated his athletic figure, arrived at the facility's front entranceway. Like other higher life-forms in the Primary Universe, Ran-tom's facial features, body contour, and extremities were human-like in appearance. Dressed in a business suit or blue jeans, he would easily pass for a human being on planet Earth.

Ran-tom looked into a face-recognition scanner and spoke his name. He could hear the hum of the security computer as it processed his appearance and voice data. "Good Evening, Commander Ran-tom. Welcome to the evening watch at SS-29. May your watch will be peaceful and uneventful," the computer said as the door at the front entranceway opened.

Ran-tom entered SS-29's main interior chamber, whose walls and floor glistened like stainless steel with the reflections from high-intensity overhead lights. After acknowledging telepathic greetings from members of the SS-29 staff, who also resembled human life-forms, he proceeded directly to the station's primary control panel, with its numerous controls and flashing lights, each color coded to indicate the operating system to which it belonged.

"Is the main sensor working properly?" Ran-tom asked ISRAN, the computer that controlled the station's operating systems. Lights on the control panel began to flash, and ISRAN responded in a monotone: "Sir, the main sensor is functioning within prescribed accuracy and energy-consumption levels."

Ran-tom then asked about the backup sensors, the power converters, the storage capacitors, and the control panel. ISRAN assured him that each of those systems was functioning properly.

"ISRAN, are your systems in good working order?" Ran-tom asked.

"Oh yes, sir, I am operating at close to 100 percent accuracy and efficiency. And thank you for asking."

Ran-tom sent a mind-imprint, a form of official communication, to the station's operations log: "All operating systems are working within design parameters; no malfunctions detected as of 27:05 hours on date 6487-42-89 in the current era." The message was recorded, and the unique frequency of Ran-tom's thought-waves served as his signature.

Ran-tom then turned and bounded up the stairs leading to his second-floor office. He closed the office door and sent a thought-message (an efficient form of communication available to most members of society) to his remote electronic secretary requesting entertainment. Instantly, a three-dimensional holographic image of a miniature 110-piece symphonic orchestra appeared on his desk. The diminutive conductor turned toward Ran-tom, bowed, and then turned back toward his musicians. When the conductor's tiny baton came down, the room was filled with Grital's 65th symphony in harmonic key no. 7.

Ran-tom leaned back in his chair and became lost in the music that captured in sound the exquisite beauty of the Primary Universe on display outside his window. The atmospheric plasma that occupies the space between heavenly bodies in the Primary Universe was exceptionally clear that night. Ran-tom could see the bright constellation known as Arreginees, the Brandus Comet with its long tail of ionized crystals crossing the lower sky, the Three Hands Galaxy with its constant blue glow, and beyond these, the infinite number of stars and solar systems that illuminated the night sky. It was a magnificent sight, a spectacular monument to beauty, peace, and order.

Midway through Grital's Second Movement, Ran-tom received a jarring thought-message from Egot, the station's chief technician. The content of the message was garbled, but it clearly conveyed a sense of urgency. Ran-tom ran out of his office and down the stairs as fast as his athletic legs could carry him. When he entered the control room, all the technicians were staring at the main monitor as if mesmerized by the data it displayed. Ran-tom pushed through the crowd until he found Egot, whose facial expression seemed to alternate between shock and panic.

"What is it? What has you so upset?" Ran-tom demanded.

Egot didn't respond orally. He couldn't. His vocal system was frozen with fear. He simply pointed to the main monitor, which told a dramatic story: In the roughly thirty minutes from when the watch began, negative energy within Section 29 had increased by 0.5 percent, moving from 49.1 percent to 49.6 percent, accompanied by a corresponding decrease in positive energy.

Ran-tom stared at the monitor in disbelief. He had an advanced degree in energy with a concentration in energy dynamics. He was a rising star in the Sensing Station hierarchy, and he knew that a 0.5 percent increase in negative energy throughout the whole universe would require an infusion of at least ten billion reins of negative energy (one rein is equivalent to 3.86×10^{12} watts of energy). That was beyond unlikely; it was physically impossible. That much negative energy could not suddenly appear out of nowhere. Searching for a rational explanation for these bizarre data, Ran-tom sent a thought-message to the station's engineering staff.

"We're getting highly unusual readings from the main sensor," Ran-tom said. "When was it last calibrated, and is there any reason to question its accuracy?"

A reply came back almost immediately: "The main sensor was recently calibrated, and our internal controls say it's functioning within prescribed accuracy levels."

Ran-tom frantically searched his memory files for a possible explanation. He soon found one. "Egot, there's no need for panic," he said in a reassuring voice. "The atmospheric plasma near us has temporarily separated causing false readings. This abnormal situation will soon correct itself."

While Ran-tom was congratulating himself for skillfully handling a sensitive situation, the main monitor showed another 0.1 percent increase in negative energy and a corresponding decrease in positive energy. The new numbers brought a collective gasp from the technicians in the room.

Egot screamed, "You have to report these data, now!"

Egot was right. Ran-tom did have to report this information to Sensing Station Command, even though he knew there had to be a logical explanation for these bizarre readings and that his superiors would probably chide him for reporting the impossible. And he had to show composure and good judgment. An officer who showed anything less in a stressful situation was likely to be placed at the end of the line for future promotions.

Ran-tom thought-messaged Shapii, his immediate superior at SS-Command: "Sir, we are getting readings showing a 0.6 percent surge in negative energy at SS-29. I suspect these are false readings due to natural phenomena, but I'm reporting them out of an abundance of caution."

"Other sensing stations are reporting similar data," Shapii replied, in a voice filled with concern. "This phenomenon appears to be universe-wide."

Ran-tom was stunned by Shapii's response. He became disoriented and grabbed a nearby chair to steady himself.

"The impossible has occurred," he mumbled to himself.

"Keep monitoring," Shapii continued. "We'll let you know more as soon as we figure this out."

The technical staff at SS-Command aggregated the incoming data from all thirty sensing stations and sent the totals to Michael, the kingdom's Defense Force Commander.

Michael, a physically imposing male life-form wearing a uniform adorned with ribbons indicating long years of service, sat ramrod straight at his desk at Universe Headquarters. He was reviewing routine security matters—mostly minor skirmishes that arose when subjects from one kingdom inadvertently crossed the border into the other kingdom without permission—when the high-alert, encrypted thought-message from SS-Command came to him on his most secure thought-frequency. Michael reviewed the message and quickly recognized what was obviously an existential threat to the Positive Energy Kingdom. He requested and was immediately granted a meeting with IAM, the kingdom's supreme ruler.

Information about the dramatic rise in negative energy was spreading like wildfire throughout the kingdom. The streets of its capital city, Infram, were crowded with life-forms. Some were hurrying home to be with family; others were leaving the city, assuming there was more safety in the outlying areas. Still others congregated near the royal palace, assuming that being close to IAM offered the most protection. Fear was turning into panic. The thought-messages coming from the general population were all variations on a central theme: This might be the end of IAM's reign; an invasion by Negative Energy Forces, led by its cruel ruler, Hasatan, was imminent; few of them would survive the attack; and those that did survive would be enslaved.

Michael transported himself along Infram's main boulevard toward IAM's palace. He had done so countless times before, but this time he was caught up in the beauty of his surroundings—the ever-blooming flowers with their brilliant colors, the graceful architecture of the buildings, the pleasing warm rays of the dual suns that illuminated the capital city. Was all this coming to an end?

He passed IAM Park, where young lions and lambs usually frolicked together on green, manicured lawns. But this time the park was eerily still. Most of the animals had taken shelter elsewhere, and those that remained stood by quietly. They sensed danger but did not know how to respond.

Michael had put on a civilian overcoat, hoping to avoid creating additional panic that might result if a high-level security official in full uniform were seen rushing to the palace. He could not, however, conceal his high energy level. Sensing Michael's power and realizing that he had to be a person in authority, a young boy with reddish hair, a ruddy complexion, and a slightly uplifted nose stopped Michael near the park entrance.

"Is it true, sir?" the boy asked. "Is it true that Hasatan will soon come and kill us all?"

Michael picked the boy up and looked directly into his eyes. Not wanting to alarm his young questioner, but not wanting to lie to him either, Michael said in his most reassuring voice, "IAM will do his best to protect us. You must have faith."

The boy seemed relieved. After being returned to the ground, he ran off to share Michael's comforting words with his young friends.

The fear in the boy's eyes filled Michael with guilt. He knew that somehow, he had failed in his most important mission—to protect the Positive Energy Kingdom from the forces of darkness. But how had he failed? What had he failed to do? As he approached the palace, he knew he would soon learn the answers to those questions.

IAM's palace is large even by Primary Universe standards—almost fifty miles wide and slightly more than one hundred miles long. Even though Michael had been inside the palace many times before, he was awed by its grandeur—the marble-like walls and floors, the windows that refracted light in the same manner as precious jewels, the elegant furnishings made from what resembled ebony or mahogany inlayed with gold and precious gemstones, the splendid visual art works, the miniature orchestras that filled the halls with symphonic sounds, the atriums awash in the vibrant colors of flowering plants. Each of these features was magnificent in its own right, but it was the total picture, how each feature blended with and complemented the others, that demonstrated the exquisite harmony that existed in IAM's kingdom.

Once inside the palace, Michael went directly to IAM's joint chambers. As he passed through the long hallways, he received another thought-message from Shapii: "Michael, our instruments say negative energy is at 49.995 percent. That's within our sensors' margin of error. Negative energy may already have crossed the 50 percent threshold. If Hasatan's hoards move quickly to take control, they will come first to our headquarters and terminate everyone here. My people are asking if they can leave headquarters, so they'll have a chance to survive. What should I tell them?"

"Let go as many as you can and remain operational," Michael replied. "You need to stay and keep a skeleton crew with you. I'm about to meet with the Supreme Ruler. If he says we can release anyone else, I'll let you know."

"Thanks. And Michael, don't sacrifice yourself for no reason. We'll need you to lead the forces that retake the universe if positive energy rises again," Shapii messaged.

Michael thanked Shapii for his concern. He appreciated the sentiment, but he knew there could be no escape for him. His extraordinary power could not be concealed. If Hasatan's forces took control of the Primary Universe, they would quickly find and destroy him, no matter where he went or how cleverly he disguised himself.

Michael opened the massive door to IAM's personal chambers and stepped inside. He braced himself for the overwhelming power surge that confronted anyone who came within IAM's presence. Three energy force fields that took human form—the Father-Creator; Dianthe, his daughter; and Serenious, the Counselor—were seated on white, overstuffed chairs positioned around a large, circular table that served as a miniature theater-in-the-round. They were watching a stage production, complete with miniature actors and stage props. Their gleaming white robes momentarily blinded Michael. He shielded his eyes to allow time for them to readjust to the intense light.

The Father rose from his chair and greeted his senior military aide: "Michael, it's so good to see you. You should visit with me more often."

In appearance, the Father resembled a human grandfatherly figure, with an upbeat, kindly face that radiated compassion and understanding. True, his face was marked with lines and creases that said he had confronted challenges to his rule in the past. But his happy, self-confident smile and the erect way he held his head suggested that his authority had never been successfully challenged, and he believed it never would be. He stood no more than five feet six inches tall. His snow-white, wispy, unkempt hair gave him an air of informality. It matched his voice, which was soft, sincere, and unassuming. Nothing in the Father's physical appearance suggested his immense power except for his clear, blue eyes. When viewed directly from the front, they sparkled with the intense light observed at the instant of an atomic explosion.

"Thank you, Excellency," Michael replied. "It's good to see you too."

"Come, join us," the Father said. "We were just watching a dramatic presentation of Adrack's fable 'The Beginning of Time.'" He pointed toward the small theater, in which miniature actors were still saying their lines, apparently unaware of the impending crisis.

"I've seen this play many times, but I never tire of it. Maltiss is playing the lead, and he does it so well. He is very talented, you know."

"Yes, sir, I'm sure he is," Michael responded. "Unfortunately, this is not a social call. I bring disturbing news. We are facing an existential threat to your kingdom, and I need your guidance. Our sensing stations are reporting dramatic increases in negative energy. At last report, negative energy had reached 49.995 percent, and it may already have crossed the 50 percent threshold. We can't explain the rise, and we can't predict where it will end."

The ominous tone of Michael's report captured the attention of Dianthe, a youthful-looking female life-form with long, silky, golden-blonde hair that contrasted nicely with her white robe. She was almost as tall as the Father. Her movements were equally graceful and regal. Her facial features strongly resembled those of her Father. She, too, radiated compassion and empathy, and her voice resonated with the same soft sincerity. She also possessed sparkling blue eyes that suggested her immense powers. Dianthe moved to her father's side and gave Michael a warm smile.

The third figure in the chamber, Serenious, was a short, balding life-form who resembled a middle-aged human male. His facial features were strong and masculine, and his skin complexion was dark, almost black. His sparkling brown eyes and playful smile suggested not only great power but also a mischievous spirit. He carried himself with grace and poise, notwithstanding a wide girth that stretched the outer limits of his robe. He, too, rose from his chair and joined the conversation.

"We've been betrayed, Michael," the Father said.

"Betrayed? Sir, I don't understand."

"More than fifty million positive-energy life-forms—life-forms I created—have defected to Hasatan. His scientists discovered a way to remove each traitor's excess positive energy and reverse its polarity, turning it into negative energy. A short time ago, Hasatan began releasing this additional negative energy into the plasma. His goal is to gain control of existence by rebalancing the universe's energy composition. And he's building a weapon, a very large weapon, which he will use to attack us as soon as he thinks he controls existence. I should have told you about this earlier, and I failed to do that. I'm sorry."

"Is there anything I can do to stop these traitors from going over to Hasatan's side?"

"Unfortunately, it's too late for that. The traitors are already in Hasatan's control."

"Sir, pardon me for asking, but how could this have happened without our Sensing Stations detecting it?"

"The desertions were cleverly arranged. Traitors were told to come to a remote section of the Great Divide, where they were infused with negative energy to neutralize their energy charge. Then, in successive waves, they slipped over the border into Hasatan's kingdom undetected.

"I gave them life. I created them out of my energy, in my image, with my values. I brought them into a kingdom where justice and reason prevail, where love is the predominant virtue, where all their needs were met. I gave them paradise, and for that, they betrayed me. Hasatan promised them a deeper understanding of good and evil, more freedom to travel about the universe, a more exciting existence, and high positions in his kingdom—all lies, of course, but the traitors believed him and went over to his side."

For a brief moment, the Father's facial expression turned dark and grim, projecting a deep inner sadness. Michael was taken aback by the Father's appearance and a little frightened. He had never seen the Father so distraught, and he was unsure how to respond. Trying to play cheerleader to the most powerful being in all existence did not seem appropriate. So, he simply asked, "Sir, is there any hope for us?"

The Father's demeanor quickly turned positive: "Michael, there is always hope. As soon as I learned of this betrayal, I asked our scientists to collect negative energy in its formative stages from the outer reaches of the universe and to convert it into positive energy using Hasatan's formula in reverse. If our scientists produce what they promised, we'll survive Hasatan's attack."

"And if they fail?" Serenious asked in a fearful voice.

"My old friend, you already know the answer to that question," the Father replied.

Dianthe put her arms around her father. "We'll get through this. It's going to be okay. Love and kindness will prevail. They always have, and they will again."

The Father gave Dianthe a hug but said nothing.

"So, our fate is in the hands of our scientists," Serenious said. "What a frightening thought!"

"Zebulous, our chief scientist, thinks he will succeed," the Father replied.

"Zebulous always thinks he will succeed," Serenious said. "That's the problem with our scientists: They all think they're omniscient and omnipotent."

The Father smiled: "Serenious, we have no alternative."

Serenious nodded his understanding.

"Michael, our scientists will only be able to convert, at most, 95 percent of this emerging negative energy before we're attacked," the Father said. "Release the remaining 5 percent into the energy plasma now."

"But that will surely raise the negative energy level above 50 percent," Michael replied.

"Yes, it will. When Hasatan sees the uptick in negative energy, he'll think he controls existence and attack us. Allow his weapon to intrude deep into our kingdom. We need to give our scientists as much time as possible to do their work. When the weapon is within fifty million miles from Infram, release all the available positive energy into the plasma. If our scientists produce what they promise, the balance of power will tip back to us, and we'll survive the attack. And Michael, Hasatan undoubtedly has spies in our kingdom. Keep this strategy to yourself as much as possible."

"Yes, sir."

"An excellent plan, My Lord," Serenious said. "But will it work?"

"We'll know very soon," the Father replied.

"Adrack's fable warns against taking action based on first impressions," Serenious said. "Let's hope Hasatan isn't watching the same stage production we're watching."

Grim smiles broke through the gloom that had prevailed in the chamber just moments before.

"Sir, by now, half our population knows about the rising level of negative energy. There is a whiff of panic in the air," Michael said. "Defense Command is asking if they can let some of their people go before Hasatan's forces arrive. What should I tell them?"

"Yes, they should release everyone," the Father responded. "This is IAM's battle to fight. And Michael, if you want to go, you may."

"You are my Lord. Where you go, I will go. Where you fight, I will fight. And if you perish, I will perish. My existence has no meaning without you."

The Father stared at his Defense Force Commander for a long moment. A warm smile replaced what had been an uncharacteristic frown.

"Thank you for that, Michael," he said. "Your loyalty gives me strength at a time when I need all the strength I can gather."

*****

The interior of the control room at the Negative Energy Weapons Laboratory was dark, the only illumination coming from monitors and lights on the control panel. Hasatan, a human-like life-form who stood over ten feet tall, looked down at the other life-forms in the room, both literally and figuratively. He impatiently paced back and forth in front of the main monitor that showed the balance between positive and negative energy in the Primary Universe, occasionally mumbling to himself. Dressed in black clothes that complemented his shiny black hair, dark eyes, and swarthy complexion, Hasatan and his arrogance were on full display, filling the room with anxiety and fear.

The younger scientists and technicians cringed whenever Hasatan looked their way. The older life-forms showed more equanimity, but they, too, were wary of Hasatan. He was notorious for momentary rages, lashing out in fury at anything or anyone that annoyed him. His subordinates were also intimidated by the plaque affixed above the control room's main entranceway. It showed Hasatan holding two negative-energy life-forms by their necks in his outstretched arms. The life-forms, writhing in pain, struggled to free themselves, but they could not do so. A smiling Hasatan seemed to delight in their agony.

"Come on, come on!" he yelled at the monitor as if it were a living organism. "Our sensors are so slow. We have pumped massive amounts of negative energy into the plasma. We should be seeing negative energy readings above 50 percent by now."

When Hasatan finished his rant, the numbers on the monitor screen began to move rapidly—49.955, 49.960, 49.965—and then still faster—49.970, 49.975, 49.980, 49.985, 49.990, 49.995, 50.000. And, finally 50.005. When the number 50.005 flashed on the screen, the whole room erupted in applause. "Finally, I'm in control!" Hasatan screamed. He could hardly control his child-like delight. For billions of years, he had been in a subordinate position. IAM had controlled the Primary Universe and set its moral tone. When disputes arose, they were resolved on IAM's terms. Yes, Hasatan enjoyed some freedom. After all, he was the supreme ruler of the powerful Negative Energy Kingdom. But even in his own palace, his powers were subordinate to IAM's. Hasatan resented IAM, but he despised IAM's lieutenants for telling him what he could and could not do. How dare they boss around the universe's second most powerful force.

But now, that was all behind him. He was in control. The thought of eliminating IAM's condescending minions sent him into ecstasy. He fantasized about the new, larger throne room he planned to build, a throne room appropriate for existence's supreme ruler. It would be the most glorious structure in the universe. He had been waiting for this day for billions of years, and now, it had finally arrived.

"Is the weapon ready to fire?" he asked.

"It is, sir," replied Jeleneous, a senior scientist dressed in black except for the gold markings on his collar identifying his senior rank, "but our readings are still within the margin of error. We must be patient; we might not yet control existence."

"But we have pumped massive amounts of negative energy into the plasma."

"Sir, the readings you see on the monitor are not precise. They are estimates and nothing more. We have to wait."

"Oh, all right, all right, I'll wait," Hasatan replied like a petulant child.

The readings continued to climb—50.014; 50.015. 50.016.

When the number 50.020 flashed on the screen, a junior scientist blurted out, "Finally, we're past the margin of error."

"Is that right?" Hasatan asked, glaring at the junior scientist. "If it is, fire the weapon, now!"

"Excellency," Jeleneous said, "we must wait until our spies tell us that all the early-stage negative energy still exists in its original form, that it hasn't been converted to positive energy. This could be a trap. We can't allow ourselves to be baited into premature action."

"Wait?" Hasatan screamed. "I've been waiting for billions of years. My moment of triumph has arrived. I am the universe's preeminent force. I can sense it; I can feel it. My coronation cannot wait another moment. Fire the weapon and the trailing rocket, so we can watch the destruction of IAM's stronghold."

"But sir, you are taking a large risk. We need to wait until..."

A laser beam from Hasatan's eyes hit Jeleneous with nearly one hundred thousand reins of negative energy. Jeleneous's outer layer exploded, filling the room with a shower of sparks. The laser quickly consumed his inner essence, until all that was left of Jeleneous were a few wisps of negative energy that briefly sparked and then went out as they drifted slowly to the floor.

"Anyone else want to challenge my authority?" screamed an enraged Hasatan.

Four junior scientists rushed to the control panel and fought with each other for the right to push the button launching the most extraordinary assemblage of destructive power the Primary Universe had ever seen.

The cylinder-shaped rocket, fully loaded with explosive material, could be seen from the weapons laboratory. Resting upright on its launching pad, the weapon stood over 800 yards high and 200 yards wide. Its outer covering was a dull black except for Hasatan's royal emblem—a flaming sword followed by the words "Bow Down and Obey" painted in red on the rocket's nose cone. Small protrusions covered the weapon's wings and tail fins. These emitted a negative-energy force field that would protect the weapon from potential interceptors. As long as negative energy was the predominant force in the Primary Universe, this weapon was indestructible. Nothing could stop it once it was launched.

Two negative-energy life-forms sitting at the far end of the laboratory—Zahn, a senior scientist, and Ondoss, his young assistant—were managing the launch. The weapon's eight large thruster engines and its nine smaller steering engines began firing in sequence. When the ship's computer confirmed that all engines were functioning properly, their power was gradually increased.

Zahn kept one eye on the launching pad and the other on a monitor that spewed out data generated by the rocket's elaborate control systems. Ondoss watched a second monitor and called out the power thresholds reached by the thruster engines. When those reached full power, flames shot out over a thousand yards from underneath the weapon. But, it did not immediately lift off its launching pad.

"This thing is overloaded," Ondoss said in a nervous voice. "It's never going to get off the ground. We'll be Hasatan's next victims."

"Be patient. It needs to build thrust against the pad," Zahn replied.

Slowly, the monstrous spaceship lifted off its launch pad and began to climb. When the rocket's speed approached one-quarter of the Primary Universe's speed of light, the ship's guidance system locked onto its target—IAM's palace.

*****

"Excellency, Hasatan has fired his weapon," Michael said.

"Thank you, Michael. Now you must excuse us." Turning to Dianthe and Serenious, the Father said: "We must unite to defend against this attack."

The three persons of IAM consist of energy force fields. When they formed a circle and joined hands, the process of merging those force fields began. It started with a low-pitched whine, but soon the sound increased in volume and pitch until it became a high-pitched scream that shattered Infram's street lights, windows, and other fragile items in or around the palace.

Slowly, the three force fields lost their individual identities and fused together into one large vessel of fiery energy that resembled a massive human form with powerful arms and legs, a bright silver complexion, and eyes that dazzled with burning energy. The figure entered a stone tower that led to the palace roof. The tower was constructed of the strongest building materials available, but it is impossible to construct a building that can fully accommodate a united IAM. As the hulking figure slowly climbed the stairs, powerful jolts of energy spun off from its form and crashed into the cylindrical walls. The walls shook, and observers on the ground below wondered if the tower would collapse. When the figure reached the top of the staircase, the door to the palace roof flew open and off its hinges. IAM stepped out onto the roof and walked slowly to the palace's eastern outer wall. There, the figure stood and peered out into space, past the nearest stars and planets, past the frothy divide where negative energy becomes the dominant power source, until it located the approaching weapon.

*****

"Excellency, the weapon is approaching the Great Divide," one of Hasatan's junior scientists announced.

Hasatan grunted his approval.

The monitor continued to show negative energy at 50.020 percent.

An image from a camera on the trailer rocket came up on the main monitor. The image was of IAM's palace.

"What's that fiery blob on the palace roof?" someone asked.

"That, my scientific friend, is the present ruler of the universe," Hasatan responded. "He has come out to do battle, and he is about to be blown to smithereens. This will be the greatest visual effect ever witnessed."

After a pause, Hasatan continued: "This is being recorded, isn't it? I want this scene played at my coronation. It will discourage anyone from challenging my authority. The destruction of IAM—how magnificent! Tell me again the damage this weapon will cause."

"It will destroy IAM, his palace, and all positive life-forms within approximately three million miles from the point of impact," replied a senior scientist.

"Oh, that's good, that's very good," an elated Hasatan replied.

"The weapon just crossed the Great Divide," someone shouted.

Someone else began calling out the distances from the weapon to its target: "One hundred thirty million miles to target, one hundred twenty, one hundred ten" and on until the number "fifty million miles to target" was called, at which time, the numbers on the energy monitor started to decrease: 50.020, 50.019, 50.018.

"What's going on?" Hasatan screamed. His gleeful look turned to concern and then to fear. "Why are the numbers going down?"

"The amount of negative energy is holding constant," someone said. "Additional positive energy is being pumped into the plasma. IAM's forces must have found a way to create additional positive energy. It was a trap."

Everyone in the room froze as Hasatan looked around, as if searching for another scientist to blame for this predicament.

"These instruments, are they accurate?" Hasatan demanded, his voice taking on an especially surly tone.

"Yes, sir, they are," someone replied.

As the group stared at the main monitor, two laser beams streamed from IAM's eyes toward the weapon.

"What's that?" Hasatan demanded.

"I don't know," a voice answered.

The data on the energy monitor continued to decrease—50.012, 50.011, 50.010—until the number 49.995 appeared on the screen.

When the readings for negative energy dipped below 50 percent, the two laser beams locked onto the weapon and held it in a vise-like grip.

"Turn the weapon away from its target," Hasatan ordered. "Bring it back to us."

Zahn manipulated several knobs on the control panel, but the weapon did not turn. He turned the weapon's remote manual guidance wheel, but the weapon still maintained a steady course.

"Excellency, I can't control it," he said. "It's being held by those two laser beams."

"Why can't you idiots design a weapon that can't be controlled by alien forces?" Hasatan screamed.

A third laser emanating from IAM appeared on the monitor screen, this one more powerful than the other two. It raced toward the rocket at the speed of light. When this laser reached its target, there was a massive explosion that illuminated the entire universe. A brilliant light flashed on the monitor screen, which then went dark. When compression from the explosion reached the weapons laboratory, the building shook violently. A wall crumbled, the roof caved in, and Hasatan and his scientists were knocked off their feet.

Hasatan was the first to get up from the floor. He brushed the dirt from his clothes and looked around to survey the damage.

"Our weapon has been destroyed," said a young scientist who had also risen from the floor.

"Of course it's been destroyed, you idiot. I am undone... undone by your incompetence!" Hasatan screamed.

A laser beam shot out from Hasatan's eyes and cut through the young scientist's outer covering. He writhed in pain before being consumed by the flames. Soon, all that was left of him were a few embers on the floor, which quickly went out. Other scientists dove behind desks and tables to shield themselves from attack.

"Excellency, you must conserve your energy," a senior scientist said. "IAM will soon send agents to destroy you. If you are to survive, you'll need all your energy. You must flee. Destroying these low-level minions isn't worth the energy it requires."

Hasatan had a dazed and confused look on his face. He suddenly looked older. His loss of energy had changed his color from black to a dismal shade of gray, his eyes had lost much of their intensity, and his voice had become tentative and less authoritative.

"Yes, you're right, I must conserve my energy," Hasatan repeated, before staggering out of the control room into the darkness.

*****

When IAM's subjects saw the flash of light from the explosion, they knew Hasatan's weapon had been destroyed. While IAM stood on the palace roof surveying the capital city for damage, cheers from the crowd below welled up and greeted the Supreme Ruler like a musical crescendo that peaks at the moment of emotional climax. IAM raised its arms to acknowledge their praise. It was a moment to savor and enjoy. There was no gloating, no victory strut, no self-congratulations, just sighs of joy and thankfulness that the forces of goodness had prevailed and would continue to lead the Primary Universe.

IAM slowly climbed down the stairway, holding the guard rail to steady itself after losing the massive amount of energy it took to destroy Hasatan's weapon. Once inside the palace, IAM began the disuniting process. When the three persons of IAM had regained their individual identities, the Father summoned Michael.

"Capture Hasatan and bring him before me," the Father said. "He has lost much of his power. He won't put up much of a struggle. In fact, finding him may be your biggest challenge."

"It will be done as you command, Excellency."

Like everyone else in the Positive Energy Kingdom, Michael was awed by IAM's display of raw power in responding to Hasatan's attack: "Sir, destroying Hasatan's weapon would have required at least twenty-five billion reins of positive energy. Have we just witnessed the full extent of IAM's power?"

The Father smiled: "Michael, it's best that you never know the answer to that question."

2.

Hasatan stood between two guards in front of the massive doors of the Positive Energy Kingdom's Great Hall. He was hunched over and barely conscious. He had been fleeing from IAM's security forces for weeks and had lost so much energy that simply transporting himself from one place to another had become arduous. His garments were torn, his hair disheveled, and his face soiled. Now, in chains like a common criminal, he was about to be brought before IAM for judgment.

He knew his existence would be terminated. He had tried to kill the king and failed. Now he would have to pay the ultimate price. But was it necessary for him to be humiliated in the process? Did his destruction have to be a public spectacle? It would have been better if IAM's security forces had summarily executed him where they found him—hiding in the hinterlands—and spared him this degradation.

The massive, wooden-like main doors of the Great Hall were elaborately carved with scenes depicting historical moments in the Primary Universe. As the doors slowly opened on their enormous hinges, the magnificence of the Great Hall came into view. Hasatan had heard rumors about the Great Hall's grandeur, but he was unprepared for the spectacular sight before him—a huge structure with what appeared to be white marble walls decorated with finely-crafted statues lavished with gold leaf and precious jewels, elegant gold chandeliers, a huge mural depicting the creation of the Primary Universe that covered the ceiling, and a long line of fluted white columns that led the eye to three massive, dazzling, gold thrones suspended in midair at the far end of the hall. The Father sat on the middle throne; Dianthe sat to his right, and Serenious to his left.

"All of this could have been mine," Hasatan thought to himself, "but for the incompetence of my scientists."

"It's time," the leader of the detail called out.

The guards stepped forward in unison. Hasatan, mesmerized by the Great Hall's grandeur, stood still. The positive-energy chain around Hasatan's neck was pulled forward beyond its insulator, and a shower of sparks poured out from Hasatan's neck onto the floor. This unexpected shock brought Hasatan out of his brief reverie, and he moved quickly to catch up with his guards.

The Great Hall was filled with IAM's nobles, who sat on either side of a wide center aisle, each in a high-back chair carved with images memorializing his or her accomplishments. There was Nomis, a powerful life-form who towered over the others in physical stature, and Werdna, his brother. There was Luap, an intellectual giant who had proposed ways to expand IAM's kingdom. There were Semaj and Nhoj, who had remained loyal to IAM through the many challenges that had arisen during IAM's long rule. There were...well, too many to mention here.

The nobles knew Hasatan's agents would have destroyed every one of them had his attack succeeded. Consequently, they showed no empathy for him as he shuffled down the center aisle, his head bowed under the weight of his chains and humiliation, to what everyone assumed would be his termination. He ignored the muffled laughs and whispered taunts. He didn't care. He had only a few moments of existence remaining. He would not spend them caring about what IAM's underlings thought of him.

The detail stopped in front of IAM's thrones.

"Take off his chains," the Father directed.

After the chains were removed, Hasatan summoned all his remaining strength. He stood erect with his head held high, as befitted the ruler of a large kingdom. He was determined not to go out like a sniveling coward.

He bowed to the three persons of IAM out of feigned fealty and then spoke in a loud, confident voice: "Your excellencies, I deeply regret this unfortunate challenge to your authority. I foolishly allowed resentment of your rule among my subordinates to get out of hand. I assure you that in the future ..."

"My wayward friend," the Father broke in. "Let's be candid with each other. The only thing you regret is that your attack failed."

Muffled laughter filled the hall.

Hasatan bowed his head with a slight smile: "My Lord, your power is exceeded only by your wisdom."

"You needn't be anxious; you will not be destroyed," the Father said. "Your loss of energy is punishment enough for your treachery."

Serenious leaned over and whispered in the Father's ear: "Is that wise? This wretch may attempt yet another challenge to our authority, and next time, his attack may be more formidable."

"I understand the risk," the Father whispered back. "But there will always be a leader of the Negative Energy Kingdom, and whoever replaced our ambitious friend here might be even more dangerous."

Serenious nodded his agreement.

For the first time since his capture, a smile appeared on Hasatan's face. He stood erect and assumed that haughty attitude for which he was well known in his own kingdom.

"Thank you, Excellency," he said confidently. "You are truly a ruler of justice tempered by mercy."

"In return for sparing you, I am imposing an obligation: The traitors you so ardently courted, you may keep them. They are yours, and you must provide a new home for them."

Hasatan quickly recognized the threat this condition imposed.

"Excellency, these traitors are positive life-forms, they belong with you," he said. "Surely, you can repair their deficiencies, both physical and moral. Because they consist mainly of positive energy, I cannot repair them. And in their present unreconstructed condition, they are untrustworthy and a threat to anyone who harbors them."

"Keeping track of these traitors will be easier for you than for us," the Father replied. "You wanted them, you worked hard to get them, and now they are yours. If controlling them becomes a problem, you can always confine them."

"But Excellency, we are ..."

"Do not argue," the Father interrupted, in what for him was a stern voice. "Be grateful you have been spared."

Hasatan stood silent as the Father, Dianthe, and Serenious rose from their thrones and departed the Great Hall. Inwardly, he bristled. IAM's will had been imposed on him once again.

"Will there never be an end to this humiliation?" he thought to himself.

As the Great Hall emptied, Hasatan mentally steeled himself for the long journey back to his kingdom, where he faced an uncertain reception by those he had deserted in a panic while attempting to save himself.

3.

Several thousand years later, which is not a long time in the Primary Universe, Dianthe said to the Father: "I hear prayers coupled with screams of agony coming from the Negative Energy Kingdom. I suspect Hasatan is abusing the life-forms who deserted us and went over to his side."

"It's a great distance to Hasatan's realm. You may be hearing nothing more than the natural sounds of the universe."

"Perhaps, but those screams seem very real to me."

"Then go to where the traitors are being held. Tell Hasatan I do not want them to be mistreated."

"Thank you, Father, I will do that."

Early the next morning, Dianthe began the long journey to Hasatan's kingdom. She soon reached a speed at which planets, suns, and moons flew by in a blurred collage of heavenly bodies. After several hours, she stopped to rest and regenerate her powers at Nunce, a small, desolate planet located just before the Great Divide. She found a comfortable resting place—a large rock that had been sheered smooth by natural forces. She sat down, turned toward the center of the Positive Energy Kingdom, spread her arms, closed her eyes, and began to absorb positive energy.

Her peaceful repose did not last very long. She heard strange voices. Nunce was uninhabited, or so she thought. Dianthe turned around and was surprised to see several negative life-forms with human-like features who were also looking for a place to rest and absorb energy. They moved lethargically, their clothes were soiled and in tatters, and their speech was slow and impaired. Their faces bore the dazed look of wartime refugees fleeing battle lines.

Dianthe called out to a male life-form who seemed to be the group's leader. His clothes hung loosely on his body, indicating that he had once been a more robust figure. But now his face was gaunt and his limbs spindly. Dianthe wondered if he was about to expire.

"Where are you going?" she asked gently, so as not to create any unnecessary anxiety in the man.

"I'm not sure, My Lady," he replied. "We're escaping from Hasatan and his inner circle. They have been draining energy from us and using it to restore themselves to full power. It started after that disastrous attack on IAM. Some of us have been drained several times; we barely have enough energy to remain alive. If we lose any more, we'll expire. But that doesn't stop Hasatan. He doesn't care if he kills us all, so long as he's restored. Can you help us, My Lady? Please help us."

Dianthe moved closer to the man and rolled back the hood of her outer cloak. Her distinctive blonde hair, fair countenance, and brilliant blue eyes came into full view.

The man fell to his knees. "Princess Dianthe, I didn't know it was you," he said. "I'm so sorry to have bothered you with our little troubles."

"Do not be afraid. I mean you no harm," Dianthe said with a disarming smile. "The planet Bense is only ninety-two thousand miles from here, close to the Great Divide. Go there, face the Negative Energy Kingdom, and rebuild your energy reserves. Then, if you can do so safely, return to your home. If doing so would be unsafe, remain on Bense. I will inform the Bense authorities that you are coming."

The old man's face brightened as if he had received new life, which, indeed, was the case.

"Thank you for your kindness, My Lady."

The other members of the group joined him in thanking Dianthe.

"Now, perhaps you can help me," Dianthe said. "Do you know how Hasatan is treating the positive life-forms who went over to his side?"

"Those poor devils are having a rough go of it. Hasatan has them confined on a small planet near a star at the outer edge of the Negative Energy Kingdom. He doesn't let anyone know how they are being treated but judging from the screams picked up by various audio sensors, it can't be good."

"Thank you. I wish you well in your travels," Dianthe replied.

Dianthe remained on Nunce until her power was fully restored. Then she continued her journey, crossing the Great Divide into the Negative Energy Kingdom, where her speed was significantly reduced—negative energy creating more resistance.

Dianthe's incursion into Hasatan's realm was soon detected by his kingdom's security sensors. Hasatan transported himself out into space to meet Dianthe.

"If you had told me you were coming, I would have met you sooner," Hasatan said, while bowing obsequiously. "What brings the fair Dianthe to our kingdom?"

"I want to see how the positive energy prisoners you are holding are being treated. I've heard their screams, and I want to see them."

"You've come all this distance to check on the traitors?" Hasatan asked incredulously.

"Exactly. Where are they being held?"

"In a facility at the edge of my kingdom. But trust me, there is nothing there that would interest you."

"I want to see it," Dianthe said firmly.

"Dianthe, it's a confinement facility. There's nothing to see. Let me show you the new architecture at my palace. It's quite beautiful. We have some splendid architects in our realm."

"The confinement facility; take me there, now," Dianthe demanded.

"All right. As you wish."

Dianthe could see the small planet where the prisoners were confined from far off. It was surrounded by black clouds that held in the heat and obscured pulsing solar rays that regularly bombarded it. As the small rotating sphere moved around star 666, those sections of the planet closest to the star broke out in flames. Screams could be heard a long way out, and those screams became louder and more intense as Dianthe and Hasatan approached.

"Why did you choose this planet for a confinement facility?" Dianthe asked. "It's so close to that star."

"It's large enough to house all the prisoners and yet far away from our population centers," Hasatan replied. "I need to protect my people from danger. Surely, you can understand that."

"Are all the prisoners held in one place?"

"No, we're holding the rebellion leaders in a separate facility up north. We don't want them to have any contact with their followers."

"Take me there first."

Hasatan and Dianthe transported themselves to the main entrance of what resembled a medieval prison constructed of limestone. The style of the building was Gothic, with pointed arches, flying buttresses, and menacing gargoyles devouring prisoners who writhed in agony before being consumed. The buildings were marked with black, vertical striping, the result of repeated exposure to flames and intense heat. Dianthe and Hasatan passed through security at the main gate and entered the prison compound. From there, Dianthe could see rows of stone barracks that extended out for miles in several different directions.

"Each prisoner is confined to a single room in these barracks," Hasatan said. "This courtyard is the last thing they saw before starting their confinement. The prisoners call this place the 'Courtyard of Sighs.' Kind of poetic, wouldn't you say?"

Dianthe didn't reply.

"Is there a particular prisoner you want to see?" Hasatan asked.

"No. Just pick one," Dianthe replied.

Hasatan entered the nearest building; Dianthe followed. The dark, dingy hallway was cluttered with trash the guards had discarded, the heat was oppressive, and a strong, unpleasant odor—the sweet smell of decay—greeted Dianthe as she stepped inside.

"What's that awful smell?" Dianthe asked.

"One of the prisoners must have expired in a nearby room," Hasatan replied. "When they expire, they leave a foul odor that lingers. When the guards opened the door to check on the prisoner, the odor must have escaped."

"Are you keeping track of the prisoners who expire?"

"Yes, of course. As I said, each prisoner is confined to a single room. The rooms are insulated, so neither sound nor telepathic communication can pass from one room to another. It's a security measure. If they could communicate with each other, they could conspire to escape."

Hasatan proceeded down the dark hallway, reading the name plates on successive doors as if looking for a particular individual. Finally, he stopped: "You'll recognize this one."

He thought-messaged a numeric code into the door lock. Dianthe heard the click as the lock disengaged.

"Most of these prisoners are docile, but occasionally, they become aggressive," Hasatan explained. "We need to be careful."

He opened the door cautiously, looking to see if anyone was hiding behind it. He and Dianthe then entered the room, which was only large enough to accommodate a table, a single chair, and a bed. The prisoner, sitting at the table, looked up slowly. He was a youthful male life-form—handsome, with dark, well groomed hair. He had a pleasant smile. The top buttons of his red prison uniform were undone, revealing broad shoulders and a barrel-like chest.

The room's walls, ceiling, and floor were covered with mirrors, so that wherever the prisoner looked, he would see himself. But the image in the mirrors didn't match the prisoner's actual appearance. The figure in the mirror was morbidly obese, its face locked into a condescending sneer, its hair unkempt, and its eyes fixed in a hateful stare.

"To justify their betrayal, these prisoners pretended to be acting out of noble motives—leading their followers to a better life in the Negative Energy Kingdom," Hasatan explained. "But they didn't care about their followers, and they certainly didn't care about those they left behind in the Positive Energy Kingdom. Their sole motivation was to advance their own selfish interests. These mirrors reflect not the prisoners' outward appearances but their inner selves. In these mirrors, the prisoners see themselves for what they really are: lazy, self-centered narcissists who indulged themselves and exploited their followers. They are depressed by the images they see, and that makes them docile and easier to control."

The prisoner began speaking in a slurred and halting manner, "Sir...may...I...leave...now?. . . I...would...like...to...leave...now."

Dianthe recognized the prisoner. He was one of the actors in a theatrical company that performed regularly for IAM.

"X-mead," she called out. "It's Dianthe. Don't you recognize me? You played the role of Ono in the stage play *A Wonderful Journey*. Do you remember?"

X-mead looked up and slowly made eye contact with Dianthe. He appeared to be confused. He frowned and rolled his eyes back in his head. Then he slowly repeated Dianthe's words: "You...played...the...role...of...Ono...in...the...stage...play...*A*...*Wonderful...Journey*....Do...you...remember?" At no time did he show the slightest indication that he understood what those words meant.

Up to that point, for Dianthe, the betrayal had been about abstract numbers: How many life-forms had gone over to Hasatan and how those defections had affected the distribution of energy and power between the two kingdoms? But X-mead's betrayal was different—it was personal. Dianthe knew X-mead. She had watched him perform on several occasions. She had spoken with him, congratulated him on his artistic achievements. He had betrayed not only a set of values, but a personal relationship with Dianthe. His treachery cut deeply into Dianthe's psyche.

"Of all people, X-mead, how could you betray us?" she asked. "You showed such great understanding of love and loyalty on the stage?"

Dianthe's voice broke with emotion, as tears flowed down her face faster than she could wipe them away. Embarrassed by her show of emotion, she turned away and struggled to compose herself.

"Are they all like him?" she asked.

"Most of them are," Hasatan replied. "It's unfortunate. These prisoners had talents. They were creative, they had initiative, and they certainly had organizational skills. After all, they delivered millions of positive life-forms to us right under IAM's nose without the positive-energy authorities knowing about it. Unfortunately, they came to us as defectors who can never be trusted. Once a traitor, always a traitor."

Dianthe stared at X-mead with a look of pity combined with contempt and then turned away.

"I've seen enough," she said. "Take me to where the other prisoners are being held."

Hasatan closed the door to X-mead's room. It slammed shut with the sound of finality that has depressed prisoners throughout time.

Hasatan and Dianthe transported themselves to the entranceway of the main facility, where the traitor-followers were being held.

"This is a very dangerous area," Hasatan warned as they reached the main gate. "Over forty-eight million traitors are confined in this facility, and they are constantly attacking each other, the guards, even me. I take no responsibility if you are injured here."

"Your concern for me is touching, and I would be impressed if I thought for a moment it was real," Dianthe said. She turned to the guard sitting in an enclosure by the entrance gate and said, "Turn off the security screen so we can enter."

The guard looked to Hasatan. "Go ahead, turn off the security screen," Hasatan grumbled.

Dianthe and Hasatan passed through the entrance gate and a tunnel that led to a large cobblestone square. The square was surrounded by buildings also constructed in the Gothic style with a substance that resembled limestone. When Dianthe and Hasatan stepped out of the shadows, they were greeted with blank stares from both prisoners and guards. The guards were easy to identify. They wore black uniforms that highlighted their brutish appearance and sullen demeanor. They mostly stood behind transparent shields that protected them from the prisoners and the hostile environment. What stood out about the prisoners, aside from their tattered red prison uniforms, was the look of terror on their faces. They moved about slowly, constantly looking at the ground as if they were walking through a mine field.

Dianthe soon saw the reason for their concern: Without warning, large flames ten times the height of the tallest prisoner shot up from between the cobblestones and engulfed half of the courtyard in fire. Members of the crowd screamed and ran to escape the flames, trampling over smaller life-forms in their way. Several prisoners did not move fast enough to avoid the flames. Their screams echoed off the stone buildings, as their bodies were tormented by fire.

After the flames subsided and the crowd stopped running, a fight broke out between two muscular prisoners, one slightly larger than the other, over some imagined slight that had occurred during their rush to avoid the flames. The two combatants slowly circled each other, looking for vulnerability. The larger figure attacked first, striking the head of the smaller life-form. The combat was brutal. Each prisoner struck the other with vicious blows.

After absorbing a particularly crushing blow, the smaller combatant fell to the ground. His attacker grabbed his arm and pulled it from his shoulder. Sparks poured from the wound. The injured prisoner struggled to get to his feet but couldn't.

The larger life-form intensified his attack. He beat his opponent with his own limb until he crushed his adversary's skull. The victim shriveled up into a smaller life-form, which then crawled away and disappeared into the crowd. The victor celebrated his brutal achievement by dancing around the square, holding his victim's limb above his head like a trophy as the crowd cheered.

During this vicious combat, the prisoners and guards stood by and watched. No one attempted to stop it. To the contrary, both prisoners and guards cheered the combatants on.

"Why didn't you stop that?" Dianthe demanded of Hasatan. "And what have you done to these creatures? They never acted like this when they were in our kingdom."

"When the prisoners were first confined, we injected them with paranoia, so they would start fighting and consume energy," Hasatan explained. "Once the fighting began, it continued without further help from us. These really are miserable creatures. They betrayed their creator, but do they see themselves as traitors? No, they see themselves as victims, betrayed by their leaders. Isn't that rich—they look at themselves as innocent victims?"

Dianthe was momentarily taken aback by Hasatan's brief flirtation with moral philosophizing, but she let it pass without comment. As the crowd dispersed, a small prisoner wearing a red cloak with a hood that covered the prisoner's head approached Dianthe.

"Be careful," Hasatan warned. "The little ones are sometimes the most vicious."

The figure knelt before Dianthe and threw back the hood, revealing a beautiful young girl. Her name was Teresa, and she resembled a human child of nine or ten with long blond hair, blue eyes, and delicate facial features that personified innocence.

"My Lady and my Savior, you have heard my prayers and come for me," Teresa said with a bright smile. "I have been here a long time. But I knew that if I kept the faith and prayed hard enough, you would come for me. I never meant to betray you. I simply followed my assigned guardians. Before I realized what was happening, I was in Hasatan's kingdom. I am so ashamed. I should have paid more attention to where my guardians were taking me and what was happening. Forgive me. Have mercy upon me."

Tears ran down Teresa's delicate cheeks as she bent down to kiss Dianthe's feet.

Dianthe was moved. She opened her arms to embrace the small life-form. But before Teresa could respond, a muscular guard came up from behind the little girl and grabbed her around her neck. Sparks flew from the contact of positive and negative energy. Teresa screamed. Her small face became contorted, as she writhed in pain. Her small body shook violently, and she visibly aged before Dianthe's eyes. Her golden hair turned gray, her smooth skin turned course. Her face became wrinkled.

"Help me!" Teresa called out. "My Lady, please help me."

Dianthe was momentarily stunned by the guard's assault on this small life-form. When Dianthe regained her composure, she screamed at the guard to release the little girl.

The guard eventually complied, and Teresa fell to the ground. By then, the young life-form was almost unrecognizable from her former appearance. In obvious pain, she crawled to the edge of the crowd where she stopped and turned back toward Dianthe.

"I trusted you," her sad little eyes said. "Why didn't you prevent the guard from hurting me?"

Teresa then turned away and disappeared into the crowd. Dianthe chased after her.

"Stop!" Hasatan shouted. "Don't go into that crowd. It's not safe."

Dianthe stopped and confronted the guard: "Why did you grab that small life-form? You knew touching her would harm her."

The guard had no idea to whom he was speaking.

"Lady, there are over forty-eight million prisoners confined in this facility," he said, nonchalantly shrugging his burley shoulders. "A few thousand become unruly and need to be forcibly restrained every day. Some are injured, but with so many prisoners, what difference does it make?"

Dianthe glared at the guard in frustration but said nothing. The guard turned and walked away, wondering why he had been reprimanded. He had never been told not to injure prisoners.

"Hasatan, you knew my Father did not want these prisoners to be mistreated, and yet you disregarded his instructions. He will hear about this."

"Let's not get all excited about nothing," Hasatan replied. "We must protect ourselves from these creatures. They're dangerous. Maybe we've gone a little overboard. We'll correct things. Give us some time."

"Find that small life-form that approached me. I want to know all about her. I want to know where she came from, who her guardians were, what she has done while confined."

"Of course, you'll have her complete personal file as soon as we identify her. We'll work with you on this. No need to get out of sorts."

"Good. Just ensure that actions meet words."

"You have my word."

Dianthe glared at Hasatan. A thousand thoughts ran through her mind, but she resisted the temptation to tell Hasatan what she thought of his "word."

"All right, I've seen enough," she told him. "Thank you for showing me around this facility. And remember, I want a report on that small life-form and what you plan to do to improve conditions at this facility."

Hasatan said he would do as instructed.

After Dianthe departed, the superintendent of the confinement facility, who was standing behind Hasatan, asked, "Excellency, do you want us to change any of our procedures?"

"You think I've lost my mind?" Hasatan said sarcastically. "I didn't want these prisoners. They were forced on me. Our confinement procedures are fine. Use them."

"What about the little girl?"

"I'll tell Dianthe she did not survive. Make up a fictitious file. Record today as the date she expired."

"Yes, sir."

As Dianthe transported herself back to IAM's palace, she bristled with anger. Her face took on a stern look, her nostrils flared, and random flames shot from her eyes.

"How could this have happened?" she asked herself. "Hasatan has been torturing these prisoners for ages, and we have done nothing to stop him. I have done nothing to stop him. And that little girl, so innocent, so trusting that I would protect her from harm, tortured and disfigured before my eyes."

Dianthe was angry, not with Hasatan, but with herself. "Why didn't I inspect this facility sooner and stop Hasatan from doing what he always does—abusing others less powerful than himself?"

Her anger helped propel her across the vast expanses of the universe at a velocity approaching the Primary Universe's speed of light.

4.

On her return to IAM's palace, Dianthe immediately went to the Father's chambers. She was agitated, and her excess energy visibly swirled around her.

The Father was startled when Dianthe burst unannounced into his quarters.

"You must be exhausted, crossing the universe in so short a time," he said to her. "Sit down and rest."

Dianthe felt no need to rest, and she was in no mood for small talk.

"It's far worse than I suspected!" she exclaimed. "Hasatan is torturing the prisoners. He has turned their leaders into passive vegetables and the followers into brutes who spend their time tearing each other apart when they aren't being consumed by searing flames from a nearby sun. It's barbarism, and we have to stop it."

"Yes, I saw it all through your eyes. I recognized most of the prisoners, including X-mead. They were all treated well in our kingdom; X-mead was treated especially well. I don't understand why they would betray us, and not only us, but also the principles on which this kingdom was built—kindness, love, compassion, justice. There must be something exhilarating in rebellion, in throwing off the bonds that bind subordinates to their superiors."

"Did you see that little girl pleading for forgiveness and praying that we bring her back to our kingdom?"

"Yes, I saw her."

"She is loyal to us. She reached out to me, and I failed to

protect her. She was disfigured before my eyes. We must bring her back to our kingdom and restore her. We must find all those who are loyal to us and bring them back."

"Are you certain this small life-form is loyal to us and not pretending to be loyal to escape Hasatan's cruelty?" the Father asked. "Dianthe, we must be careful. If we take back traitors who only pretend to be loyal to us, they might organize another rebellion on behalf of Hasatan, and the next one might succeed. If that were to happen, Hasatan would destroy us and massacre our leaders. Millions of loyal subjects would die. He would enslave those he doesn't eliminate. The Primary Universe would become a dark place; love and reason would no longer be the universe's most powerful forces. I will not risk that for life-forms who voluntarily left our kingdom and have now discovered they don't like their new lives with Hasatan."

"Just bring back the ones who are truly loyal to us. Surely you can identify them."

The Father did not respond. He turned away from Dianthe and looked out his window at the nearest suns and planets. After a long pause, he said, "Unfortunately, I can't tell which of the traitors, if any, are still loyal to us."

"Father, please don't joke about something this important."

"I'm not joking, Dianthe."

"Father, there is nothing in all of existence that escapes your attention. You know when the smallest creature in existence falters. You know each of your subjects by name, you know the number of hairs on each of their heads. How could you not know who among the traitors has remained loyal to us?"

"When I created these life-forms, I wanted their loyalty to be freely given, not programmed or coerced. To achieve that end, I gave each of them free will—the freedom to remain loyal to us and the freedom to turn against us. To encourage their loyalty, I planted in each of them a seed to remind them that they should be loyal to their creator, and that goodness is preferable to evil. That seed is not eternal, however; it can be destroyed. If a life-form turns against us, his or her seed will die.

"I wanted to be a trusting father. I didn't want to be constantly looking over my shoulder to see who remained loyal to us and who did not. So, I denied IAM the ability to look into their minds and hearts to determine if their seed was still alive. Yes, I have great power, but that power includes the ability to deny myself knowledge."

Dianthe was dumbfounded. Was there really something in this universe that was unknown to the Father? In her whole existence, since she was formed out of the Father's energy, she had never even considered such a possibility.

"Denying myself this knowledge nearly destroyed our kingdom," the Father continued. "Had Hasatan collected a few more reins of negative energy, our reign would have come crashing down around us like a meteor shower. We dare not become careless in safeguarding our security or the Rule of Love—the principle that has guided the administration of our kingdom since its beginning—will be lost."

"Can't you reverse this denial and grant IAM access to this information?" Dianthe asked.

"Unfortunately, I can't reverse it. It's fixed for all time. Aside from this young girl, did any other deserter come forward and ask for forgiveness?"

"No, but there was no opportunity for anyone else to come forward. And besides, the guards would have stopped anyone who tried."

"So, this small life-form may be the only one of Hasatan's prisoners who remains loyal to us, and we can't be sure about her."

"She was the only one who dared to come forward. But there might be millions of prisoners who remain loyal to us. We must test them all to ensure that loyal subjects do not suffer further from Hasatan's cruelty."

"Every traitor, including this little girl, deserted us and went over to Hasatan voluntarily. They chose their path."

"This little girl was simply following the guardians whom she trusted. She never meant to betray us. She is not a traitor. And that may be true for other prisoners as well."

"She knew where she was going. She was not taken there against her will. She could have refused to go and cried out for help if her guardians tried to force her. She is not without blame, Dianthe."

"When she left us, she was a young, immature life-form, unsophisticated in the ways of the universe."

"She was mature and sophisticated enough to understand that she was leaving our kingdom and abandoning us."

"Father, you gave life to these prisoners. They were formed out of your energy in your image. They have lived under your rule. Many have personally served you. Deep within each of them is your sense of right and wrong. We cannot simply abandon them to an infinite existence of torture and misery. Fairness and mercy cry out that we give them a chance to prove their loyalty."

"Fairness and mercy cry out that we protect those who have remained loyal to us and our values. The deserters all knew they were leaving our kingdom and that doing so would endanger our rule. That much is clear. However, I do not want the deserters to suffer unnecessary cruelty for all eternity. I will instruct Hasatan to stop mistreating them."

"Hasatan will promise to make improvements. He'll make cosmetic changes and then continue to mistreat the prisoners. He despises them; they are a constant reminder of his failed attack on our kingdom and the problems that failure caused for him. He will never treat the prisoners fairly. We must find a way to test all the prisoners and bring the loyal ones back to our kingdom," Dianthe pleaded.

The Father did not respond. Instead, he looked out his window into space, as if the solution to this conundrum might be written on a distant planet. He did not want to grant Dianthe's request. Testing all the prisoners would be an enormous undertaking, and he sensed it would be a futile act—that few, if any, loyal prisoners would be found. But it was obvious that Dianthe wasn't going to change her mind about the need to test all the traitors.

"Love has always been a mainstay of your kingdom," Dianthe continued. "Love is kindness, it is forgiving, it extends a hand to those in trouble. How can we remain true to our core beliefs and turn away from a small life-form who prays for our help? Yes, taking prisoners back to our kingdom involves some small amount of risk. But does our love retreat at the first sign of danger? Is it timid? Does it lack the power to persevere in the face of peril?"

A small tear ran down the Father's face; he wiped it aside.

"Father, I have upset you," Dianthe said. "Please forgive me."

The Father put his arm around his only child.

"No, you didn't upset me," he said. "I am just so proud to have a daughter who is unsurpassed in her love for others. We will find a way to test the prisoners' loyalty. They do not deserve a second chance, but as an act of grace, we will give it to them."

5.

About six months later, the Father, Dianthe, and Serenious were seated on the terrace adjoining their shared chambers. They were admiring the rising of the dual suns.

"It is another glorious day in the Primary Universe," the Father said, "a day suitable for an important announcement: I have a plan for testing the loyalty of those who went over to Hasatan."

"Father, that's wonderful news!" Dianthe exclaimed. She had begun to wonder if she would ever hear those words. But now, the Father's announcement relieved her of a heavy burden—the guilt she felt for failing to check on the condition of Hasatan's prisoners for so many years. But now there was hope for young Teresa and all those who had kept the faith that their creator would never abandon them.

Serenious did not share Dianthe's enthusiasm.

"And if we find any that have remained loyal to us, then what?" he asked.

"I will bring them back into our kingdom," the Father said.

"Are you sure you want to do that for creatures who deserted us and nearly brought our kingdom down, and us with it?"

Yes, I'm sure. My daughter has persuaded me that forgiveness is more powerful than vengeance or excessive caution."

"I accede to your wisdom, Excellency," Serenious replied in a voice filled with reservations.

"My plan requires that we create a new universe in another dimension," the Father said.

"Creating a whole new universe in another dimension would be a huge undertaking. Is that really necessary?" Serenious asked.

"Unfortunately, it is. A valid test of the deserters' loyalty requires that they not remember their prior existence. If they realize they are being tested to determine where they will spend eternity, they will proclaim loyalty to us even if their only loyalty is to themselves."

"And inserting the traitors into a new universe in another dimension will achieve that goal?"

"Yes."

"How will this test work?"

"We will create hosts called "humans" who will be able to survive in this new universe. We'll place the deserters in these hosts and record the hosts' behavior over their lifetimes. The resulting data will tell us who has remained loyal to us and our principles and who has not."

"The hosts' actions will be informative, but I assume we'll also be able to examine the traitors' inner thoughts to identify the intent guiding those actions," Serenious said

"Unfortunately, not," the Father replied. He then explained how for all eternity he had denied IAM the ability to examine the deserters' inner thoughts about loyalty to their creator.

Like Dianthe, Serenious was taken aback by the Father's reply. He struggled to grasp what seemed like the impossible.

"How will you create this new universe?" he asked.

"Before I answer that question, the three of us must agree that we will not intervene in this new world either to preordain future events or to interfere with events that are unfolding. Natural forces must be free to function as they might, and the deserters must be free to live their lives as they choose. How they exercise that freedom will tell us if they are loyal to us or not. If we intervene and thus reveal our existence, we will bias the test results, and this experiment will become a very elaborate but useless exercise."

Serenious immediately agreed.

Dianthe did not respond.

"Dianthe," the Father said. "We cannot proceed unless we have your agreement."

"Our loyal subjects in the Positive Energy Kingdom regularly pray to us, giving thanks for their blessings and requesting help to solve their problems," Dianthe said. "Teresa, the child-like prisoner, prayed to us while confined in Hasatan's hell. If she and other loyal prisoners are transferred into a new universe, they will continue to pray to us, especially when they find themselves in difficult situations. To answer those prayers, we may need to intervene in this new world to change the course of future events. Are we going to ignore those prayers?"

It was an insightful question, and the Father paused for a moment before replying.

"We will answer all sincere prayers in an appropriate manner," the Father said. "And if that requires intervening in the material universe on occasion, we will do so, but only in subtle ways where our interventions can also be viewed as the result of natural phenomena."

"Will we be able to travel ahead in time to observe how the test will unfold in this new universe?" Dianthe asked.

"Traveling ahead in time is always energy intensive, and it will be especially energy intensive in the material universe. For that reason, we should do it sparingly; but yes, traveling ahead in time to observe future events in this new world will be possible," the Father explained.

Dianthe was pleased with these answers. She had concerns about this experiment: What if it began heading in the wrong direction? Would IAM not intervene to guide it back on course? "If we can travel ahead in time to observe if the test is serving its purpose and if we are willing to intervene in the material world if that becomes necessary to protect the test's integrity, I agree."

"Good, then we can proceed," the Father said. "I will use energy from the Primary Universe to create this new world. More precisely, I will take energy from our universe to create "matter," which is what this alternative universe will consist of."

"Matter?" Serenious repeated with a perplexed look on his face. "I'm not familiar with that term."

"That's because matter does not exist in the Primary Universe," the Father said. "Everything of substance in our universe, including ourselves, consists of a force field held together by positive and negative energy. But in this new universe, everything of substance will consist of matter made from energy. I will show you."

The Father wiped excess energy from his brow and compressed it in his powerful hands until it became silica, soda ash, and limestone. Under the intense heat caused by the Father's firm grip, these materials joined together to form a drinking glass. The Father repeated this procedure to form hydrogen and oxygen atoms, which he combined to form water. The water flowed from his hand into the glass, filling it. He held the glass up to the light and stared at it. The intensity of his gaze caused the water to boil and vaporize. Once outside the glass, the water vapor cooled, causing a gentle rain that refilled the glass.

"This is matter," the Father said, handing the glass to Serenious. "This is what the material universe will consist of."

"Sir, that was quite impressive," Serenious replied as he reached out to accept the glass. He and Dianthe studied the glass and its contents as one might study foreign substances, which is exactly what glass and water were to Serenious and Dianthe.

"This glass feels strange," Serenious said. He dipped his finger into the water. "And that feels stranger still."

While examining the glass, Serenious held it at an angle. Some of the water spilled out of the glass onto the floor and splashed up onto Serenious and Dianthe. They both jumped back in surprise.

"Water from the material universe will not hurt you," the Father said while trying not to laugh.

"We have liquids in our universe," Serenious said. "We also have containers to carry them. But this water and glass feel very different to me. Why?"

"Because they have a high level of mass. As you know, everything in the Primary Universe is made up of electrical charges that come together to form force fields. These force fields have low levels of mass, and as a result, they move at very high speeds. To create this new universe, I will use similar building blocks made of energy—what the deserters will call 'electrons,' 'protons,' and 'neutrons'—to create what they will call 'atoms.' And I will surround these atoms with a force field that will give them extra mass, the heft you felt when you held the glass."

"To what end?"

"This additional mass will slow everything down in the material universe, including the defectors' intellectual processes. It will reduce their ability to recall their betrayal and game this test."

"Where will you get the energy needed to construct these building blocks? And how will you form this new world?"

"I will show you." The Father snapped his fingers, bringing up a holographic image of the entire Primary Universe. Small streamlets of energy, both positive and negative, began flowing from every star and planet, from every moon and meteorite, and from the atmospheric plasma that occupies the space between these celestial bodies. Small streams of energy joined other small streams to form small rivers, and small rivers joined together to create larger rushing rivers of energy. At the confluences of these energy flows, the energy changed color from an indistinct gray to a brilliant silver that glistened in the sunlight.

These large rivers ultimately flowed onto IAM's palace grounds, where they all joined together to produce one enormous, gushing torrent of energy that surged across a temporary bridge and cascaded down into a newly created void in another dimension. This void was the beginning of a new universe, a material universe—the universe that would someday include planet Earth. Once this transfer of energy was complete, powerful lasers emanating from the Father's outstretched hands compressed this energy into a single particle of matter, smaller than a single atom. An instant later, this tiny speck expanded with unimaginable force, throwing primitive matter and cosmic rays across the vast expanses of this new creation.

This violent expansion caught Dianthe by surprise. She shrieked and jumped back from the hologram.

"Sorry, I should have warned you that was coming," the Father said. "What you just witnessed will, indeed, be a powerful event, so powerful that its cosmic echoes will be heard billions of years in the future."

The image in the hologram changed to what appeared to be a murky, boiling cauldron of indistinct mush.

"I'm seeing something, but what is it?" Serenious asked.

"You're seeing a primordial soup," the Father explained, "a mixture of primitive matter and radiation. For many years, this soup will remain extremely hot. But eventually, it will cool enough to allow subatomic particles, then atoms, and finally molecules to form. Let's jump ahead in time about a billion years."

The image in the hologram showed a universe consisting of vast regions of nearly empty space with occasional large dust clouds. Some of these clouds were tinged yellow. Others were slightly illuminated.

"What are those?" Serenious asked, pointing to one of the clouds.

"Concentrations of space dust made up mainly of what humans will call 'hydrogen and helium atoms.' These concentrations will be called 'nebulae,'" the Father explained.

"Are they significant?" Serenious asked.

"Oh, they're vital," the Father explained. "I will create a force that humans will call 'gravity.' Gravity will pull these atoms together until they collapse in on themselves, creating large furnaces that will be called 'stars.' The largest of these stars will use a fusion process to burn hydrogen and helium atoms at extremely high temperatures, creating more complex elements that will be called 'carbon,' 'magnesium,' and 'iron' among others.

"When the largest of these furnaces burn through their fuel, they will explode, throwing these more complex elements into space. Eventually, this space debris—'space junk,' if you prefer—will be pulled together by gravity to form planets, moons, and everything else made of matter, including the human hosts themselves."

"This is all quite fascinating," Serenious replied.

The Father replied with a smile.

"I sense the presence of something I don't see," Serenious said, staring at the hologram.

"You're sensing what humans will call 'dark matter' and 'dark energy.' Less than five percent of the energy we transfer into this new dimension will make the full transition into matter. Most of this energy will stall somewhere in the process and remain in a suspended state. But dark matter and dark energy will serve a useful function: Their gravity will help stabilize this new universe."

"Father," Dianthe said, "what will this universe look like when it's ready for the hosts?"

A new image appeared in the hologram. It showed a vast universe containing more than a trillion stars and several times that many planets and moons.

"Oh, how beautiful!" After studying the image for several moments, Dianthe said, "This alternative universe looks familiar to me."

"It should," the Father replied. "It's a mirror image of the Primary Universe, only it's matter based and in a different dimension."

"Is it necessary for this new universe to be so large with so many stars and planets?" Serenious asked. "Wouldn't a smaller universe meet our needs?"

"For planets to come into existence and for life forms to evolve into suitable hosts, this new universe will need to remain stable for billions of years. The Primary Universe has remained stable throughout the ages. I copied its structure to avoid experimenting with a new design and all the potential problems that would entail. This project is already very complex. I didn't want to make it more so."

"Transferring energy from one universe and dimension to another and changing it into matter seems like a relatively straightforward process," Serenious said.

"Just the opposite," the Father responded. "Creating a suitable universe out of energy will be a complex process involving many intricate calculations. If we get any of these calculations wrong by even the slightest amount, we will fail to create a stable universe in which the human hosts will be able to survive."

"For example?" Serenious asked.

"Matter will need to be distributed in exactly the right amount throughout the universe: Too many particles of matter per unit of space and the universe will eventually collapse in on itself and self-destruct; too few and stars, planets, and galaxies will never form.

"Gravity will need to be precisely the right strength: Too weak, and stars will never form; too strong, and stars will constantly crash into one another, producing a universe too violent to survive. If gravity is too strong, the typical star will last, on average, only a short period of time (10,000 years) and life-forms the size of humans could not exist—they would be crushed by the force of gravity.

"Life-forms will need to be protected from excessive radiation. I need to ensure that radiation is not too strong wherever in this universe I place the first life-form.

"The force I create to balance the interaction of negative-charged electrons and positive-charged protons will need to be the right strength. If it is .0000001% too weak or too strong, complex molecules needed for life—carbon, iron, and oxygen—will never form.

"Neutrons will need to be exactly 1.00137841870 times heavier than protons. If there is the slightest deviation from that number, molecules needed for life will not form.

"If what humans will call the 'strong nuclear force' is a smidgen too strong, hydrogen will not fuse slowly into deuterium and helium, and all the hydrogen in the universe will be consumed within minutes of the universe's creation. Without hydrogen, this universe will be without water—a substance essential for life.

"What humans will call the 'weak nuclear force' will need to be the right strength to allow stars to provide energy in the form of sunlight to the planets that rotate around them. Without this energy, life will not be possible.

The ratio of matter to antimatter will need to favor matter by at least one part per billion or matter will not form.

"For nitrogen and carbon to form, the beryllium isotope, which has a half-life of 0.0000000000000001 of what humans will call 'seconds,' will need to locate and take into itself a helium nucleus before decaying. If that doesn't happen, this new universe will consist exclusively of hydrogen and helium, and human life will not be possible. And if the ratio of ..."

"Okay, okay!" Serenious exclaimed. He had tried to follow the Father through what seemed like an endless maze of complexity, but the terms, indeed the very concepts that would be at work in this new universe, were so foreign to him that he finally gave up. "I get the picture. You'll need to fine tune this universe to create a suitable environment for a successful test. And that won't be easy."

"Exactly right," the Father replied. "I have reviewed my calculations several times. I think my analysis is correct. If I'm wrong, we'll know soon enough."

"Pardon my saying so, Excellency, but this exercise is getting very complicated."

"Well, it's going to get even more complicated," the Father replied. He pointed to a collection of stars that would someday be called the "Milky Way Galaxy." "Do you see the medium-size star toward the outer edge of this grouping? Now look at the third planet out from the center star. That's where we will conduct our test."

"That hot, beat-up hunk of rock?" Serenious asked.

The Father laughed: "Yes, it's a little beat up now from being hit by space debris, but I will put a stop to that at the appropriate time. And, yes, it will have to cool."

"What makes this planet special?"

"It will have enough mass to have a magnetic field, and it will develop an atmosphere. These two features will help protect humans from deadly solar radiation. The planet's orbit around its sun and its relatively constant axial tilt will keep the planet's surface temperature within a moderate range during the time of our test. And this planet will have all the elements needed to support human life—carbon, hydrogen, nitrogen, oxygen, phosphorus, and sulfur, among others."

"About these life-forms called humans that will serve as hosts for the traitors, how will they be created?" Serenious asked.

"When this planet cools, I will place a one-cell life-form on it," the Father said. "This small life-form will grow and evolve into more complex life-forms through a process humans will call 'evolution.' After about 4.1289 billion Earth years, this one-cell life-form will evolve into suitable hosts for the deserters."

"Why start with a simple life-form that will take so long to develop; why not start with something more advanced?"

"If we start with a life-form in the middle of its evolutionary development, the deserters will know something beyond natural phenomena produced it. That will suggest the existence of an extra-terrestrial creator and that will bias the test results. But if we start with a simple, single cell, the deserters will assume it was produced by natural phenomena—lightening striking a pond with the right mix of atmosphere and chemicals and *voila*, life."

"Father, this first life-form will be anything but simple," Dianthe said. "To survive, it will need to identify and bring through its outer membrane water and nutritious food in sufficient quantities to survive. It will need to convert that food to nourishment and excrete waste. It will need to avoid the dangers of a hostile environment, repair injuries, and ultimately reproduce itself. These are complex functions. To perform them, this first life-form's intelligence system, its little brain, will need to possess and process"—Dianthe paused to do the calculation—at least 3.27698 billion units of information. How could anything this complex be produced by random acts of natural phenomena—lightening striking pond water indeed? The prisoners will eventually see through that contrivance and recognize life as something provided by an outside force, an active creator. Won't that bias the test?"

"Actually Dianthe, to survive, the first life-form's intelligence system will need to possess and process, at a minimum, 3.19356 billion units of information," the Father said. "But no, the prisoners whose seeds of loyalty have died will not see life as evidence of a creator."

"Dianthe makes a compelling point," Serenious said. "When the traitors consider the complexity of this first life-form, they'll ask themselves, "If natural phenomena could produce something this complex, why haven't those same natural forces created other equally complex items, like miniature computers, adroxes, or advanced communication devices?"

"Trust me, both of you. Prisoners whose seeds have died won't ask themselves that question," the Father said.

"Excellency, if this universe must be fine-tuned to support human life," Serenious said, "won't that fact alone suggest the existence of someone doing the fine tuning? Natural forces in the Primary Universe have never fine-tuned anything."

"The prisoners whose seeds have died won't make that connection," the Father said.

"This universe will be expanding, and it will contain residual evidence of a dramatic expansion during its early existence. Won't those facts suggest that there had to be a beginning of this universe, a moment of creation, and that something or, more precisely, someone had to start a chain of events that eventually created humans and all the stuff that surrounds them?"

"These defectors do not see reality," the Father replied. "They see what they want to be true. That is what led to their betrayal. They convinced themselves that life with Hasatan would be better than life with us. How naïve! Hasatan doesn't treat his own angels very well. Why would he treat these defectors any better? But the defectors believed Hasatan's lies because they wanted them to be true. Those whose seeds have died will believe there is no creator other than natural phenomena because they want that to be true. But you have a point. Something as complex as a life-form, even Earth's first life-form, would not likely result from natural phenomena. So, I will cover this planet with many different life-forms—viruses, fungi, bacteria, plants, insects, birds, fish, mammals, creatures large and small. Life on this planet will be so abundant that the deserters will take life for granted. They will see nothing special in it."

"Ah, a very clever strategy, sir," Serenious said.

"Father, what will these human hosts and their surroundings look like?" Dianthe asked.

A new image appeared in the hologram—that of a large freshwater lake that would someday be called the "Sea of Galilee." Small waves caught the bright sunshine and reflected shimmering images toward a shoreline lined with majestic palm trees swaying in a gentle breeze. At the lake's northern end, large patches of *Anemone coronaria*, a brilliant red flower, turned the ascending shore line into a stunning red carpet. A small boat bobbed in the waves about a half mile from the western shore. On board, three stocky fishermen struggled to haul in a net filled with squirming fish.

"Oh, how spectacular," Dianthe said. "What Earth year am I looking at?"

"Counting from the year this planet will come into existence, you are looking at Earth year 4,543,762,014," the Father replied.

"Those fishermen—their facial features, their bodies, their extremities, the hair on their heads—they look like us," Dianthe said. She looked at the balding Serenious and said, "Well, they look like some of us."

Serenious forced a polite smile.

"And that big fisherman in front of the boat, the one they're calling Simon, he looks exactly like Lord Nomis," Dianthe continued.

"Yes, these life-forms are patterned after us. I saw no reason to create new appearances," the Father replied.

"This planet is so fascinating. I want to see more of it," Dianthe said.

"Feel free to do so," the Father replied.

"May I join you?" Serenious asked.

"Of course," Dianthe replied.

"Excellency, do you have the design for this planet in a form that we could take with us to use as a guide?"

The Father thought-messaged his complete plan for planet Earth to Serenious and Dianthe.

After reviewing it, Dianthe and Serenious transported themselves forward in time to the Earth year shown in the hologram. They landed on a bluff overlooking what would someday be called the "Gulf of Alaska." Dianthe spotted three whales swimming north. The whales—two adults and a youngster—had begun their journey in the Southern Ocean, where the young whale was born. They were headed to their summer home in the North Pacific, where they would feed mostly on krill to restore body fat consumed during their long journey north.

"According to the Father's plan, these graceful swimmers will evolve from land animals," Dianthe said.

"Just then, a huge piece of ice broke off from a nearby glacier and fell into the ocean with a stupendous roar.

"That was impressive," Dianthe said.

"Yes, it was. Natural forces will seem so powerful to these humans that some of them will worship nature as a god," Serenious said.

Dianthe and Serenious transported themselves inland and came to rest on the South Summit of what someday would be called "Mount McKinley" and then "Mount Denali," at 20,310 feet, one of Earth's highest mountains. Five large glaciers dressed its slopes in a modest white gown of snow and ice. To the north between the mountain and a large lake, a large bull moose was feeding in a verdant meadow. The moose's well-developed antlers represented a formidable threat to any would-be attacker, but the bull seemed unconcerned about that possibility.

Looking north and east, Dianthe spotted a young grizzly sitting upright on its hind quarters in the shallows of what humans would someday call the "Kuskokwim River." The bear was trying to catch salmon swimming upstream to their spawning grounds. Time and time again, the young bear lunged at a leaping fish, but each time, the fish was faster than his swipe, and he came up empty. Finally, a large salmon jumped right into his outstretched paw. The young bear brought the wriggling fish to his mouth with an unmistakable look of accomplishment.

"This region of Earth looks like the polar region of our home planet in the Primary Universe," Dianthe said. "But this high peak, this protrusion from the land's surface, is a strange phenomenon. We don't have anything like this on our planet. What could create such a thing?"

"The collision of two land masses," Serenious responded. "We don't have these in the Primary Universe because when land masses collide in our world, they simply suffuse into one another. But in this new world, because it consists of matter, these gigantic collisions will occur, creating what will be called 'mountains.'"

"Is the rest of this planet this beautiful?"

"Let's see for ourselves."

The two transported themselves south over a vast expanse of ocean. Dianthe spotted a chain of islands that would someday be called "French Polynesia." She pointed to one of the chain's smaller islands that featured a towering peak rising 3960 feet above sea level.

"Look, another landmass collision creating a mountain on this tiny island," Dianthe said.

"According to the Father's design, this mountain will be created, not by the collision of two land masses, but by a volcano spewing out hot lava under the sea," Serenious said.

"This island is so beautiful. And the waters surrounding it are so clear, they resemble the Great Mensa Sea," Dianthe said after landing on one of the island's sandy beaches.

"Yes, even humans, with their limited optical systems, will be able to see everything living in these waters," Serenious responded.

"I don't see any humans on this island," Dianthe said.

"Humans will not get here for hundreds of Earth years," Serenious replied.

Two dolphins swam close to shore, raised their heads out of the water, and looked directly at Dianthe.

"Those fish are smiling at me," Dianthe exclaimed. "How extraordinary!"

"Actually, those aren't fish. They're dolphins—mammals," Serenious replied.

"Whatever they are, they have a lovely smile."

"Our high energy levels attracted them. They are curious creatures with highly developed, complex brains. In fact, the Father considered using them as hosts for the traitors before choosing humans."

"Everywhere I look on this planet, I see beauty." Dianthe said. She then transported herself north and east, across an ocean, a landmass, another ocean, and another landmass until she arrived at what would someday be called the "Wadi Desert in the Hashemite Kingdom of Jordan." She landed on a high sand dune. Serenious soon joined her.

"These large waves of sand resemble the ocean waves we saw on our way here. Only they lack motion. And listen."

Serenious cocked his head. "I don't hear anything," he replied.

"Exactly. There is nothing to catch the wind and make a sound—no humans, trees, or vegetation. There is just peace and silence. Isn't it wonderful? This planet is beautiful even in its most desolate places."

"Your Father does excellent work," Serenious replied. He then transported himself north and west to a landmass in the shape of a boot that extended out into a large sea and then onto a city near the East Coast of that landmass.

"This large city will rule an empire that will control much of the Western World during Earth year 4,543,762,014," Serenious explained. "This city will be called 'Rome.'"

"It's an impressive city for any age," Dianthe said. "Look at that large oblong stadium inside the city? There must be over 150,000 life-forms inside that structure."

"That is the 'Circus Maximus.' It will be used for chariot races, although it will have other uses as well, like executing people." That comment caught Dianthe's attention, and she asked herself, "Would people be executed in this new world?"

Dianthe and Serenious moved to the city's outskirts, where Dianthe saw a meadow filled with wild roses. She descended to the meadow and picked a bloom. Sniffing the flower as she caressed it to her cheek, Dianthe said, "This looks like a flower in our palace gardens. Isn't it beautiful?"

After agreeing that they had seen enough, Dianthe and Serenious traveled back in time to the Father's side.

"Father, your fine hand is evident throughout this creation, from the Arctic to the tropics, from the most populated areas to the most desolate." Holding up the rose she had just picked, Dianthe continued, "And look at this flower. Its color is so vibrant; its fragrance, so sweet, its petals, so soft; its design, so pleasing to the eye. Anyone who holds a flower like this in her hand will know there has to be a creator-god."

Serenious chimed in: "This planet, indeed this whole universe, is extraordinary. Elegant in design, mathematically precise, a masterpiece of construction, and beautiful beyond description. Did you intend for it to be so?"

"Durinzo, the palace artist, warned me that if I designed a universe and a planet, I would make them too beautiful," the Father replied. "He was right, of course."

"When humans develop the technology to look around this universe, they'll see what natural phenomena can produce—massive burning furnaces called stars; desolate, lifeless planets with little or no protection from the sun's radiation; planets made of gasses without any firmament; comets traveling through space with no capability of supporting life; moons devoid of anything but rock," Serenious said. "Out of the more than four trillion planets in this universe, they will see that Earth is unique in its beauty and its capacity to accommodate life. Surely, they'll realize there had to be something beyond natural phenomena that made it so."

The Father finally lost his patience. "Listen to me, both of you," he said sternly. "Yes, this new world will have a surface beauty. But it will have other features that do not suggest a kindly creator."

The Father opened another hologram. It showed the rolling hill country of Southern Africa and a mother impala suckling her young calf. The mother became distracted and fell behind the herd. She did not notice the pack of hyenas stalking her. Suddenly, the largest hyena sprang from the tall grass and attacked the young impala. The mother tried to fend off the attacker. But when three other hyenas pounced on the calf, pulling it to the ground, she realized she was no match for these predators, and she abandoned her offspring. The hyenas ripped the young animal apart and began to devour it. Initially, the hyenas fought among themselves to determine which animal would eat first. Not surprisingly, the largest animal prevailed. At the end of their feast, the sated hyenas, blood dripping from their mouths, wandered off to sleep.

"Do you understand what you have just observed?" the Father asked.

"Father, that was horrible," Dianthe protested. "That poor little innocent animal. Are we going to allow things like that to happen in this new world?"

"This new universe will not run according to our values," the Father explained. "Here, survival will depend on the strong preying on the weak. Brute force, not love and kindness, will control. The deserters whose seeds have died will feel comfortable in this world because it will match their own values. Deserters carrying a live seed, if there are any, will be horrified by this world's brutality. They will yearn for a different world with different values. Earth will provide an excellent environment in which to test the deserters' commitment to love and kindness, and thus their commitment to us."

Dianthe and Serenious said they understood.

"To create this new universe, we'll need to use all the surplus energy available in the Primary Universe," the Father continued. "But that won't be enough energy to conduct this experiment. The three of us will need to contribute some of our own energy to repower the deserters and transfer them into this new world."

"I will supply all the additional energy needed," Dianthe insisted. "I asked for this test; I should be the one to power it. You can restore me to my present state over time."

"You don't have enough energy to repower all the deserters," the Father said. "If you tried, your energy would decrease to a dangerously low level from which we might not be able to restore you. I will not allow you to be placed in that situation. Each of us will contribute a third of the additional energy needed to run this trial."

"I'm willing," Serenious said.

"As am I," the Father said. "Both of you need to understand that, even with the extra energy we supply, there will be barely enough energy to power this test and not much energy available to deal with intervening factors."

"Intervening factors! What intervening factors?" Dianthe asked.

"Like whatever Hasatan might do," the Father said.

"Hasatan!" Dianthe exclaimed. "Are we going to allow him into this new universe?"

"A universe constructed solely of positive energy would be unstable and quickly self-destruct. We'll need to use both positive and negative energy to build this new world. And if we use negative energy, Hasatan will be present. There is no way around that."

"If Hasatan is allowed into this new world, he will try to manipulate this exercise to serve his own purposes," Dianthe said.

"I suppose he might try."

"Hasatan may not want to let the traitors out of his control for fear they would report his atrocities. On the other hand, he may see this test as an opportunity to get prisoners loyal to him back into our kingdom to serve as spies," Serenious said.

"All that is possible," the Father conceded.

6.

The images of Hasatan's cruelty to the prisoners lingered in Dianthe's mind: The flames that branded the prisoners and left them screaming in agony, the cruel combat between two prisoners which left one barely alive, the horrific disfigurement of a beautiful young girl. It was cruelty without purpose, cruelty for the sake of cruelty, and Hasatan delighted in it.

IAM had never paid much attention to how Hasatan treated his angels. They were Hasatan's, he created them out of his energy, and he was given freedom to treat them as he pleased. But for Dianthe, the prisoners from the Positive Energy Kingdom presented a different situation: These life-forms were created by the Father. Dianthe knew many of them by name. Some had personally served her. Others, like X-mead, had entertained IAM. She could not ignore their misery, even though they may have betrayed her trust. Seeing Hasatan mistreat the prisoners was difficult to accept. But the thought of him entering this new universe and using his powers to bias the test that would determine where the prisoners would spend eternity was something she could not abide.

And so, during the next gathering of the three persons of IAM, she declared, "We must limit Hasatan's ability to bias the tests results. If allowed free rein in the material world, he will create mayhem and chaos, and we will be blamed for the resulting misery and suffering. Humans will reason that a loving god would never allow mass misery to exist and that its presence is proof that there is no god, or if a god does exist, she's either a sadist or she doesn't care about her creation. Follow me ahead in time to the second day of the seventh month of Earth year 4,543,763,905 (July 2, 1916) to a place that will be called 'Serre, France,' and I will show you an example of the misery Hasatan will create."

The Father and Serenious followed Dianthe through time to Serre and then to a battlefield near this picturesque French village. It was the second day of what would become known as the "Great War's Battle of the Somme," a battle that would last more than four months and kill or injure more than a million men. The battlefield near Serre had once been a tranquil, verdant meadow where dairy cows enjoyed lush grass. But now, that meadow had become "no-man's land," marked in the west by British trenches and in the east by German fortifications. The area around the British fortifications still retained some of its pasture-like qualities, except, of course, for the trenches and the barbed wire. But the area around German positions had become a moonlike landscape devoid of any life. For several days prior to July 1, British artillery had pounded German positions up and down the German line with more than 1.7 million artillery shells in anticipation of a British attack. The results near Serre were dramatic: What had once been stately trees were now upright poles denuded of leaves and branches. What had once been lush pasture was now a cratered stretch of churned earth lacking a single living blade of grass.

Early on the morning of July 1, British troops were told that this massive artillery bombardment had destroyed German defenses and that they would experience light resistance while attacking the German line. But the German positions near Serre were heavily fortified, and the Germans had sustained light losses from the shelling. When British infantry began their charge, German machine gunners opened fire, and the slaughter began. The guns were silent now. The two armies had tacitly agreed to allow medical personnel to search the battlefield for survivors, but few were found. It had rained that morning, and small streamlets of water, stained red by the blood of a thousand ashen-colored corpses, trickled down the hillside into a small stream that ran to the Somme River.

The story of the battlefield could be seen in the faces of the fallen. Some showed steely determination as they charged enemy lines; others showed the terror men felt when German machine guns opened fire; still others were contorted by the anguish that wounded men endured before they died. The bodies of the dead had begun to decompose in the warm afternoon sun. The stench of decomposing human flesh blanketed the battlefield.

Wearing the white uniforms of medical personnel, the Father, Serenious, and Dianthe wandered through the battlefield, trying not to step on the corpses or body parts that littered the landscape. Dianthe paused sporadically, examining the faces of the dead, as if she were looking for someone. Finally, she found the object of her search: British Sergeant Winston A. Rollins. In his mid-thirties, Rollins had been a career soldier who had, as a younger man, fought in the Second Boer War. He was a happy-go-lucky warrior who delighted in pointing out that his initials—W.A.R.—were well suited to his profession.

A small gold medallion inscribed with the Latin phrase *Deo et Regi Fidelis* ("Faithful to God and King") hung from a chain around his bull-like neck. The medallion was a gift from his mother, an Irish Catholic who did everything she could to beat religion into her son's thick head. But Rollins's faith in a supreme being was, simply put, a casual thing. He wore the medallion as a good-luck charm. He had survived several vicious battles during the Boer war and was convinced that either the medallion or the luck of the Irish had protected him. But on July 1, both his luck and his protection had run out. He lay on his back with a bullet hole in his forehead. The bullet had tumbled after impact and taken off the back of his skull.

There was only a slight scowl on his otherwise handsome face, suggesting that death had come instantaneously and without pain.

Dianthe reached out and touched the sergeant's muscular arm, which was tattooed with a heart and the words "To All the Girls I've Loved." "Sergeant Rollins," Dianthe called. The sergeant sat up with a dazed look on his face. His prominent blue eyes slowly focused on the three figures standing before him. He studied them for a moment and then scanned what he could see of the battlefield. He grimaced at the sight of the many corpses, their faces locked in grotesque, empty stares, their contorted bodies lying in unnatural positions.

"Oh, my god!" he said. "My whole company is here, and every one of them...dead. There's Johnny Campbell, the young father who was so proud of his twin sons, and Michael O'Flaherty, who was hoping to get back to Dublin to marry his childhood sweetheart, and Robert Strawn, who had promised his mother he'd be home by Christmas. They're all gone. Did we at least win this battle? Was there a point to this madness?"

"Neither side won this battle, Sergeant," Serenious replied.

Rollins continued to survey the battlefield. "How did I survive this, and how long have I been unconscious?" he wondered out loud. He examined his body, his arms, legs, and trunk, but saw no wounds. He was unaware that the back of his head was gone.

"This battle took place yesterday, about thirty hours ago," Serenious replied.

"Somehow, I got through this; God be praised," Rollins said. His expression suddenly turned to sadness and then to despair. "What am I saying?" he exclaimed. "God be praised? Look at this carnage. Look at the faces of these innocent young boys! Look at their pain, their fear. Can there be any better evidence that there is no god than this battlefield? Look at it! Would a merciful god ever permit anything this monstrous to happen?"

The sergeant grabbed Dianthe by the arm. "If there's a god, he's a monster who writes his name in the blood of innocent young boys." He pulled on the gold medallion around his neck until the chain broke. Then he threw the medallion as far away as he could. Tears streamed down his face. "God be praised? What a cruel joke!"

Rollins looked at Dianthe and said, "If you wanted to help the wounded, you should have been here earlier. From the looks of these bodies, you're not going to find anyone alive now. They've been out here bleeding and dying for a full day. But search—by all means, search. And if you find someone still alive, yell, and I'll help you carry them to your field hospital. You'll need help." Nodding toward the Father and Serenious, he said, "These two guys won't be able to carry a wounded man very far."

"Oh, they're stronger than they look," Dianthe replied.

"Yes, we exercise regularly. We're really quite capable," Serenious added with a mischievous smirk on his face.

"Sergeant, you need to rest. It was a difficult battle; you've earned some rest," Dianthe said. She gently touched the sergeant's arm. Rollins lay back and resumed his original position. His blue eyes glazed over and stared into emptiness.

"Hasatan will delight in this carnage and its unmistakable message—that confusion and chaos rule the universe, not a loving creator," Dianthe said.

"I fear that Dianthe is correct," Serenious said. "Anyone who goes through this horror, even traitors carrying a live seed, will turn away from their creator for allowing this to happen, if not for causing it. And the story of this battle will likely destroy the seed in the faithful for generations to come."

The Father smiled: "Both of you are mistaken. Prisoners who have remained loyal to us will not suddenly lose their faith because they come face to face with monstrous evil. They will not attribute the sins of man to the will of their creator," he said, as he walked a short distance to the body of a British soldier who had been shot through the chest.

"Private Strawn," the Father called out. Strawn sat up and looked around. Seeing the Father, Strawn's face shown with wonder and joy. He called out in an excited voice, "My Lord and my God. I knew if the worst happened, you would come for me."

"A Father's love for his children is eternal, my son," the Father replied.

"I know that, sir. Father, may I ask a favor? Would you comfort my mother and tell her it's all right? I'm in your hands, and it's all right. She'll be so upset when she learns what happened. She's always doted on me. I'm her only child, you know. My father died two years ago. I'm all she has left. And now she'll have no one. She'll take this real hard unless you comfort her."

"I'll comfort your mother and give her peace," the Father said. "She'll be joining you soon; she doesn't have much time left on earth. But now, you need to rest. It's not yet time for you to come home."

"Yes, thank you, Father. One more thing, please bring all these men home? They're all good men. They did the best they could out here. Our artillery was supposed to take out the German machine guns, but that didn't happen. When the machine guns opened fire on us, no one turned and ran. We all continued with the attack. But it was very hard...the enemy mowed us down like blades of grass...human blades of grass. It was very, very hard."

"Yes, I know, but that's over now," the Father replied in a gentle voice that momentarily broke with emotion. "We'll see about these other men, but now, you need to rest." Strawn smiled at the Father, Dianthe, and Serenious. He returned to his original position, closed his eyes, and remained motionless.

"Coming face to face with monstrous evil, the worst evil that Hasatan can impose on this new world, may not destroy a seed that is strong," said Serenious. "But what about a seed that is just barely alive? Could events in the material world extinguish a seed that is weak?"

"A weak seed might be destroyed by what it encounters in the material world," the Father replied. "But that is unlikely."

"But it is possible," Serenious said.

"Yes, it's possible," the Father conceded.

"So Dianthe is right to be concerned about Hasatan's ability to create mischief in this world."

"I suppose she is."

"Is the opposite true? Might a prisoner, whose seed died before entering the material world, become loyal to IAM after viewing events in this universe?"

"Again, that's theoretically possible but unlikely."

"One more thing. You denied yourself the ability to look into traitors' minds, yet you knew Private Strawn was carrying a live seed?"

"Strawn will come from a family of church goers; that was a clue. He will regularly pray to us even when he is not exposed to danger; that was another clue. And he died with a smile on his face. Obviously, he trusted us enough not to fear human death. That was also a clue."

"Oh, so you guessed?"

"Not really," the Father said, smiling. "If a prisoner with a live seed is in your presence, you will feel the seed's power. And if a prisoner whose seed has died is in your presence, you will sense the seed's absence. But that will only happen if a prisoner is in your presence."

7.

Once every 10,452 years, a spectacular celestial event takes place in the Primary Universe. Five of the universe's brightest stars come into perfect alignment from the perspective of IAM's palace. When these stars are so positioned, their overlapping energy fields produce magnificent visual effects that illuminate the night sky with waves of brilliant colors—purples, blues, greens, and reds—that pulsate as the stars continue to move in their orbits.

One such celestial event occurred on Primary Universe date 357⁹ ZMC-8623-37-20. It was a balmy evening. The scent of lilac perfumed the air. As darkness silently crept over the palace grounds, the gathering crowd grew restless. The younger life-forms were particularly impatient. Some of them had never witnessed this celestial wonder. At exactly 29:00 hours, it began: The stars formed a straight line pointing toward IAM's palace, and the night sky was awash in vivid color. The "oohs" and "aahs" from the crowd increased in volume with each slight change in color. This dramatic show lasted, at most, fifteen minutes, but it was enough time for every observer to permanently store these awe-inspiring images in his or her memory bank. When the stars were no longer aligned, and the night sky returned to normal, groans of disappointment could be heard.

The Father, Dianthe, and Serenious watched this show from the palace terrace. "The beauty of this celestial event is unsurpassed in the night sky," the Father said. "The heavens become a canvas on which natural forces paint beautiful images for all to see."

Sensing that the Father and Serenious were in an accommodating mood, Dianthe said, "Father, I want you to send me into this new world, so I can explain your plan for redemption—that we will welcome back to our kingdom all who remain loyal to IAM, without any punishment being imposed on the deserters for leaving our realm. As our interaction with Sergeant Rollins showed, Hasatan and his angels will fill this new creation with misery, discouragement, disappointment, and lies about the purpose of human existence. A counterbalance is needed: A clear, powerful voice to rebut those falsehoods, a voice to explain that the only way the prisoners can be reconciled to their creator is through loyalty to IAM and our principles. Nothing else will save them. I want to be that voice."

A rapid increase in the energy pulses emanating from the Father telegraphed that he was neither pleased nor persuaded.

"If a 'clear voice,' is needed, Serenious can inspire one of the deserters to provide it," the Father said. "There's no need for you to enter this universe."

"To rise above the din of false information, this speaker must avoid being trapped by trick questions, persevere in the face of danger, and speak with authority," Dianthe replied. "Serenious can inspire wisdom and courage in a speaker, but not beyond the limits imposed by that speaker's humanity. I need to perform this mission. And besides, if I am in this new universe when the transfer of my energy occurs, the transfer will be more efficient than if my energy is drained from me here and then transferred into this new world."

Sensing the growing tension between Dianthe and the Father, Serenious interjected, "Dianthe is right about that—the energy efficiency part, I mean."

The Father ignored Serenious's comment. "How would you perform this mission?" he asked Dianthe.

"I would enter this world as a humble person, born of a lower-caste woman, in a remote location. While assuming a low profile, I would teach the traitors about the true way to be reconciled to their creator. My presence can be arranged so it will not compromise the integrity of this test."

"Where would you enter the material universe?"

"In a small country called 'Judea,' which is located on a land bridge between two great continents. Many prisoners who appear to be loyal to IAM will live in this area. I can sense the aggregate power of their many seeds of loyalty.

The Father looked to Serenious for confirmation.

"I believe that's correct. I, too, sense the combined power of their seeds," Serenious replied.

"And when would you enter this world?" the Father asked.

"When my teachings can be recorded and widely disseminated," Dianthe replied. "Perhaps three thousand Earth years after humans devise a system of writing. By then, human writing will be able to express complex thoughts. And by then, there will exist a dominant empire that will help disseminate my teachings to many nations."

"You want your teachings to be widely disseminated while you assume a low profile," the Father said with a distinct edge in his voice. "How can that be?" Straining to control his temper, he continued, "The more I hear of this idea, the less I like it. Dianthe, your presence in this world would add so many complications to this test."

"They can be managed," Dianthe insisted. "When almost all my power has been drained and used to bring Hasatan's prisoners into this new world to be tested, I will experience what humans will call death. While I am in a dormant state, you can repower me and gradually return me to my present condition."

"I have designed this new world so that evidence of IAM's existence will be evenly balanced with the evidence that IAM does not exist. Defectors carrying a live seed will look at this evidence and see IAM and hope for reconciliation with their maker. Defectors whose seed has died will look at exactly the same evidence and see superstition and nonsense. If you enter this world, you will distort that balance."

"Hasatan will be in this world, and he will distort that balance. I would simply correct whatever distortions he causes so that the evidence is, once again, evenly balanced."

"If you take on a human side, with all its limitations, you will not think logically," the Father insisted.

"Why not?" Dianthe asked.

"Human emotions will influence your judgment. You will respond to human problems emotionally, not analytically. And you will use your powers in ways that will prove you are not of that world."

"Father, my dominant half will always be in control. I would exercise my power discreetly."

"Unfortunately, because of your human side, you would not." Serenious again interrupted to break the rising tension: "A technical point: If Dianthe wants to be taken seriously in Judea three thousand Earth years after human writing begins, she will have to enter this universe as a male life-form. Female life-forms will not be taken seriously in that place at that time."

There was a long pause. "Oh, all right, I'll enter as a male life-form if that's what's necessary," Dianthe said, in an uncharacteristically sharp tone of voice.

"Dianthe, if you take on human form, with all its intellectual frailty, you will use your powers in frivolous ways," the Father said. "Transport yourself ahead in time to noon on the seventeenth day of the ninth month of Earth year 4,543,762,016 (September 17, 0026) to a large house in the City of Cana in Galilee where a wedding celebration is underway. You will better understand my point."

Dianthe soon found herself behind storage boxes in an isolated corner of the basement of a large house that belonged to one of Cana's more prominent citizens. The basement room was normally used for ceremonial washing, but on this day, it was filled with wedding guests of lower standing in the community. Dressed in a plain, unadorned robe and headscarf, Dianthe casually walked out into the main part of the room and blended into the crowd.

Like everyone else in the room, her attention was soon drawn to a man, thirty-one years of age, standing in the center of the room. His height—almost six feet tall—made him stand out in the crowd. His appearance lacked refinement: His beard and shoulder-length dark hair were not trimmed. The calloused hands and thick forearms of a workman, perhaps a stonecutter or a carpenter, protruded out from under his robe. His coarse clothing was faded and torn in places.

The man was from Galilee, a poor, backwoods area. That fact alone suggested he lacked education and urban sophistication. But there was evidence to the contrary—elegant facial features, and dark, penetrating eyes that seemed to look deep into the essence of anyone who came near. There was also his patrician bearing—the erect posture, the authoritative voice, his encyclopedic knowledge of religious texts, and his unmistakable charisma. He was a fascinating person, and everyone that passed by could not resist staring at him, if only for a moment. On the surface, he seemed cheerful, returning every smile that came his way. But at a deeper level, there was an unmistakable melancholy about the man. Whether this sadness was for the people with whom he came in contact or for himself and his future was unclear.

Dianthe worked her way through the crowd to observe more closely the man she would become if she entered the material universe.

Rebecca, an attractive woman in her late teens with dark hair, sparkling brown eyes, and a welcoming smile, approached the same man from the opposite direction. She was also dressed in the simple clothes of a person of lower class.

"Jesus, I'm glad you came to the wedding celebration. I haven't seen you in Nazareth for some time. Have you been on a journey?" Rebecca said, while letting the front of her dress fall open to reveal her ample cleavage.

"Yes, I have been away from Nazareth recently," Jesus replied.

"You need to settle down...and think about important things," Rebecca said coyly.

"Like what?" Jesus asked.

"Like getting married and having children. Your friends say you are well past the age when you should be married," Rebecca replied.

Mary, a handsome woman in her mid-forties, stood in another corner of the room, talking to a female friend she had known during childhood but had not seen in many years. Mary had been watching her son and Rebecca out of the corner of her eye. Mary suddenly broke off the conversation with her friend, went to her son, grabbed him by the arm, and pulled him away from Rebecca.

"Have nothing to do with that woman," Mary told him. "Throwing herself at you like that. Shameful. That was shameful."

"Mother, she means no harm," Jesus replied in a soft, quiet voice.

"Let me be the judge of that," Mary said.

"Yes, Mother," Jesus replied.

"I just learned that the groom's father is about to run out of wine," Mary said. "More people than expected have come to the wedding feast. Can you help?"

"It's not yet time for me to reveal who I am."

"I know but running out of wine will embarrass our host. He is a kindly man; he helped your father find work on occasion. I hate to see him embarrassed. Surely, you can help."

"If that's what you want, Mother."

Mary summoned several servants. "Do whatever my son tells you," she told them.

Six large stone jars, each capable of holding between twenty and thirty gallons of water used for the Jewish rites of purification, stood in one corner of the room. Pointing to the jars, Jesus said to the servants, "Fill them with water."

When the jars were filled, Jesus said, "Draw liquid out and serve it to the chief steward for the wedding." After the steward tasted the wine, he called the bridegroom and the bridegroom's father aside and said, "This wine is superb. I have never tasted anything like it. It is far superior to what you served at the beginning of this celebration. Why did you wait so long to bring out this extraordinary wine?"

The bridegroom looked at his father. The dumbfounded look on his father's face said the chief steward was not going to get an answer to his question.

After Dianthe transported herself back to the Father's side, she said, "I agree, making wine for a wedding feast would not be the best use of my powers. But few people would know what took place at this wedding."

"If you enter this world and interact with human hosts, your human side will lead you to perform thousands of so-called miracles," the Father explained. "You will make the blind see, the lame walk, the lepers clean; you will bring the dead back to life. Once the afflicted learn that simply touching your robe will provide healing power, they will come to you in large numbers. Some will walk, some will crawl, and some will be carried by friends. And every one of these healing acts will indicate that your powers are from a different world."

"Father, I will try to control my human instincts."

"I know you will try, but the point is, you will not succeed. And what purpose would these miracles serve? These hosts will be fragile creatures. You might temporarily restore the afflicted to good health, but infirmities will soon return. And they will all experience human death. While their imperfections might cause them discomfort during their earthly lives, compared with eternity, their ills will be short-lived."

"Father, these miracles, these acts of kindness, will show the prisoners that their creator still loves them, even after their treachery and betrayal. The power of demonstrated love will nourish the seed in those in whom it is weak and maintain it in those in whom it is strong."

"But these miracles will likely bias the test results and increase the chances that we would bring disloyal life-forms back into our kingdom," the Father replied.

"At the time Dianthe proposes to enter this world," Serenious said, "many so-called magicians will use fraud and deception to claim they possess supernatural powers. If Dianthe performed miracles, she would be one of many who appeared to have supernatural powers. Most people would dismiss her, or should I say him, as another religious crackpot or con artist. In my judgment, Dianthe's performing miracles in Judah would not necessarily destroy the integrity of this test."

"You may be right about that, but there is another problem," the Father said. "Dianthe, as your energy flowed from you into this material world, you would become more and more unsure of your mission and more vulnerable to attack."

"Vulnerable to attack!" Dianthe exclaimed. "No matter how much power I lose, I would still be many times more powerful than any human."

"I'm not concerned about danger from humans; I'm concerned about danger from Hasatan. As your power declined, Hasatan might catch you in a weak moment and convince you to do something harmful to you and to us."

"You think Hasatan would be able to find me laboring as a carpenter in Nazareth?"

"Because of your extraordinary power, Hasatan would find you no matter how you dressed or where you hid. Travel ahead in time to the early morning of the last day of the third week of the seventh month of Earth year 4,543,762,017 (July 17, 0027) to the synagogue at Capernaum, a town along the northern coast of the Sea of Galilee and observe."

Dianthe soon found herself sitting on a stone seat in the rear of the synagogue watching a religious service. She was dressed in a robe and head scarf that concealed her sex and identity.

Several weeks before, news had circulated widely that Jesus of Nazareth would attend this religious service and speak as a guest teacher. As a result, the synagogue was filled to capacity with worshippers and those wanting to learn more about this Jesus of Nazareth. Uzziah, who was leading the service, finished the main prayer and then invited Jesus to speak. Jesus rose from his seat and turned toward the congregation. He had spoken only a few words when a half-crazed man sitting next to Dianthe stood up and growled in a staccato-like cadence: "Let us alone, thou Jesus of Nazareth! Have you come to destroy us, to wield the sword of IAM's judgment? I know who you are—the holy one of God. You cannot fool me in your simple clothes."

Jesus looked at the man and said, "Be silent and come out of him."

One of Hasatan's lesser angels, a green, translucent creature with the head of a lizard and large wings, slithered out of the man's mouth. With a hateful look on its face, the creature glared at Jesus for a long moment, saliva dripping from its chin. It screamed that Hasatan would punish the village for inviting Jesus to speak at the synagogue and then flew out of the building through a side window.

Members of the congregation rushed to windows to watch the creature fly up and disappear into the clouds. All eyes then turned toward Jesus, who remained silent. This quiet interlude did not last long. Uzziah ran out of the synagogue, and the whole congregation followed. He and the others began telling everyone in Capernaum what had occurred. At first, no one believed them, but when revered leaders of the community, including Abijah, Obed, and Boaz, all told the same story, the villagers became convinced that something miraculous had occurred in their midst.

Dianthe waited until the synagogue was empty and then transported herself back to the Father's side. The Father greeted her with, "Rest assured, if you enter this new world, Hasatan will find you."

"When he does, I will reject whatever he attempts," Dianthe said. "Please, observe through my eyes."

Dianthe projected herself forward in time to the desert east of Jerusalem. It was early in the afternoon of the sixth day of the eight month of Earth year 4,543,762,016 (August 6, 0026). She hid behind a large rock to observe Jesus as he prayed. The temperature was high. Jesus had been fasting in preparation for what he would have to endure in the future. He was hungry, thirsty, and weak—almost delirious.

Suddenly, Hasatan appeared out of a puff of black smoke. He swaggered to where Jesus had knelt to pray and sat down on a nearby rock. Squinting because of the bright sunlight, which he detested, Hasatan looked down at Jesus.

"If you are who you think you are," he said, with ridicule dripping from his tongue, "you don't need to purify yourself. You're already pure. Turn these stones into bread and eat. Satisfy your human need for food," Hasatan said, as he took a bite from an apple he was carrying.

"Hmmmm, tasty. I never realized how good these are," he said, offering the apple to Jesus. "Here, take a bite."

"Earthly food alone does not sustain; only the power of the Father," Jesus replied.

"Have it your way," Hasatan replied. He picked Jesus up and carried him to the highest point in the temple in Jerusalem. From there, Jesus could see the Kidron Valley, the Garden of Gethsemane, the Mount of Olives, and the surrounding areas.

"Jump," Hasatan said. "If you are who you think you are, IAM's angels will catch you and prevent your destruction on the rocks below. If not, your miserable little existence will be over, and so will your suffering."

"Hasatan, what do you seek—a demonstration of the Father's love for me? And if there were such a demonstration, would you no longer try to influence this test to determine which of your prisoners have remained loyal to us?"

Hasatan ignored the question. Instead, he took Jesus to a high place in the heavens, from which Jesus could see not only the material universe but also the Primary Universe and all adjoining universes.

"Look at all of existence," Hasatan said. "Isn't it magnificent? If you join your powers to mine, we'll be the most powerful force in all existence. This will all be ours. You will no longer be subordinate to your father. You will no longer be lectured by him, corrected by him, told what to do or say. Instead, you and I will rule all of creation. Our thrones will sit side by side in a magnificent throne room. Every life form, including your father and Serenious, will bow down before us. If you pass up this opportunity, it will never come again."

"Is this how you lured the traitors away from our kingdom, with false promises of power and glory?" Jesus asked. "I am my father's child. Why would I ever betray the preeminent force for good in all universes?"

"You fool. You will always be subordinate to your father. You will always be his lackey."

"I am happy to serve my father in any role he chooses."

"Oh, spare me the platitudes. You are not what you pretend to be—the obedient child. You are simply weak and timid. And you will always be weak and timid. Go back to your father. Do his bidding. You don't have either the imagination or the strength to rule all of existence." With that, Hasatan left as he had come, in a puff of black smoke.

Dianthe returned to the Father's side, saying, "I will always reject Hasatan's attempts to turn me against you."

"There would be another problem if you enter this new world," the Father said. "Have you considered what your earthly death would be like?"

"No, I haven't looked that far ahead," Dianthe replied.

"You should. It may change your mind. At the time you propose to enter the material world, religious life in Judea will be controlled by two groups—the Sadducees and the Pharisees. The Sadducees will operate the temple in Jerusalem, the center of religious life in Judea. They will not believe in an afterlife. They will teach their followers that to live a blessed earthly life, they will need to make ritual sacrifices to IAM, which the Sadducees will perform on temple grounds for handsome fees.

"The Pharisees, on the other hand, will believe in a life after human death. They will profess that the pathway to 'heaven' is slavish adherence to a long list of rules, most of which they will write. These rules will control virtually every aspect of human life: What to eat, how to worship, how to interact with others, how to groom oneself, how to conduct business.

"If you teach humans that the pathway to eternal life with their creator is neither ritual sacrifice nor slavish adherence to esoteric rules but simple loyalty to IAM, if you go about healing human infirmities with strange powers, you will represent an existential threat to both religious orders. They will find it necessary to get rid of you. They will have you put to death, and the preferred way to eliminate rabble-rousers at that time and place will be crucifixion. Do you know what that would be like?"

Dianthe shook her head in the negative.

"You will be whipped and taken to a place where criminals and rebels are put to death. Your executioners will use iron spikes to nail your hands and feet to a wooden cross," the Father said. "The cross will be stood upright, with one end planted in the ground. You will hang there until death relieves you of your agony. For a while, you will be able to hold yourself up by your legs, so you can breathe. But eventually, your legs will become fatigued and then only your arms will support you. But your arms will not be strong enough to support your body for very long. You will soon fall forward and die from asphyxiation if you don't die from shock first.

"Travel ahead in time to midday on the fifth day of the fourth month of earth year 4,543,762,020 (April 5, 0030). That will be the day of your execution. I want you to see what crucifixion would be like. I want you to observe the pain your human body will suffer."

Obediently, Dianthe travelled through time and arrived on a pathway leading to the top of a small hill called "Golgotha," located a short distance outside the Jerusalem city wall. Dianthe was dressed in a hooded cloak that concealed her identity. She climbed the hill and merged inconspicuously into the small crowd that had come to witness Jesus's execution.

A gray, angry sky hung over the city, and a foul odor lingered over the hill. For years, the Romans had used Golgotha, which translates as "the skull," to crucify the condemned. If an appropriate bribe was paid or other special arrangements made, those executed were taken down from their crosses and given a proper burial. If not, their bodies remained nailed to their crosses until their rotting remains fell to the ground. Roman execution details often kicked human skulls and large bones down the hill to clear a place to rest until their day's work was done. Nonetheless, the top of Golgotha was covered with small bones and other remnants of human life.

When Dianthe arrived at the top of the hill, she saw that two men had already been nailed to wooden crosses. One, a small man, alternated between screaming in agony and complaining that he was a victim of injustice. The other, a larger man, quietly moaned in anguish. He seemed to be praying for forgiveness for the sins that had brought him to this end.

Jesus stood off to the side of the pathway, alone, waiting to be crucified. His cloak rested on his shoulders. Thorns made into a crown had been jammed into his brow, and his face and neck were stained with dried blood. A large wooden cross lay on the ground.

Balbus, a stocky, scarred, middle-aged Roman soldier wearing an off-white, blood-stained woolen tunic, ordered the only child of the Father to lie on the cross with arms outstretched. Jesus, in a mild form of shock, meekly complied. Balbus roughly tied Jesus's arms to the cross beam with a coarse rope. He ordered two of his men—Aelius and Lukas—to hold Jesus's right hand against the cross beam so his hand wouldn't move.

"Get a spike and bring it here," Balbus yelled to Gaius, a young soldier who had been rescued from fighting in wars in Northern Europe by an influential Roman relative. Gaius was also dressed in a tunic, but his was of a finer wool, more suitable for warmer climates.

Gaius picked up a seven-inch iron spike that was lying on the ground and offered it to Balbus. Instead of accepting the spike, Balbus handed a heavy hammer to Gaius, saying, "Here, you're going to do this one."

"But I've never done this before," Gaius protested.

"Just do what I tell you."

"I can't do this."

"What's the matter? Afraid because he claims to be a holy man? I've crucified them all—holy men, rabble-rousers, thieves, revolutionaries. The nails go through them all the same."

Aelius and Lukas both laughed.

"Shove the spike through his hand into the wood," Balbus ordered. "Start right where I'm pointing. At the base of his thumb."

This was Gaius's first execution detail. He was nauseous after watching the other two condemned men being nailed to their crosses. He was trying hard not to give in to his weak stomach—the Roman Army did not look kindly on signs of weakness from its soldiers—but the sheer inhumanity of nailing a human being to a wooden cross was taking its toll, not only on the two men already crucified, but on Gaius as well.

The young soldier forced himself to place the iron spike's sharp point where Balbus was pointing.

"Now, push it through his hand into the wood so his hand won't move when you hammer it," Balbus said.

Gaius pushed the nail, so it barely pricked the skin on Jesus's hand.

Balbus let out a disgusted grunt. He shoved Gaius aside and then put all his weight behind the spike and pushed it through Jesus's hand until it came to rest against the wooden crossbeam.

Jesus moaned.

"Now quick, hammer it," Balbus ordered.

Gaius struck the nail with the heavy hammer and the spike was driven deep into the soft cedar wood. This procedure was repeated for the left hand.

"Now this is the tricky part—nailing the feet," Balbus said. "If you make a mess of this, you won't be able to nail the feet so they stay fastened to the cross. You understand?"

Gaius nodded that he did.

Balbus grabbed Jesus's left leg and placed it on a small platform that had previously been nailed to the cross. Aelius held the left foot against the platform while Balbus placed Jesus's right foot on top of his left. After checking to see that the feet were correctly aligned, one on top of the other, Balbus drove the spike through both feet using all his weight and strength. The spike came to rest against the wooded platform. Jesus cried out in pain.

"Quick, drive the nail home," Balbus demanded. Gaius did so, and the nail went through the wooden platform into the cross.

Gaius turned pale. He could no longer control himself. He fell to his knees and began vomiting.

"You're a disgrace to the Roman Army," Balbus said. He ordered Aelius and Lukas to lift the top of the cross and drag it to a previously-dug hole. Using a rope tied to the top of the cross, the other two executioners pulled the cross up to a vertical position while Balbus held the base steady until it fell into the hole with a thud. Jesus cried out in anguish, as the weight of his human body strained against the nails and rope.

Jesus said in a whispered voice, "Father, forgive them for they know not what they are doing."

Dianthe carefully watched every detail of the crucifixion. She vicariously felt the pain as each nail was hammered into the cross. She became sick to her stomach and weak, unable to watch her own execution. She turned away from the three crosses and faced the city wall while trying to compose herself.

The Father, who had been watching the execution through Dianthe's eyes, admonished her, "Don't turn away. You need to see how your proposed entrance into this universe would end."

Dianthe obediently returned her attention to the three crosses.

After crucifying Jesus, his executioners cast lots for his clothes. Balbus took a small leather bag from his pack. The bag contained three stones, each polished and marked with a Roman symbol: One stone was marked with the symbol for the sun, another for Earth, and the third for Mars. Balbus laid the stones out in front of his subordinates. Then, in order of rank, each soldier selected a stone. As the senior member of the detail, Balbus chose first. He selected the stone marked for Mars, which had a distinctive oblong shape. Then Aelius and Lukas selected a stone. Balbus put the stones back into the leather bag. He shook the bag, turned it upside down, and opened the bag slightly. The stone marked for Mars fell to the ground

"I'll take the sandals, mine are falling apart," Balbus said.

"Funny how the stone you select is often the first to fall," Aelius said.

"Are you saying I cheated?" Balbus said in a threatening voice, while placing his right hand on his dagger.

Aelius had no desire to challenge the battle-hardened Balbus. "Not at all," he said. "I'm simply congratulating you on your good luck."

Balbus smiled but said nothing.

A crowd had gathered at the execution site. It contained the usual number of homeless, dirty, malodorous street people who came to every execution hoping to witness some entertaining event marking the end of a human life. But this crowd was larger than usual; it included priests and Pharisees, who stood as far away from these street lowlifes as they could.

After Jesus was crucified, several priests and Pharisees came forward to taunt him. "If you are the son of God, come down from the cross, and we will believe," they sneered.

Emboldened by the example of these religious leaders, Jesse, one of the street people, came forward to taunt Jesus. He had overheard several priests say that the sign nailed to the top of the cross identified Jesus as the "King of the Jews." Pretending he could read the sign, Jesse scoffed, "King of the Jews. Some king you are. Don't you know the only kings around here are the ones the Romans pick. Are you stupid or something?"

Jesus looked down at Jesse. Despite his pain, he smiled. The expression on his face was one of kindness, compassion, and empathy. It said, "I understand your fear and frustration. I understand what it means to be despised by everyone around you. But you are not despised by everyone. I love you."

That was not the reaction Jesse expected from someone experiencing an agonizing death. Jesse fell back, as if knocked off his feet by an unseen force. He quickly scrambled back to his feet, all the while staring at Jesus. He mouthed the words, "Who are you? Are you really the son of God?"

Wonder and then fear gripped Jesse. He turned and ran to the nearest city gate. Before passing through it, he turned back to the three crosses and mouthed the words, "Forgive me, Holy One."

Mary, Jesus's mother, and Mary Magdalene, a long-time member of Jesus's inner circle, stood in the background and looked on in horror as human life slowly left their Lord. His mother was dumbfounded as she tried to understand what had gone wrong. It was not supposed to end like this. Her son was not supposed to be beaten until he was virtually unrecognizable and then nailed to a wooden cross like a common criminal. She had personally witnessed his powers; she knew they were real. And now he meekly hung on a cross waiting to die. She prayed for her son to come down from the cross and start his earthly rule.

John, the only disciple of Jesus who dared come to Golgotha, stood silently before the cross, eyes riveted on his Lord. "How could it end like this?" he wondered. "Where are all the people Jesus healed? Where are the people who lined the streets of Jerusalem, cheering and laying down palms just a few days earlier?"

During Jesus's thirty-three years, four months, and three days in the material world, he would supply a major portion of the energy needed to power the experiment that would test where the traitors would spend eternity. He had taught through sermons and demonstrated by his actions the way to salvation. But now, his mission in the material world was almost complete. Human death was near. He was weak. He had lost much of his energy. His mind was spinning out of rational thought. In his confusion, he cried out, "My God, my God, why have you forsaken me?" Then peace came upon him, and he whispered, "It is finished." His bloody head fell forward, and human life left him.

The soldiers had been ordered to ensure that the three crucified men were dead and taken down from their crosses before the beginning of a special Sabbath. At about 4:00 p.m., Balbus used a heavy hammer with a long handle to break the legs of the other two men, but when he got to Jesus, he said, "This one's already dead." To be sure, he picked up his spear and drove it into Jesus's side, through the pericardium sac that surrounds the heart and into the heart itself. Jesus's body did not move. The ultimate sacrifice was already complete.

Dianthe wandered around Golgotha waiting for the crowd to disperse so she could return to the Father, unseen. She was disoriented and in a state of shock. For the first time and in vivid detail, she had witnessed what she would have to endure to enter the material world to teach the defectors the path to salvation. She now also understood the level of human depravity reached by at least some of the defectors, having observed it firsthand in her own horrific execution. She was saddened and depressed, and that is how she returned to the Father's side.

In a stern voice, the Father said, "Now you know what crucifixion would be like. Whatever gave you the idea that I would allow this—that I would allow my only child, my precious daughter, part of the triumvirate that rules the universes, to be brutalized with the most painful human death possible at the hands of those who betrayed us? Like an indulgent father, I have always given you what you asked. But now, you ask too much. I will never agree to this!"

This last sentence was spoken with a determination and

intensity the Primary Universe had never witnessed before. When the Father finished, everything in the Primary Universe came to an abrupt stop. Time, literally, stood still. From the largest stars and planets to the smallest electron; every life-form, every moving particle in existence stopped, awaiting the Father's next words.

Dianthe trembled from the Father's powerful admonition and from witnessing her own bloody sacrifice on the cross.

"And what do you think this painful human death would accomplish?" the Father demanded. "Surely, most traitors will view your crucifixion as evidence of your frailty, not your love. You saw the religious leaders mocking you while you hung on that cross. Entering the material world is such a preposterous idea, I can't believe you ever harbored it."

"The prisoners who carry a live seed will see my crucifixion as a great sacrifice made on their behalf, a sacrifice neither earned nor deserved but given out of love and grace," Dianthe gently replied. "They will see my death as dramatic evidence of IAM's boundless love for his children. They will marvel that the ruler of all existence would allow his only child to enter the material world and be put to death for showing them the way to salvation. Yes, those in whom the seed has died will look at my crucifixion as a sign of weakness, the end of a political rabble-rouser who was punished according to the legal customs of the day. In this way, my sacrifice will be consistent with your test design: That the evidence of IAM's existence be evenly balanced with the evidence that there is no creator."

The Father looked at Serenious and said, "Please say you don't agree with that."

"Forgive me, Excellency, but I believe this is Dianthe's decision to make, not yours and not mine," Serenious replied.

"Dianthe, why can't your life in this material world be a little less dramatic? No miracles, no sermons, no confrontations with religious authorities, no triumphant entry into Jerusalem. Just spend your days as a carpenter and let your energy flow into this new universe during your human lifetime without incident," the Father asked.

"Hasatan would not allow that to happen," Dianthe replied. "He would provoke a confrontation that revealed who I am and why I entered this world."

"Dianthe is right about that," Serenious said.

"There is another problem with your crucifixion," the Father said. "Just before your human death, you would be weak and confused. Your human side would be dominant. You would no longer fully understand the true nature of your mission. If your human death occurred in an obscure location away from Jerusalem, Hasatan might not find you because of your low power level. But if you are crucified on Golgotha, just outside Jerusalem's city wall, Hasatan surely would find you. If he attacked you on that cross, I would have to terminate this trial and return all the traitors to Hasatan's control."

"Why would Hasatan attack me when I am close to human death and my power reserves are very low?" Dianthe asked. "What would that gain him?"

"Predicting Hasatan's actions has never been a useful exercise," the Father said. "But if he thought he could destroy you by overwhelming you with negative energy in your weakened condition, he might try if for no other reason than to take revenge on IAM for successfully resisting his attack."

"Can this test be designed to avoid my crucifixion?" Dianthe asked.

"Unfortunately, not. To prevent the Romans from executing you in this painful way, we would need to radically change the thinking of the many influential deserters who will help determine your human fate. That could not be accomplished without undermining the test's validity," Serenious explained. "I'm sorry Dianthe, but if you enter the material world as you propose, you will be crucified."

"I understand," Dianthe said stoically, "but I feel I must do everything in my power to give Teresa and prisoners like her, who are now suffering at Hasatan's hands, a chance to come home, a chance to regain paradise. Father, I know my entrance into this material world poses challenges, but I say again, whatever problems it creates can be managed."

Turning toward Serenious, the Father asked, "Do you agree?"

"I do," Serenious replied.

The Father looked at Dianthe with a father's loving eyes. He saw her innocence and her determination to bring loyal life-forms back to their kingdom. In a voice that was barely audible, he said with obvious sadness in his voice, "If this is what you feel you must do, I will send you into this material world, even though it means you will be crucified. But I will not watch you suffer on that cross."

Dianthe's smiled: "Thank you, Father. I am grateful for your love and your trust. I will do my best to honor both."

The Father smiled but said nothing.

After this discussion, the Father, Serenious, and Dianthe went their separate ways. The Father returned to his personal chambers. The images of Dianthe's future crucifixion stuck in his mind. Everywhere he looked—at the artwork on his walls, at the stars and planets outside his window, at the images in his memory bank of Dianthe as a young life-form—he saw his precious daughter bleeding and dying on a rough wooden cross. He tried to will away that image, but it persisted in his consciousness. Finally, the most powerful force that ever was, is now, or ever will be, simply bowed his head and wept.

8.

Later that same day, when the three persons of IAM were again together in their common chambers, Dianthe said, "Father, my crucifixion and human death will bring despair to my earthly followers."

"It most certainly will," the Father replied.

"To minimize that harm, I would like to be repowered and brought out of my dormant state within three Earth days of my sacrifice," Dianthe said.

"Why so soon?"

"So, I can quickly show my Earthly followers that I rose from the dead as I promised I would."

"We cannot restore you to your present condition in three Earth days, but we can restore you to a form your followers will recognize in that short period of time."

"That would suffice."

"Do you have your resurrection planned out?"

"I do. Please observe through my eyes."

Dianthe transported herself through time to the first day of the week following the crucifixion. She materialized behind a hedge in a small garden that contained the tomb where Jesus's body had been laid. The tomb was owned by Joseph of Arimathea, a wealthy man and an admirer of Jesus. The time was an hour before dawn.

Four Roman soldiers were in the garden. Their assignment was to ensure that no one broke into the tomb and carried away Jesus's body. While three soldiers slept, Marcus, the junior member of the detail, wearily paced back and forth in front of a large circular stone that covered the tomb's entrance. It was a clear night; the sky was filled with bright stars. There was a gentle breeze from the east.

To pass the time, Marcus kept repeating to himself an epic poem about a brave Roman soldier who died to protect the honor of his family name and to protect Rome from hostile invaders from the north. He had learned the poem as a young boy, and he repeated it on occasions like this when he was alone with his own thoughts.

Suddenly, the ground below Marcus's feet began to quake. Out of the corner of his eye, he saw the stone covering the entranceway to the tomb begin to move. He ran to the stone and pushed against it. But it kept moving. He planted his feet against the root of a nearby tree and pushed against the stone with all his strength. But it continued to move.

"Wake up," he screamed to the other soldiers, "and help me!"

Soon, all four soldiers were pushing against the stone, but it kept moving anyway. When it had moved enough to reveal the inside of the burial chamber, the soldiers could see a bright light coming from inside the tomb.

"What's that?" Marcus yelled.

"The holy one has come back to life to avenge his death on us," another soldier replied.

That thought caused the soldiers to panic. They ran out of the garden, leaving their swords and shields behind.

Later, just after dawn, three women—Mary Magdalene and two of her friends—entered the garden. They were carrying spices and perfumes to anoint Jesus's body. When they arrived at the tomb, the stone that had covered the entrance was lying on its side several paces from the tomb's opening.

Cautiously, the women peered into the tomb and saw an angel, a human-like figure with a golden complexion wearing a brilliant white robe. The angel was sitting on the stone where Jesus's body had been laid.

"You are looking for Jesus," the angel said. "He is not here. He is risen and is with the living, not the dead. Go and tell his disciples."

The frightened women ran out of the garden. Mary Magdalene ran a short distance and then stopped. She knew this was good news: Her Lord had risen from the dead. But the confusing, emotionally draining events of the last several days finally caught up with her, and she sat down and began to cry.

As she wept, a hooded figure approached her. "Woman, why are you crying?" the figure asked.

Assuming it was the gardener, Mary responded, "If you have taken my Lord's body, please tell me where you have laid him."

The figure replied simply, "Mary."

She instantly recognized the voice. There was only one like it. "Teacher," she called out.

Mary reached out to embrace her Lord.

"Do not touch me, Mary. My power is at a high level. If you touch me, you will suffer harm. Instead, go tell Peter and the others not to despair, that I have risen from the dead as I said I would."

Later that same day, Jesus's disciples, except for Judas and Thomas, huddled together in a large room behind a locked door. They were terrified that the authorities might be searching for them and that they also would soon be arrested and sentenced to die by crucifixion.

Suddenly, a brilliant light appeared in the room. Jesus stepped out of the light. Wearing a dazzling white robe, he appeared in human form with a golden complexion and well-groomed hair and beard.

"Do not be afraid," he said. "The scriptures have now been fulfilled by my death and resurrection."

Jesus explained that he was sending the disciples out into the world to explain the way of salvation to all who would listen. He breathed on the disciples, conveying the power of Serenious's guidance to them, and then disappeared.

Later that same day, Thomas rejoined the group. When told that Jesus had appeared to the disciples, Thomas replied, "Until I put my finger where the nails pierced his hands and put my hand into his side where the spear was run through, I will not believe."

A week later, the disciples, including Thomas, were in the same locked room. Jesus appeared to them again, and this time he sought out Thomas. Holding out his hands, Jesus said, "Put your finger in the holes left by the nails." Opening his robe, he said, "And put your hand into my side and feel the wound left by the spear."

Thomas fell to his knees and cried out, "My Lord and my God!"

Jesus said to the disciples, "Thomas believes because he has seen the print of the nails and the mark left by the spear. Blessed are those who have not seen these things but yet believe."

Jesus then disappeared from the room and returned to the Father's side.

"Do you want to appear to anyone else?" the Father asked.

"Yes," Dianthe replied. She then transported herself to the road that led from Jerusalem to Emmaus, a small town located seven miles northeast of Jerusalem. The time was late afternoon of the first Sunday following the crucifixion. Two followers of Jesus, Cleopas and Alphaeus, were walking on the road toward Emmaus. They had heard rumors that Jesus had risen from the dead, but the last few days were so confusing and chaotic, they didn't know what to believe. Dianthe assumed the identity of Jesus. Wearing an outer garment with a hood that covered his head and concealed his identity, Jesus came up from behind the two men and joined them.

"What are you discussing?" he asked.

"The recent events in Jerusalem," Cleopas replied.

"What events?"

"Have you just come from Jerusalem and are not aware of the events that occurred there?" Alphaeus said.

The hooded stranger shrugged his shoulders but did not reply.

"Jesus of Nazareth, a prophet powerful in word and deed, was handed over to the Romans, who crucified him," Cleopas said. "We had hoped he would free Judea from Roman oppression, but obviously that was not to be. But this very morning, the city was alive with rumors that Jesus had risen from the dead and appeared to several people."

"We don't know what to make of this," Alphaeus added.

The hooded man explained that the prophets had foretold Jesus's death and resurrection, and he rebuked the two men for not paying sufficient attention to scripture.

When the three men reached Emmaus, Cleopas said to the stranger, "The day is almost spent. Stay the night with us. You are obviously a man of great learning. We want to hear more of your teachings. You can continue your journey tomorrow."

The stranger agreed to stay the night.

Later, the three men sat at a table in Cleopas's home. When servants brought fish and bread, the stranger took the bread, gave thanks, broke it, and gave it to his hosts. He then removed the hood that covered his head. Alphaeus and Cleopas instantly recognized Jesus. They fell to their knees. Cleopas called out, "My Lord and my King!" Jesus smiled and then disappeared.

"We must hurry back to Jerusalem and tell the disciples that we have seen the Lord," Cleopas said.

The Father, who was observing these events through Dianthe's eyes, asked his daughter, "Do you want to appear to anyone else?"

"Yes, I want to appear to several others, but one of these is special to me."

Dianthe transported herself to a garden next to the Roman barracks in Jerusalem. It was late in the evening of the fifth day after Jesus's crucifixion. Gaius, the young soldier who had helped crucify Jesus, sat alone on a bench, reflecting on the crucifixion and the events that had followed.

The four soldiers who had run away from the tomb had each received twenty lashes for deserting their post. They were nearly executed. What saved them from a painful death was that they all told the same story, down to the smallest detail about the ground quaking, the stone moving, and a bright light shining from inside the tomb. And they told that story with an intensity and sincerity that was impossible to dismiss.

When the four soldiers returned to their quarters, the barracks came alive with discussions about the meaning of the events at the tomb. Each soldier had his own theory about what these events meant, and these theories ranged from the imaginative to the fantastic. All four soldiers believed that Jesus must have been a holy man, perhaps a prophet. Balbus did not. He maintained that the guards' story was a well-rehearsed, self-serving fantasy concocted by the soldiers to explain away abandoning their post, and that Jesus was nothing more than a backwoods troublemaker who had met an appropriate end.

Gaius did not know what to think. He continued to wonder if he had helped crucify a holy man and if the gods would punish him for this wicked act. As he sat on a bench, his head throbbed with guilt and fear. Unable to eat a full meal since the crucifixion, he felt weak. He had hoped these miseries would disappear as the days moved on, but his suffering had only increased. Feeling the need to wretch, he fell to his knees, but there was nothing in his stomach to bring up. Knowing he could not go on like this, he resolved to do the honorable Roman thing: If his condition did not improve by tomorrow, he would take his own life.

As he stared at the ground in front of him, it suddenly became bright as if it were midday. He looked up and saw Jesus, again in a glorified form. Gaius was overcome with fear. He assumed that Jesus had come to punish him, perhaps with an excruciating death, as payback for Jesus's painful crucifixion. Gaius tried to crawl away. "Do not be afraid, Gaius" Jesus said. "I came to forgive you, not to punish you. You were part of a plan conceived in heaven many years ago. You played your assigned role as best you could. It was a difficult role for you. You are a kind and gentle person, and in your own way, you showed kindness to me. I will always remember that."

Gaius was too awestruck to speak. He trembled with fear. His only response to Jesus's words was a nod to acknowledge that he had heard them.

"And Gaius, do not take your own life. Live and tell your descendants that I have blessed you and them," Jesus said.

These words finally brought peace to Gaius, and he regained enough composure to say calmly, "Thank you, Holy One."

Jesus smiled and then disappeared.

After Dianthe returned to the palace, Serenious said, "These appearances will be powerful moments that will help spread Dianthe's message of salvation to all peoples. So, I regret having to raise a technical problem with bringing her back to consciousness within a few days of her execution."

"What's the problem?" the Father asked.

"Jesus's body will be wrapped in a burial shroud. Repowering the body in that short period of time will require sending a large amount of energy through the burial cloth. That transmission will burn an image of the body into the shroud, providing evidence of a connection to an extraterrestrial power source."

"That would be a problem," the Father said.

"But there is a solution," Serenious said. "After Dianthe leaves the tomb, I will tinker with the shroud, so its age can never be determined."

"Ah, Serenious always has a solution to any technical problem," the Father said.

9.

The Father's plan to create a material universe in which to test the deserters' loyalty was imaginative, well-thought-out, and complex. And it raised many questions in Dianthe's mind. Those questions took on special significance since she would be entering this new world and interacting with the defectors. She wondered what to expect from them. So, the next day, when she and the Father were together, she asked, "When I'm in the material world, will I be able to tell which of the prisoners retains a live seed?"

"If a defector with a live seed is in your immediate presence, you'll sense its power," the Father replied.

"And if the prisoner is not in my presence?"

"There will be another sign."

"What will that be?"

"Prisoners with a live seed will show the ability to love others; actually, they will show the ability to love something besides themselves."

"That's it, the ability to love others?"

"In most cases, those in whom the seed has died will love themselves above all else. But those carrying a live seed, even if it is weak, will feel compelled to care for others, to put others first, to sacrifice for others if that becomes necessary."

The Father opened a hologram. The date was the fourteenth day of the fourth month of Earth year 4,543,763,901 (April 14, 1912). The RMS Titanic, the largest, most luxurious passenger ship of its day, was steaming across the North Atlantic at a high rate of speed, given its location—an area where icebergs were frequently sighted. The Titanic was on its maiden voyage. It had left Southampton, England, four days before en route to New York City. Aboard were 913 crew members and 1,317 passengers, including some of the world's most wealthy and prominent citizens. The Titanic was said to be unsinkable. It had sixteen watertight compartments that could be sealed off with remote-controlled doors to retain the ship's buoyancy, if that became necessary.

The evening of April 14 was clear, with light winds. The moon was bright, the ocean glassy calm, the sky filled with stars. Visibility was excellent. The clock on the highly-varnished center console in the ship's bridge struck 23:39 hours when lookout Frederick Fleet cried out, "Iceberg, right ahead!" Robert Hitchens, an experienced helmsman, immediately turned the ship to port. The 883-foot ship turned but not quickly enough given its high rate of speed. The Titanic collided with an iceberg that ripped a gaping hole in its starboard side. Seawater poured into five of the watertight compartments. The Titanic was constructed to remain afloat if up to four compartments flooded. A fifth compartment flooding with seawater meant the ship was doomed.

Because the Titanic was thought to be unsinkable, it carried only twenty lifeboats, enough for only half of its passengers and crew. And its crew was not well-trained in lifeboat procedures. The result was predictable: After the ship struck the iceberg, chaos ruled. Most of the lifeboats were not filled to capacity before being lowered into the ocean. Lifeboat 1, with a capacity of forty passengers, was lowered with only twelve people aboard. Lifeboat 7, with a capacity of sixty-five passengers, carried only twenty-four. When the last lifeboat was ready to be lowered, it was almost full; one empty seat remained.

Harold, an elegantly dressed first-class passenger and a prominent businessman from Chicago, Illinois, was about to climb on board that last lifeboat. His wife, Clara, dressed in nightclothes under a pink, embroidered silk robe, was already on board, sitting three rows back from the bow on the starboard side. Before Harold could climb aboard, Roxanne, a young woman with a third-class ticket, ran up to the lifeboat. Her washed-out dress was low cut, revealing an ample bosom. She reeked of alcohol and had difficulty pronouncing words.

"I've got two little children that need me," she screamed in a Cockney accent. "Let me on this boat." That was a half-truth. She did have two little children by two different lovers, but she had left her children in London with relatives and run off with a third man who promised to take her to America.

"She's not a mother; she's a tart," Clara observed. "Look at how she's dressed."

Harold stood still, as if frozen by the winter chill of the North Atlantic.

"Harold, get in this boat!" Clara demanded. "You can't sacrifice yourself for the likes of her! You have three children who need you! I need you!"

"I'll find another lifeboat," Harold replied. "The rule is: women and children first. I couldn't live with myself if I didn't give her that seat."

"Harold, look around!" Clara screamed. "There are no more lifeboats! They've all been launched. You'll die if you don't get on this boat."

"And if I do take this last seat, she'll die," Harold replied.

The other passengers in the lifeboat stared at Harold, wondering what he would do. The ship suddenly lurched as waves began to wash over the Titanic's bow. An older woman seated in the stern of the lifeboat yelled, "Oh, for God's sake, lower this boat before we all drown!"

Harold said nothing. He stepped aside so Roxanne could board. His face showed a strange mixture of fear and satisfaction.

The young woman passed by him without so much as a smile or a thank you. She sat down next to Clara, who moved as far away from her unwelcome fellow passenger as she could.

The crew member in charge of the lifeboat yelled, "Lower away!" The huge vessel lurched again as the bow sank below the ocean surface. The crew quickly lowered the lifeboat.

"Harold, my poor brave Harold," his wife sobbed. "He will never see his children grow up. He will never see his grandchildren. Why does he have to be so brave?"

Harold frantically searched the ship for another lifeboat, but Clara was right. They had all been launched. By then, Harold knew he was not going to survive. But a strange thing happened. Feelings of panic left him. He became calm and serene amid the pandemonium that surrounded him. A young seaman with a panicky look on his face approached and grabbed the handrail near where Harold had positioned himself.

"We will soon see our creator," Harold said, putting his arm around the seaman. "Will you pray with me?"

The young seaman nodded in the affirmative.

"Heavenly Father," Harold began, "we thank you for all the blessings you have given us during our lifetimes: Family, friends, good health, good fortune, the beauty of ocean sunrises and sunsets, but foremost, our faith in you. Thank you for parents who shared their faith with us."

As the bow continued to sink below the ocean's surface, the giant vessel's stern continued to rise. Now the stern was at a forty-degree angle to the water. Harold and the seaman had wedged themselves behind an upright metal stanchion that was part of the railing system, so they were able to keep from falling forward. Others were not so fortunate. Many who had been holding onto the stern railing lost their grip. Screaming in terror, they slid down the main deck toward the submerged bow and then either fell into the Atlantic or smashed into structures forward that were not yet submerged.

A young frightened mother, carrying an infant, tumbled toward Harold. He reached out to grab her, but her body was several inches beyond his reach. He watched the young woman descend the length of the ship and smash into a railing near the bow with great force. The child flew out of its mother's arms into the sea, while the mother's broken body jammed into the railing. Harold, a devout Catholic, exclaimed, "Oh, my God," and then crossed himself. He continued his prayer.

"If it be your will, Father, let us both somehow survive this disaster. If not, please be with us. Let the end come quickly. Please be with everyone who remains onboard this ship. And although none of us is deserving, bring us all home to eternal salvation. We pray for those who will live on after us—our families and friends. Let them accept our departure without bitterness. Help them lead successful lives according to your will. And when their time comes, let us be reunited with them in heaven."

Dianthe stared intently at the image. "Did you feel a power surge?" she asked Serenious.

"I did," Serenious replied. "And it came from within the hologram. You know, there's something odd about the seaman crouching next to Harold. He is a little too perfect for that role."

At 02:20 hours, April 15, 1912, approximately two hours and forty minutes after striking the iceberg, the large ship lost buoyancy. It began to sink, slowly at first and then rapidly, its bow knifing through the water on the way to its final resting place at the bottom of the Atlantic. Just before the water reached Harold, the young seaman changed his appearance. His clothes became a gleaming white robe, his hair became wispy white, his eyes became brilliant spotlights of pure energy. The seaman had transformed into the Father.

"Harold, today you will be with me in paradise," the Father said, as he carried Harold up toward heaven moments before the ship's stern slipped below the ocean waters.

The hologram closed, and the Father rejoined Dianthe and Serenious.

"A well-to-do man willing to sacrifice his life for a stranger of a lower social class," Dianthe said. "That is a beautiful demonstration of love for others. Surely, his seed is alive."

"It would appear so," the Father said. "Harold will not want to sacrifice himself. But defectors carrying a live seed will find it difficult to turn away from others in need."

"Harold deserves credit for a brave, sacrificial act," Dianthe said. "But looking at his life before this fateful event, I see he'll not live a life consistent with IAM's principles. He will enter into some questionable business deals, and on occasion, lie to his business associates and customers. He will violate many of your rules, yet you intend to bring him back to our kingdom. Tell me again: What criteria will be used to judge these prisoners?"

"There will only be one criterion: If prisoners demonstrate that they are loyal to IAM—that they believe in IAM and look to us for salvation—I will bring them home," the Father said.

"That's all?" Dianthe asked.

"That's all."

This answer gave Dianthe comfort. It was in line with her own thinking about what the test for salvation should be. Dianthe then asked a related question: "Will I be able to recognize a prisoner whose seed has died?"

"If that prisoner is in your presence, you'll sense the seed's absence," the Father said.

"And if the prisoner is not in my presence?"

"Be wary of prisoners who delight in finding fault in others and condemning others for their failings," the Father replied. "If their principal concern is their own comfort, prestige, and authority, if sacrificing for others makes no sense to them, they probably no longer carry a live seed. Consider this."

A hologram appeared. The time was 6:30 pm on the twentieth day of the twelfth month of Earth year 4,543,763,930 (December 20, 1941). The place was Chelmno, a small town along the Ner River in German-occupied Poland. On the outskirts of town, a German SS unit had built a facility to murder large numbers of Jews and other "undesirables" as part of the Third Reich's "final solution" to ethnic impurity.

The hologram focused on the modest, two-bedroom temporary home of Otto and Frieda Hess. The home was spotlessly clean and orderly, the coffee cups in the cupboard stood in a perfect line, the books in the bookshelf were neatly arranged in descending order, from the largest volumes on the right to the smallest on the left. The home and its contents were a metaphor for an orderly world that may have existed in Poland prior to the German occupation but no longer existed in late 1941.

Otto sat at a dining room table, hunched over a stack of papers. He looked out of place in his Nazi SS uniform, which was several sizes too big for him. Forty-five years old, Otto was a German businessman from Lodz, Poland, a small city south of Chelmno. He had been temporarily impressed into the SS unit at Chelmno because of his accounting skills.

Otto's German ancestors had lived in Lodz for more than one hundred fifty years. In 1941, the family operated several businesses in the city, including a bank, a dry goods store, and a bakery. Otto's uncle, Frederick, ran these family businesses. To build good will with the German occupiers, Frederick had arranged for an early Christmas banquet for senior German officers stationed in and around the city. At the banquet, held on Saturday, December 13, it was Otto's misfortune to sit next to Colonel Herbert Lange, the Chelmno Camp Commander. Lange was desperate to find someone who could prepare accurate reports to send to Berlin on the number of persons murdered each day at Chelmno.

After a few glasses of wine, the otherwise reticent Otto began bragging about his accounting skills, saying he could design an accounting system for any need. When Lange heard this, he thought he might have found the solution to his problem. He informed Otto that he was being given the honor of temporarily serving in the German Army and participating in the Fuhrer's quest to build a superior race that would someday rule the world. He also informed Otto that a staff car would be at his home at noon the next day to take Otto, Frieda, and a few belongings to Chelmno.

The Nazis were obsessive recordkeepers. By design, they did not keep official records on the number of people killed in their death camps, because they did not want that information to become part of Third Reich history. Since Chelmno was exclusively a death camp, the camp staff did not include anyone with accounting skills, and there were no written procedures describing what information should be included in the death reports that were not to be kept.

Because Chelmno was the first death camp in Poland to attempt murder on a large scale, Reichsführer Heinrich Himmler and the Führer, himself, wanted accurate and detailed information about the camp's capacity to kill prisoners and dispose of their remains. Lange was ordered to report such information to Berlin on a daily basis. He prepared his reports using information provided by his staff. Berlin sent several of these reports back to Lange, saying they were "insufficient in detail" and in some places "inconsistent with other data," such as the capacity of trains bringing prisoners to Chelmno. Lange was told that Berlin was losing patience with his performance and that he had better find someone who could prepare accurate and complete reports, or he would soon find himself at the Russian Front.

When Otto arrived at Chelmno, Lange explained the purpose of the camp, and he gave Otto copies of his initial reports and Berlin's responses. Otto was shocked and nauseated at the mass murder of innocents, and he summoned the courage to tell Lange that under no circumstance would he participate in this atrocity. But Lange was a desperate man determined not to experience the harshness of the Russian winter. He told Otto that if he refused to help the SS, Otto's extended family would be taken into custody and that each day he remained uncooperative, one of his family members would be hanged, beginning with the youngest child. Lange also told Otto that he must not disclose information about the camp to anyone and that if he violated that order, Lange would personally cut Frieda's heart out of her body in Otto's presence before killing him.

Lydia was Otto's favorite niece. She was a beautiful four-year-old girl who called him "Uncle Ottie." In his mind's eye, he saw his niece bravely standing on a scaffold, handing her executioner her favorite doll and making him promise that he would take care of it. The hangman placed a noose around the girl's little neck and pulled the rope tight. The trap door opened, and the little girl fell out of sight.

The image was too much for Otto, and he began to cry.

"Spare me the emotions," Lange said. "Just tell me you'll do it."

"Yes, I will do it," Otto replied, "and may you burn in hell for this."

Otto worked late every evening preparing detailed reports on the number of prisoners killed at the camp each day. The numbers were broken down into categories—sex, age group, Jews and non-Jews, time required to receive and process incoming prisoners, time required to gas them and incinerate their remains, valuables collected (including gold fillings), and other information that Berlin wanted. He also prepared a cover letter summarizing the pertinent details for Himmler and the Führer. These documents were carried by special courier to the nearest airfield and then flown directly to Berlin each morning.

On the evening of December 20, Frieda, dressed in a dowdy housedress, was cooking dinner. Frieda did not know what the SS was doing at Chelmno or how Otto fit into the operation. Otto told her he was keeping records on military equipment. Frieda was cooking a meat-and-vegetable stew, whose sweet aroma filled the small house, when a young man in his mid-twenties burst through the front door without knocking. It was the couple's only son, Frederick.

Frederick resembled the perfect Aryan: He stood more than six feet two inches tall, with a narrow waist and broad shoulders. He had muscular arms from years spent as a member of a rowing club. His thick blond hair had a slight curl that gave his appearance an artistic flair. His blue eyes dominated handsome facial features, and he possessed a warm and welcoming smile that charmed everyone he met. He carried himself erect, his head held high, and he walked with a slight swagger, like the knights and noblemen who once ruled this part of Northern Europe.

Ever since their son's birth, Frieda and Otto had idolized Frederick and shamelessly doted on him. They lived modestly so they could send him to the best schools in Europe, including Heidelberg University. They hoped someday Frederick would take over the family businesses, and they were alarmed when he, too, was impressed into the German army.

When Frederick came through the door, Frieda rushed to embrace him. Otto was more reserved in his greeting.

"Frederick, what are you doing here, and why aren't you in uniform?" Otto asked. "Did you get permission from your commanding officer to visit us?"

Frederick stared at his Father, surprised to see him wearing an SS uniform. "I have joined the resistance," he replied.

"You have deserted the German army?" Otto said with alarm.

"You heard me."

"The SS run the facility here at Chelmno. If you are captured, you'll be shot. If you are discovered in our home, your mother and I will be shot. If you decided to desert the German Army, why did you come here? And how did you find us?"

"Your neighbor in Lodz, Mrs. Holtzman, told me where you were. I've come here to take pictures to show how the SS is using the three gas vans on the old estate outside of town. My orders are to get the film to the West—to the Americans or the British."

"Why do you want to do that?" Frieda asked.

"Ask your husband. He can tell you," Frederick replied.

"What do you mean, 'Ask your husband?' Otto is your father."

"All right, Father, tell her what the SS is doing with those gas vans."

Otto appeared flustered. He didn't reply.

"What's the matter, Father, lost your voice?"

"Otto, what is he talking about?" Frieda demanded.

"I don't know what he's talking about," Otto insisted.

"My dear father is part of an SS unit that is using those vans to murder Jews. They're killing men, women, even young children. Can you imagine the horror? Little girls holding their dolls being gassed to death?" Frederick said.

Frederick walked toward his father and picked up one of the papers lying on the dining room table. After scanning the document, he said, "He's keeping detailed records for the SS Command in Berlin on the number of Jews killed here each day."

Otto grabbed the paper out of Frederick's hands.

"Otto, is this true?" Frieda asked with a worried voice.

Otto's silence confirmed that it was.

Turning to his mother, Frederick said, "I must leave now. He's right. Being here isn't safe, either for me or for you. But I wanted to see you again, perhaps for the last time."

Frieda began to cry. "Don't say that. Of course, we will see each other again, when this damn war is over," she said.

"I need to go," Frederick said, embracing his mother and gently kissing her on the forehead. He made his way to the front door, opened it slowly to see if anyone was in sight, and then left the cottage without once looking back at his father. As he walked down the front walkway, he was startled by the presence of three figures—the Father, Dianthe, and Serenious— all wearing dark overcoats. Frederick assumed they were SS. He drew his pistol. Pointing it at the three, he demanded, "Who are you, and what do you want?"

"We are not SS, Frederick," the Father said. "We're here to help you."

"I don't need your help."

"Actually, you do. And your father needs help even more. Go back to him. Tell him you love him and want to help him."

"He isn't my father. He's a mass murderer and a monster."

"He's a bookkeeper who was impressed into the SS against his will and ordered to come here. He had no choice. And now, he's trapped."

"Why are you defending him? He's part of a machine that is murdering thousands of innocent men, women, and children. He no longer deserves to be called a human being."

"You are his son, his own flesh and blood. Help him rather than condemn him...before it's too late."

"Get out of my way, you old fool. Can't you see injustice when it's staring you in the face?"

"Very well," the Father said.

As the Father, Dianthe, and Serenious stepped aside to allow Frederick to pass, a single shot rang out from inside the Hess cottage. Seconds later, Frieda burst through the front door; her hands and apron were bloody.

"My Otto has shot himself, my poor Otto has killed himself," she screamed.

Neighbors came running out of their cottages to see what had happened. They tried to console Frieda, but there was no consoling her over the loss of her life partner of twenty-eight years.

"It's just as well," Frederick mumbled to himself. "He didn't deserve to live."

"Frederick, have you no remorse over the death of your own father, the man who sacrificed so much so you would enjoy a good life?" the Father asked.

"I told you, he's not my father." Frederick turned and disappeared into the darkness, and the Father, Dianthe, and Serenious transported themselves back to IAM's palace.

"Dianthe, once you enter this new universe, you will meet many Fredericks," the Father said. "They will pretend to be righteous, but it will be a false righteousness. Their real aim will be to advance themselves by dragging down everyone around them. If you stand in their way, they will trample over you."

"Aren't you being too hard on Frederick?" Dianthe asked. "After all, Otto will help perpetrate one of the greatest crimes in human history. Surely that deserves condemnation."

"Yes, it does. But Otto will be a bookkeeper, not a murderer," the Father explained. "He will also be a kind and clever man, who will take risks to help others. He will convince the camp commander that he needs twenty assistants—Jews who otherwise would be murdered —to collect the data presented in his reports to Berlin. Twenty helpers will be more than needed, but Lange will be so relieved that Otto's reports pleased Berlin that he will go along with Otto's demands. Otto's replacement will no longer carry on this deception, and ten of those who were spared by Otto's actions will die."

"So, you believe Frederick's condemnation of Otto is misplaced?" Dianthe said.

"For those who carry a live seed, love and forgiveness will come before condemnation," the Father said. "Those whose seeds have died will delight in condemning others for their faults and failures. Indeed, they will enjoy seeing others stumble and fall; it will make them feel superior. Hypocrisy is also at work here. Japatha, the prisoner who will occupy Frederick's body, was a leader in the great betrayal. Listen to a conversation that took place between Japatha and Nontin immediately before the great exodus to the Negative Energy Kingdom."

A hologram opened showing Japatha and Nontin in the latter's quarters in the Positive Energy Kingdom.

"Nontin, are you with us or not?" Japatha asked. "You have to decide."

"Yes, I'm with you."

"Well then, why are you hesitating? You should be heading to the Great Divide by now, so you can be processed and then slip over the border at the appropriate time."

"I'm still trying to get comfortable with the idea that, if this revolution succeeds, Hasatan will likely terminate many positive life-forms that have befriended and helped me. I feel I owe them something. They are innocent. They have done nothing wrong."

"But they have done something wrong. They've failed to recognize our superior talent and properly reward us for our contributions to this kingdom. They lack imagination and boldness. They are a timid people who prefer order and stability over fairness and justice. They are an inferior people, and they will have to pay the price for their inferiority. We will soon be the new masters of all universes. We will belong to a special race, a confident, daring people of superior talent and intellect. And you and I will hold high positions and live in luxury in this new kingdom. If a few inferior life-forms must perish for us to achieve that goal, so be it. We can't allow them to stand in the way of our destiny."

"I suppose you're right."

The hologram closed.

"Amazing!" Dianthe said. "Frederick condemns his father for furthering, under duress, the same goals he enthusiastically pursued during the great exodus."

"When you are in the material universe, teach the defectors that they were not put on earth to judge others, but to be judged," the Father said. "In fact, teach them to pray that they be forgiven only as they forgive others."

"Father, the prisoners will not be able to meet that standard. If they pray to be forgiven only as they forgive others, they will be praying themselves back into Hasatan's hell."

"I will not hold them to a standard they cannot meet. But saying that prayer over and over again may help them understand that, if they want to be forgiven for the universe's ultimate sin—turning away from their creator—they must forgive others who sin against them. Also teach them that, while they must forgive the sinner, they must not ignore the sin. Forgiving others does not mean turning a blind eye toward evil."

10.

"Father, during my ministry in this new world, I will have disciples, followers who will pledge their loyalty to me," Dianthe said. "Will I be able to trust them?"

"One of your disciples will betray you," the Father replied. "He will point you out to the authorities who will apprehend you. When that happens, your other disciples will flee. One will deny he ever knew you. Your disciples will come from the deserters' ranks. They are imperfect creatures. You should not be surprised if one of them is disloyal."

"I have not looked forward in time to determine the loyalty of each of my disciples. Who will betray me?"

The Father opened a hologram. The image was of Jesus's twelve disciples sitting around a large table in an austere, second-story room. The time was the day following Jesus's triumphal entrance into Jerusalem, when thousands of cheering citizens had welcomed Jesus and his followers into the city on what would become known as "Palm Sunday." The disciples had just finished their evening meal and were drinking wine. Jesus was not among them. The atmosphere in the room had turned jovial. The disciples were enjoying thoughts of earthly glory, an easier existence, a better life. The conversation turned to which of the twelve would become the greatest disciple.

"Maybe it will be me," said Simon Peter, a tall man with broad shoulders, muscular arms, a masculine face, long unkempt hair, and a full beard. "The Lord, himself, called me a rock and said he will build his church on me."

"Simon, you're headstrong, impetuous, a common man, and a fisherman," said Matthew, a tax collector. "Has anyone ever heard of a fisherman becoming a great leader? You're all habitual liars," he added with a hearty laugh.

"Matthew is right, the future leader of our movement will not be a fisherman," said Andrew, another tall, young, bearded man with a powerful build. "But it won't be a tax collector either. Lying may come naturally to fishermen, but to tax collectors, it is an acquired skill developed only after years of practice."

More laughter rang out. "Perhaps Thomas," Simon Peter said. "He is thoughtful, a critical thinker. He even looks like our Lord. Yes, I'll wager it will be Thomas."

"I am too much the skeptic," replied Thomas, a man with handsome facial features and hair that had recently begun to turn gray. "Perhaps Bartholomew. He is honest and trustworthy. Our movement will need such men to survive."

"I am a simple man who does not aspire to greatness," Bartholomew replied. "No, it will not be me. Perhaps, one of our political activists: either Simon the Zealot or Judas. One of them will be the greatest among us."

"The Zealot is more likely to get us all crucified than to move our movement forward," said Simon Peter. "It will be Judas, handsome and articulate, a patriot who is crafty and wise to the ways of the world. Judas alone among us has the wisdom to navigate between the shoals of Roman arrogance and the Sanhedrin's insecurity."

Andrew stood and shouted, "A toast to Judas. May he lead well!"

The other disciples stood and joined in the toast. Raising their drinking cups, they said in unison, "To Judas."

Judas rose slowly from his chair. He stood out from the others in the room. He was clean shaven and strikingly handsome. He was well groomed and dressed more elegantly than the others. He obviously paid attention to his appearance. Judas clearly enjoyed the accolades coming his way. He smiled and then chose his words carefully: "Thank you for your confidence in me, my brothers. History will tell whether this praise is well deserved."

The group cheered and then went on talking about other subjects. The hologram closed.

"Now do you know who will betray you?" the Father asked.

"The loudmouth Peter seeking power?" Dianthe responded.

"No, not Peter. At a critical time, he will deny you, but he will not betray you."

"Matthew, the tax collector seeking financial reward?"

"No, not Matthew."

"Who then?"

"It will be Judas."

"Judas?" Dianthe repeated the name. "Quiet, thoughtful Judas?"

"Yes, Judas, perhaps too quiet and too thoughtful," the Father replied.

11.

"After my sacrifice, my followers will organize an institution to honor me and preserve my teachings. It will be called the 'Christian Church.' Will it be a positive force in the material world?" Dianthe asked.

"Like all institutions run by defectors, your church will have serious weaknesses," the Father said. "Some church leaders will be full of IAM's love; they will sacrifice for others and be admired for their kindness and compassion. Others will be seduced by Hasatan's angels. They will avoid the hard work it will take to expand your church and, instead, insist on living leisurely lives of luxury in palatial residences filled with fine art and elegant furnishings. They will be full of judgment for those around them and be feared and despised by their parishioners. Their actions will weaken your church."

The Father opened a hologram that scanned the city of Seville, Spain, and came to rest on the Cathedral of Saint Mary of the Sea. When completed, this Cathedral was the largest and most beautiful Christian church building in the world. It was designed to demonstrate Seville's wealth and its dedication to Christian principles. But it was not always used in ways that were true to its designers' intent.

The time was 10:00 a.m. on the fourth day of the tenth month of Earth year 4,543,763,549 (October 4, 1560). A trial, part of the Spanish Inquisition, was about to begin in one of the building's spacious halls. The Inquisition in Spain began as an effort to eliminate heresy and ensure orthodoxy of church doctrine; by 1560, it had become an instrument to repress would-be reformers.

The accused, Juan Vazquez, manacled in iron chains, sat by himself at a table facing a religious court. He was accused of heresy, of being a sympathizer of Martin Luther, who had openly criticized the leadership of the Catholic Church. Vazquez was a wealthy man with large land holdings. He was also a generous man who had given away large sums of money, not only to the church, but also to many in need. He was admired by everyone who knew him. Unfortunately, he was also a candid and trusting soul, and that had led to this trial. In an unguarded moment, Vazquez had written a letter to someone he thought was a friend. In the letter, he said, "I am grateful for the protestant reformers, especially Martin Luther, for their criticisms of our Catholic Church, and I hope their criticisms will bring about reform." The person who received the letter gave it to Archbishop Fernando Arias, the leader of the archdiocese, in hopes that this act of treachery might protect him from becoming the target of a future investigation.

Vazquez's fate was in the hands of two inquisitors—Pedro Garcia and Ferdinand Ortiz—and a *calificador*, Father Juan Diez, whose job it was to determine if the accused's alleged misconduct constituted a crime "against the faith." All three men were church bureaucrats who made up for a lack of intellect and talent with fierce loyalty to the church's hierarchy.

The prosecutor, Juan Mendez, a slender man whose gaunt face continuously wore a sinister smile, seemed well suited to a proceeding that could result in a man being burned alive. By then, Mendez had sent so many accused heretics to their deaths that burning human beings alive had become relatively routine for him. He sat at the prosecutor's table calmly reviewing his notes, waiting for the signal to proceed, which came at exactly 10:05 that morning.

Mendez stood and faced the Inquisition panel. "This is a simple case," he said, "because the evidence of this man's heresy is written in his own hand." Mendez waived Vazquez's letter like a matador trying to attract a bull's attention. After reading the offending parts of Vazquez's letter, he placed it on the table in front of Garcia, Ortiz, and Diez with a dramatic flair. He then invited the three to read it for themselves.

"He does not deny writing this letter," Mendez said. "What more evidence do you need? Vazquez is grateful for the heretics that have struck at the heart of our holy Catholic Church. He is grateful for Martin Luther, who called our holy leader the antichrist. Juan Vazquez is a wealthy man, and wealthy men often think they can do what they want and say what they want. This inquisition must demonstrate that heresy like Vazquez's cannot be tolerated. Do you agree?"

The two inquisitors and the *calificador* nodded in the affirmative.

"The penalty for heresy is death," Mendez said. "Is that your sentence?"

All three said that it was.

Vazquez was never asked if he had anything to say in his defense. He knew nothing he could say would change the verdict, and he was too proud to beg for mercy.

After the verdict was announced, two uniformed guards grabbed Vazquez by his arms, lifted him out of his chair, and began leading him to the door.

Archbishop Arias was sitting in the back of the hall, watching the proceedings. Arias and Vazquez had known each other since they were young boys. They had played together and attended the same church school. Arias had always resented Vazquez for his wealth, his fine clothes, his special tutors, and the popularity his family enjoyed in the community. Arias had waited years to find evidence that might support a charge of heresy against Vazquez. When he received Vazquez's letter praising Martin Luther, he immediately demanded a trial.

This proceeding was one of many Arias had initiated. He had aggressively brought charges of heresy against prominent citizens and, upon conviction, seized their wealth. He had sent part of his booty to Rome and kept part to further his own luxurious life style. Rome had accepted these contributions without once asking why so many of Seville's leading citizens had suddenly turned to heresy after leading pious lives.

Vazquez was led toward the exit. When he came to where Arias was sitting, he stopped.

"I forgive you Fernando," he said, "and I pray that our Lord will forgive you. I will burn for a few short moments. I pray that you will not burn for all eternity."

"Get this heretic out of my sight," Arias snarled.

"You missed your calling, Fernando," Vazquez added, before the guards could pull him away. "You should have been an actor. You have great talent for it."

A large crowd had gathered in the public square to witness Vazquez's execution. Most knew that Vazquez was a pious man of strong faith, but no one dared challenge his death sentence for fear they would meet a similar fate. Many in the crowd were praying for a miracle—that somehow an angel would come down from heaven and spare Vazquez from a painful death.

The guards led Vazquez to the center of a public square, where he would be burned. Executioners wearing black clothes and black hoods to cover their faces began tearing off Vazquez's outer clothes before tying him to an upright stake.

"You once helped my family with a gift of money," one of the executioners whispered in Vazquez's ear. "It paid for doctors who saved my sister's life. When I push your head back against the stake, look up like you are praying to heaven and open your mouth. I will slip in poison tablets that will take you before you feel the flames."

"I pray you, good friend, do not endanger yourself," Vazquez replied. "The pain from the fire is short lived."

"Do exactly as I say," the executioner advised, "and no one will see me slip in the tablets."

Vazquez did as instructed. While tying a rope around his prisoner's shoulders, the executioner pushed Vazquez's head back against the stake and deftly slipped several poison tablets into Vazquez's open mouth. Vazquez struggled to swallow the tablets, but he finally got them down. He smiled at the man who had just risked his own life to repay a family debt. "Thank you, my friend," Vazquez whispered, "and may God bless you for this act of kindness."

The day had begun with a bright sunrise. But by 10:30 a.m., dark billowing clouds had drifted in from the east and cast dark, ominous shadows over the city. A cool chill was felt by the crowd. Church officials wondered if a heavy rain would fall and interfere with the execution.

After Vazquez was tied securely to the stake and wood spread around his feet, church officials read the long indictment for the crime of heresy and the sentence. Then they signaled the executioners to light the fire. The flames were kept low while Vazquez succumbed to the poison. His body shook slightly before he passed into unconsciousness and then death. More wood was then added to the fire until the flames engulfed Vazquez's lifeless body.

When Vazquez's shoulder-length hair caught fire, a woman in the crowd screamed. Her husband quickly covered her mouth before church officials could identify her.

Most of the crowd left the square when a gentle rain began to fall.

The image in the hologram changed to Archbishop Arias's luxurious office following the execution. Fine oil paintings and silk tapestries hanging from the walls complemented the elegant furnishings that filled the large room. A massive desk made from Spanish Walnut, inlaid with various decorative woods, occupied the center of the room. The archbishop sat behind the desk, wearing an ankle-length black cassock. A large, solid-gold cross hung from his thin neck. Arias had a nervous habit of continually fondling the cross with his hands, which left a coating of dirt and body oil on the religious icon. As a result, the gold had lost its luster. In this condition, it was an apt metaphor for the archbishop's faith in his creator.

A handsome young priest wearing an unadorned black cassock that matched his jet-black hair stood in front of the desk. The young priest was obviously distraught. His eyes watered with tears; his voice broke with emotion.

"I have heard Juan Vazquez's confession, and I know he was not an evil man," he said. "Surely, you also know he was a faithful believer in our Lord. He should not have been convicted and sentenced to death."

Before Arias could respond, his secretary entered the room and said, "Pardon my interruption, Archbishop, but I need to know if you would like your personal furnishings moved into the home formerly owned by the heretic Juan Vazquez before the legal transfer of his property to the church can be completed."

Arias smiled: "Yes, of course, make the move immediately. Why leave such a fine house empty? It is better that it be in the service of our Lord."

"Very well, sir, I will direct that your furnishings be moved today," the secretary replied.

The young priest glared at Arias and, in a contemptuous voice, said, "So that's why Juan Vazquez had to die. So, you could take his large house and make it your own."

Arias slammed his fist down on his desk. "Watch your tongue, you fool, lest the fire take you as well," he said angrily. "You must learn to show respect for your superiors. For that malicious comment, you will scrub floors for the next year as your penance." Arias rose from his desk. Turning his back to the young priest, he walked to a window and opened it to allow fresh air into the room.

A letter opener with a long, steel blade extending from a jewel-encrusted ivory handle rested on Arias's desk. This magnificent piece had been given to Arias by another nobleman seeking protection from the Inquisition's wrath.

The young priest stared at the letter opener and asked himself, "Was this the solution, perhaps the only solution, to the evil that was corrupting the archdiocese?" He slowly picked up the letter opener. It felt comfortable in his hand, like it belonged. He silently walked toward the archbishop.

"You're not a servant of our Lord," he said. "You're a monster, masquerading as a man of God." Arias turned quickly to face his young accuser. He saw the steel blade flash in the sunlight an instant before it plunged deep into his chest. Arias tried to strike his assailant, but his frail arm was no match for the muscular younger man. There was a muted scream for help from Arias, but life left him quickly, almost as soon as the young priest pulled the blade from his chest. Small flames flared from Arias's eyes and then quickly went out as his lifeless body sank to the floor.

The guard stationed outside Arias's office rushed inside.

"The archbishop has fallen ill. Summon physicians," the young priest said, before turning away and then stabbing the blade into his own heart. As he fell to the floor, there was no sign of pain on his handsome face. To the contrary, he died smiling.

Dianthe stared at the two bodies lying on the floor in Arias's office. "Will it really get that bad?" she asked as the hologram closed.

"Are you surprised?" the Father said. "Your church will be run by deserters, the same life-forms who deserted us and almost brought our kingdom down and us with it. Did you expect them to act with love and compassion because they put on priests' clothing?"

"But they will fall so far. And part of my church will become corrupt. The flame that flared from Arias's eyes before his earthly death means that one of Hasatan's angels will become an archbishop in my church. And this young priest, so idealistic, so committed to the church, will become a murderer. What explains this rapid descent into evil by members of my church?"

"When these life-forms were in our kingdom, their values and loyalty were reinforced by those around them who shared our values. But when they were confined by Hasatan, their worst instincts were reinforced by other prisoners who had similar moral failings."

"This young priest? What should be done with him?" Dianthe asked.

"Isn't he an interesting case, confronting evil in the only way he could and doing so at the cost of his own life?"

"Father, you're not thinking of bringing him back into our kingdom, are you?"

"Actually, I am. He chose the only way available to stop an evil that was corrupting your church. Serenious, send this traitor through the material world in a second host after his death as a priest. And send me the file on his second life. I want to judge him myself."

"Yes, Excellency," Serenious replied.

"Will this injustice to Juan Vazquez be the worst of it?" Dianthe asked.

"Unfortunately, not. Your church, once unified, will split into many factions, each claiming to be the one true faith. These factions will make war on each other, torturing and murdering members of other groups, all in your name. This will go on for many years, draining strength that could be used to build your church. Don't expect institutions run by those who turned their backs on us to reflect IAM's values."

"But it seems like this church is reflecting Hasatan's values."

"Your church will reflect the defectors' values and their inability to love one another."

"Is there more bad news about this church that I should know?"

The Father opened another hologram. It showed Melk Abbey, a Benedictine monastery located on the Danube River between what is now Vienna and Linz, Austria. The date was the eleventh day of the first month of Earth year 4,543,763,748 (January 11, 1759). The image in the hologram focused on the interior of the abbey's church. What appeared was perhaps the most ostentatious display of wealth ever conceived of by the mind of man. Walls and ceiling displayed the lavish use of gold leaf and polished marble. Crosses and statuary made of gold, adorned with precious gems, provided a spectacular background for the exquisitely sculptured marble high alter. Magnificent frescoes depicting angels and heaven graced the ceiling. The elevated pulpit and sounding board, both covered with gold leaf, resembled a golden cocoon. The church's interior design was intended to introduce worshipers to the glories of heaven. But for many, it had the opposite effect: The collection of so much fine art, gold and so many precious gemstones in one place overwhelmed the viewer with its ostentatious show of opulence.

"Contrast this with how the common people in the surrounding countryside, who were expected to contribute resources to help support the abbey, lived at that time," the Father said.

The image in the hologram changed to the modest home of Joseph Loos, a one-room structure with a dirt floor, two beds, a table, four stools, a leaky roof, and a fireplace that provided heat and the means for cooking food. Joseph was a serf and his home was in the manor owned by his earthly lord, Adolf Mach. The time was 5:00 p.m. The setting sun had cast dark shadows over the Loos's household, which was in keeping with the feeling of despair that had gripped the Loos family.

The previous winter had been brutally cold at Melk, and the following spring had been very dry. As a result, crops had done poorly during the 1758 growing season. By the winter of 1758, starvation was common in the land. Joseph had carefully rationed food to get his family through the winter to the next growing season, but that meant he often went to bed hungry. On this day, he and his family were on the edge of starvation. Since early fall, he had lost twenty pounds. His children, who were always slender, were now emaciated. Joseph could not bring himself to look at their gaunt faces and spindly limbs; it was too painful. He wondered if he and his family would survive. And if he did survive, would he be strong enough to work his master's lands and the small plot of land set aside for his use during the next growing season?

On this day, Joseph looked up the hill at the abbey, with all its splendor and opulence. He did not see beauty or the creator's munificence. Instead, he saw a god that demanded so much for himself and left so little for his people.

The hologram closed.

There was a long pause, during which no one spoke. Finally, in a voice filled with disdain and with tears streaming down her face, Dianthe said, "The humble nature of my birth and life in the material world apparently will not make much of an impression on those who claim to be my followers. How could they do this? How could they so abuse their authority? How could they exploit their followers in this way?"

Neither the Father nor Serenious responded. There were no answers to Dianthe's questions, other than the obvious: The deserters who had lost the seed will be suffused with a self-indulgent narcissism that will not change after the great betrayal.

"I now see that millions of humans will suffer and die because of church leaders' greed for power and riches," Dianthe said. "Perhaps this noble experiment will achieve nothing. Perhaps all the prisoners should be returned to Hasatan. Will my church offer any bright lights in this dark world?"

"There will at least be one shining light," the Father said, as he opened a hologram that depicted Kolkata, India on the ninth day of the first month of Earth year 4,543,763,945 (January 9, 1956). The hologram scanned the densely populated city on the east bank of the Hooghly River, until it came to rest on an abandoned Hindu Temple that had been turned into a hospice for the poor and destitute. The time was 8:00 a.m. A Roman Catholic nun, dressed neatly in a white cotton *sari* with blue trim, was speaking in broken English to a small group of young women who had volunteered to work at this facility, where the poor and afflicted could depart the material world with a minimal amount of human dignity.

The speaker was forty-five years old and fluent in five

languages. She was plain looking; nature had not adorned her with attractive facial features. Her chin was not well shaped, her nose turned down in an unappealing way, and her skin was not smooth. She looked older than her years. She was born in Macedonia and given the name Anjezë Gonxhe Bojaxhiu. Now, she was addressed simply as "Mother Teresa."

What came across in her appearance and speech was a total, unwavering dedication to demonstrating God's love for the despised and unwanted in the world. There was no hesitation in her voice; she didn't resort to affectation or false flattery. Her statements were wise, as well as honest and straightforward. The power of her personality and her dedication to caring for those in their final hours of human existence knew no compromise. She was a leader. Had she been born into another host, she might have risen to the highest levels of government or the business world. But she was satisfied to run an organization that cared for the wretched and despised in their final hours.

"If you join our staff, your task will be to help people who lived like animals to die like angels—loved and wanted,"[1] she said. "Each morning, you will search Kolkata for the dying and bring them to this facility. You will bathe and feed them. You will administer drugs to help them with their pain, if we have such drugs. And you will help them die with dignity, according to the rituals of their faith: Catholics will receive last rites, Hindus will receive water from the River Ganges, and Moslems will have the Quran read to them."[1]

"Mother Teresa, shouldn't we be trying to convert to Christanity all who come here and are close to death—to save them from the fires of hell?" a surprised young woman asked.

"Witness the love of Jesus Christ to the dying and pray that the Holy Spirit will bring them to Christ in their last hours,"

---

[1]   These two quotes of Mother Teresa appear here with the permission of Karen Spink, author of *Mother Teresa, An Authorized Biography* published by Harper Collins (1998).

Teresa replied. "That is all we can do. The Holy Spirit must do the rest."

The hologram closed.

"During her lifetime, Mother Teresa's organization will grow to a force of more than four thousand workers running similar facilities all over the world," the Father said. "She will be awarded the Nobel Peace Prize. Speaking in broken English, she will accept that prize in the name 'of the hungry, of the naked, of the homeless, of the crippled, of the blind, of the leprous, of all those people who feel unwanted, unloved, uncared, thrown away of the society, people who have become a burden to the society, and are ashamed by everyone.'[2] Teresa will be that bright light of Christian love that you hoped would maintain your church."

"I am grateful that at least one member of my church will be filled with love for others," Dianthe said.

"Dianthe, do you recognize the defector who will reside in the host called Mother Teresa," the Father asked.

"No, should I?"

"Do you remember the young life-form who approached you in Hasatan's prison, the little girl named Teresa who resembled a fairyland princess?"

"That's her?"

"That's her. Hasatan lied to you when he said she had expired."

---

2   The quote from Mother Teresa's "Nobel Acceptance Speech" (1979) appears here with the permission of the Nobel Foundation.

12.

By then, Dianthe had begun to realize that sinister forces in the material world would threaten the survival of her church—weak leaders more concerned with their own prestige and power than with spreading the faith, infiltration by Hasatan's angels into leadership positions, resistance to the true message created by the allure of materialism, among other things. "Would my church survive in this world?" she wondered. "And if it failed, how would that impact the test to judge the prisoners' loyalty?" She put these questions to the Father.

"Your church, at least in its institutional form, will become weak and may not survive. That would be unfortunate, because it would eliminate something that holds the community of believers together," the Father said.

"I have a plan to prevent such a failure," Dianthe said.

"Yes, go on."

"I would like, with Serenious's help, to inspire three well-placed individuals to build a strong foundation for my church to help ensure its long-term survival."

"Have you selected these individuals?"

"I have. The first is Akim, son of Nahshon. In early human history, defectors who carry a live seed will understand that they have become estranged from their creator and are in need of redemption. But as time goes on, they will see salvation in earthly terms. They will look for a messiah to lead them to earthly glory, to victories in battle, to the creation of a just and powerful government ruled by enlightened leaders, a government that will protect them from their enemies. I would like Serenious to inspire Akim to turn the people away from thoughts of earthly glory toward a messiah, who will enter the world and show them the true way to be reconciled to their creator. In other words, I want Akim to prophesize me."

"That seems like a worthy idea, and I am willing to help," Serenious said. "But I'm not familiar with an influential prophet named Akim, son of Nahshon"

"I don't recall that name either," the Father said.

Dianthe smiled: "Akim's words will be attributed to another man, one of Judea's most prominent prophets, a man named Isaiah. I would like Serenious to bring about the following."

Dianthe opened a hologram that scanned the city of Jerusalem during the late afternoon of a spring day during Earth year 4,543,761,343. The image scanned the city and came to rest on a small house near the gate called "Sha'ar Ha'ashpot" in the city's southwest corner. This was the home of Akim and his wife Jessica. Akim had been a disciple of Isaiah. When old age had taken its toll on the holy messenger, and he no longer had a firm writing hand, Akim became his secretary, recording his thoughts and prophesies. Isaiah had several disciples, but Akim was his favorite. Akim did not share his master's zest for confrontation. Nor did he have the gift of prophesying. But he did have a skillful writing hand and a way with words and phrases that appealed to the old prophet.

On this same day, Manasseh was celebrating his fiftieth year as King of Judah. Several months earlier, Manasseh had grown tired of Isaiah's constant criticism of his rule for permitting, if not encouraging, the worship of various gods in addition to IAM, and he had Isaiah put to death. In fact, he ordered that Isaiah be sawed in half. To stop the spread of Isaiah's ideas and writings, Manasseh also ordered that Isaiah's disciples be put to death, and most were. To protect and preserve Isaiah's prophesies, some of which had yet to be recorded, a priest named Eliakim hid Akim from the king's guards. Akim and his wife were given new identities and a small home in Jerusalem in which to work.

Akim looked every bit the scholar that he was—a tall, spindly figure with dark hair, sunken eyes, a lean face, and an intense countenance. On this afternoon, Akim was seated at his small, cedar desk trying to remember some of Isaiah's exact words when he heard a knock at his door. He got up from his desk and peered out through a crack between the door's vertical boards. When he saw Eliakim, he removed the crossbeam and opened the door.

"You needn't barricade yourself in like this," said Eliakim, a good-natured, jovial man with a round face, mostly gray hair, and a wide girth that stretched the limits of his outer robe. "The king thinks all of Isaiah's disciples are dead, but if his guards came for you, they would not be stopped by this flimsy door or your crossbar."

"I suppose you're right, but I feel safer when the door is closed and the crossbar is in place."

"I came by to tell you that I like what you wrote several days ago. I'm sure Isaiah would have approved, had he lived to see this day. Your former master may be the greatest of all the prophets. He promised a messiah who would restore Judah to its rightful place among the great nations of the world, a wise ruler who would govern his people with justice and compassion. That would be a welcome change from the toad who now rules over us and defies the commandments given to Moses. Your writings are giving hope to our people."

"I pray that I am up to this task."

"You have written well, so far," Eliakim said before leaving.

Later that evening, Akim sat at his desk working by the light of his oil lamp. Suddenly, the room became bright, as if it were midday. Akim turned toward the light and saw a figure emerge from its brilliance. It was Serenious."

"Do not fear, Akim, I mean you no harm," Serenious said.

Out of the corner of his eye, Akim glanced at his front door, the only entranceway into his small home. The door was closed, and the crossbeam was still in place. Akim was overcome by fear. His eyes grew wide, his lips quivered, and his hands began to shake. "Who are you?" he asked in a fearful voice.

"Who I am is not important" Serenious said. "Pick up your pen. I am going to help you describe the messiah, the one for whom you and your people are waiting."

Akim obediently picked up his pen, dipped it into his ink jar, and brought it to his parchment scroll. To Akim's astonishment, his arm began to move without him directing it. Words appeared on the scroll:

"He hath no form nor comeliness; and when we shall see him, there is no beauty that we should desire him.

"He is despised and rejected of men; a man of sorrows familiar with suffering.

"But he was wounded for our transgressions; he was bruised for our iniquities, and with his stripes we are cleansed of our transgressions.

"He is brought as a lamb to the slaughter, and as a sheep before her shearers is dumb, so he openeth not his mouth.

"... he was cut off out of the land of the living.

"And he made his grave with the wicked, and with the rich in his death."

Akim stared at the words he had written. "These are not my master's words," he said.

"These are the words your Lord wants you to write," Serenious replied.

Akim recoiled in shock: "Who are you that dares speak for the living God?"

"I told you; who I am is not important. What is written on this parchment is important."

"But this is not the messiah we are waiting for. We want someone like King David, a man of power, who will restore our nation to greatness. We don't want a weakling, a suffering servant, a lamb led to slaughter. A lamb will not deliver us from the Assyrians in the North, the Babylonians in the East, the Egyptians in the South, or the Greeks in the West. We need a strong leader to rally our people. If we are conquered, our men will be slaughtered, and our wives and daughters will become slaves and concubines. We were slaves once. We do not want to be in slavery again."

"Your people may want a warrior king, but what they need is a messiah who will show them the way to be reconciled to their creator. Great nations come and go, great armies come and go, but you and your creator are eternal beings. You must look beyond the fleeting present to the everlasting. You must tell your people about this messiah, what he will be like and what he will suffer, so your people will recognize him when he comes. You have been selected for this important task; it is a great honor, Akim, son of Nahshon."

Akim did not respond. He didn't know what to say.

"I leave you now. You have my blessing. Shalom." With that, Serenious stepped back into the light's brilliance and disappeared. The room returned to the dimness of Akim's oil lamp.

Akim sat at his writing desk, trying to fathom what had just occurred. His hands were shaking, his heart raced, and his mind was a collage of frightening thoughts that paralyzed him. Try as he might, he could not make sense of what had just occurred. He felt his forehead. Maybe he was hallucinating from illness. Or worse yet, maybe he was losing his mind. Was the task of writing for the great prophet too much for him? Perhaps he had fantasized this whole episode. But the new words on the parchment that stared back at him were no fantasy. They were real.

There was a knock on Akim's door early the next morning. It was Eliakim.

"I know it's early, but I had a dream last night that you had written something especially insightful, and I have come by to read it," Eliakim said.

Akim had not slept at all the night before. He was exhausted and greeted Eliakim with incoherent mumbling. Finally, he blurted out, "I didn't write anything last night."

"Akim, I can see new words on the parchment," Eliakim

said, as he picked up the scroll and began to read.

Akim was fully conscious now. He stared at Eliakim, waiting for the explosion he was sure would come.

"Akim, your writing is much improved," Eliakim said. "In fact, it is very beautiful. In all my days, I have never seen writing this beautiful."

Akim did not try to explain how the new words came to be written on the scroll. He feared Eliakim would think he had lost his mind. Instead he asked, "Are you satisfied with this writing?"

"Yes, it is very good," Eliakim replied. "I must go now. I have a busy day. We are preparing the temple for Passover." With that, Eliakim smiled and departed.

Akim couldn't decide what was more mysterious: The stranger who had appeared and controlled his hand, or Eliakim's failure to react to writing that was radically different from the teachings of his prior master.

When Eliakim departed, Akim's wife, Jessica, entered the room. She was startled by Akim's appearance—pale, visibly shaking, breathing heavily, with terror-filled eyes. She had never seen him so frightened, even when the king's guards were searching for Isaiah's disciples.

"Are you all right?" she asked. "You didn't come to bed all night."

"I don't know if I'm all right" he replied. "I honestly do not know."

The hologram closed.

"Dianthe, you have chosen well," the Father said. "Akim will, indeed, help build a strong foundation for your church."

"Thank you, Father."

"Who else have you chosen for this task?" the Father asked.

"A man who first persecuted my followers," Dianthe said.

"His name?"

"Saul, Saul of Tarsus."

"What do you want him to do?"

Dianthe opened a hologram.

The time was early afternoon on a spring day in Earth year 4,543,762,023 (April 5, 0034). The place was a road leading to Damascus, an ancient city east of the Mediterranean Sea located on a plateau 2,230 feet above sea level. Damascus was bounded by Mount Qassioun on the west and desert on the east. The river Barada and an elaborate system of man-made canals supplied the city and surrounding agricultural areas with water. The sweet fragrance of flowering fruit trees masked the sour smells of city life.

By Earth year 4,543,762,023, Damascus had been conquered by the Assyrians, Hittites, Egyptians, Greeks, Romans, and Jews, among others. All of them had left their mark on the city's culture. Damascus was located along caravan routes to the Mediterranean, Arabia, cities along the Euphrates, and beyond to China. Foreigners were seen on its streets and in its eating places and inns. As a result, Damascus had become one of the world's wealthiest and most cosmopolitan cities, willing to tolerate a wide range of ideas and religions. For this reason, a small group of Jews fearing persecution in Jerusalem because they had become followers of Jesus had chosen Damascus as their new home.

The hologram came to rest on five travelers resting by the side of the road about three miles from Damascus's southern gate. The group's leader was a short, well-dressed man with broad shoulders and dark eyes that peered out from a friendly countenance. He had red hair and a ruddy complexion. He walked slightly hunched over, the result of a birth defect. The man was a Jew, and he went by two names. When interacting with other Jews, he called himself Saul of Tarsus. When interacting with non-Jews, he used his Roman name—Paul.

Like his father, Saul was a Pharisee, and he referred to himself as "a Pharisee among Pharisees." He was intimately familiar with the Halakha, the labyrinth of Jewish laws, regulations, and interpretations that controlled virtually every aspect of Jewish life. Like other Pharisees, he believed in life after death, and like other Pharisees, he was fanatically devoted to following Jewish law as the way to achieve eternal salvation.

As a young boy, Saul had attended the Hillel School in Jerusalem, where he had studied under Gamaliel, one of the intellectual giants of the first century. Saul had received a broad education at Hillel, not only in religion, but also in classical literature, philosophy, and ethics. He was a brilliant student who stood out from his peers; his towering intellect was obvious even at a young age. Saul was also a gregarious extrovert, which helped him overcome the fact that he suffered from epilepsy, regarded at the time as demonic. He was a Roman citizen in a Roman world, and that provided him with rights only a few enjoyed.

The other men accompanying Saul—Aran, Ehud, Gershom, and Natan—were his friends and admirers. They had joined him on this trip to ensure his safety. The group had been resting for several minutes. They had walked from Jerusalem, more than one hundred fifty miles to the south, in seven short days, and they were exhausted. But the walls of Damascus were in sight. "Let's press on," Saul said as he stood up. "I can see the southern gate. If we walk swiftly, we'll be inside the city wall before dusk."

Saul took several steps and then felt for a leather case he kept close to his heart.

"We can't lose this," he said to Aran. "It contains the letter from the high priest directing us to find the Christian filth hiding in Damascus and bring them back to Jerusalem to stand trial. Christians, what a strange group, worshipping a backwoods rabble-rouser who was put to death by the Romans as a common criminal. Dying on a cross. Is that evidence of divine powers?"

Saul fondled the leather case and then continued to mumble about the odd nature of this new religion called Christianity.

Saul's four companions were also weary. But they too wanted to be inside the southern gate by nightfall, so the four men struggled to get to their feet and began to follow Saul. The group had walked about a hundred yards when the clouds parted and a bright light from above shone down on the men, blinding them. Saul lost his balance and fell to the ground. Then he heard a gentle voice: "Saul, why do you persecute me and my followers?"

"Who are you?" Saul asked fearfully.

"I am Jesus," the voice answered. "It is my followers you have imprisoned and put to death."

Saul's eyes grew large, and his pulse began to race. He had persecuted Christians for several years. Some of those had been put to death, others imprisoned. Saul feared that his life was about to be snuffed out by the divine power he had often ridiculed.

"What would you have me do, Lord?" Saul asked.

"Get up and go into Damascus," the voice replied. "There, you will be given an assignment."

Saul tried to get up, but he stumbled and fell again.

"I can't see," he told his companions. "I've been blinded by that light. Help me up."

Aran helped Saul to his feet.

The sun was continuing its slow but steady march toward the western horizon, and Saul knew that, in his infirm condition, he would be walking slowly.

"We must get to Damascus before dark as best we can," he said.

His companions took turns leading Saul along the road. Saul stumbled and fell several more times, but each time he got up and continued along the road leading to the city's southern gate, which he and his companions passed through in late afternoon. Once inside the city wall, they went to a private home owned by a Christian.

They remained at this home for three days. On the third day, Saul heard a knock on his bedroom door.

"Who's there?" he called out.

A voice replied, "I am Ananias. I have come to restore your sight."

Saul got up from his chair and walked towards the door.

He felt along the wall until he found the door latch, which he raised, opening the door. "I've been anxiously waiting for you," Saul said in a happy voice.

"My instructions were to come on this day," Ananias said, as he led Saul back to the room's only chair. "Sit down," Ananias instructed. He placed his hands on Saul's face and prayed: "If it be your will, Lord, return sight to your servant."

Saul blinked, and what looked like scales fell from his eyes.

"I can see!" Saul shouted, as he stood up and embraced Ananias. "Oh, thank God, I can see!"

"Saul of Tarsus," Ananias said. "The son of the living God has chosen you to know his will and be his witness in this world."

Saul's demeanor quickly changed from joy to unease.

"How can this be?" he said, raising his hands. "These are forever stained with innocent blood. How can I be a witness to the true light?"

"That is not for me to say," Ananias replied.

"But I am not worthy," Saul replied, his voice filled with emotion. "Of all the believers in this world, I am the least worthy."

"None of us is worthy in God's sight, but he forgives us. Now kneel, be baptized, and accept God's grace and forgiveness," Ananias said.

Saul knelt, and Ananias poured water on his head while saying the words, "I baptize you in the name of the Father, Son, and Holy Spirit. Now the Holy Comforter is with you, my brother in Christ."

Saul struggled to understand this new God who forgave sin without retribution. He had a deep understanding of the scriptures handed down to the Jews, which were based on thousands of years of history and learning. He knew the teachings of the prophets: Where there was sin, there had to be punishment to wipe the slate clean. Adam and Eve were banished from the Garden of Eden for disobeying their creator. Israel was taken captive to Babylon for disobeying the prophets. But this Jesus was willing to forgive sins without punishment or suffering. It made no sense to him. Nevertheless, Saul assumed that in the future, he would better understand what this Jesus expected of him.

The hologram closed.

"Saul will start nineteen churches that will establish a Christian presence in the Mediterranean world. He will write letters to many of these churches that will guide Christian understanding of the faith for thousands of years," Dianthe explained. "In service to IAM, Saul will be imprisoned and flogged. He will often go without water or food. He will be shipwrecked on three occasions. Eventually, he will be martyred by beheading."

"Saul's letters are insightful, informative, honest, and above all, never wavering in their dedication to your ministry," the Father said. "Another excellent selection. Who is your third choice?"

"Flavius Valerius Constantius, known as Emperor Constantine," Dianthe replied.

"A Roman emperor instead of a church leader?" the Father asked. "That's an interesting choice."

"During Christianity's early days, Roman emperors will suppress the Christian faith and put many believers to death in brutal ways," Dianthe explained. "Constantine will stop this suppression and adopt Christianity as his personal religion. That will ensure the survival of Christianity in the western world for at least seventeen hundred years. Allow me to show you how this will come about."

Dianthe opened a hologram. It showed a Roman army of over forty thousand men marching south toward Rome on the Via Flaminia. The army was led by Constantine, a thirty-two-year-old charismatic military leader blessed with handsome facial features, including a high forehead, bright hazel eyes, an aquiline nose, and a well-chiseled chin. Constantine had been a soldier all his adult life, and his military bearing was unmistakable. He sat upright on a splendid white horse. His highly polished body armor, gleaming in the bright sunshine, accentuated his powerful arms and barrel chest. His helmet rested gracefully on his head, as if it were the Roman crown he hoped soon to wear. The date was the twenty-seventh day of the tenth month of Earth year 4,543,762,301 (October 27, 312).

Constantine's spies had reported that Maxentius, Rome's ruler at the time, was positioning a much larger military force, almost eighty thousand men, near the Milvian Bridge, which spanned the Tiber River and led directly into Rome. But these reports did not discourage Constantine. He had successfully attacked larger forces before. His men were combat-hardened and well-motivated. They all looked up to Constantine as if he were a god, and they all were willing to lay down their lives to see him become the Roman emperor.

The thirty-four-year-old Maxentius was Constantine's polar opposite: He had a slender neck, sleepy eyes, a modest build, and a face that wore a perpetual sneer, giving him the appearance of a petulant child about to throw a tantrum. Before becoming emperor, Maxentius had not served in any important military or administrative position. His principal claim to be Rome's ruler was that his father had once ruled Rome. Maxentius had seized the crown during a power vacuum, when other stronger leaders were away fighting wars. He had bribed military leaders in and around Rome to help him in his grab for power. But after becoming emperor, he had shamelessly exploited his position, and the citizens of Rome had come to despise him. There had been riots against his rule in Rome and in Carthage. Maxentius had declared war on Constantine to build support for his rule, but that tactic hadn't worked. He remained so unpopular that ordinary citizens taunted him during public events.

When Maxentius learned that Constantine's army was approaching Rome, he consulted an oracle and was informed that an enemy of Rome would soon perish. Maxentius took that to mean he would survive and Constantine would be killed. On that advice, he led his forces out of Rome and across the Tiber River to do battle with Constantine's approaching army.

The 27th was an unusually warm day for late October. The hot sun was beating down on Constantine's army, requiring it to stop frequently for water and rest.

At midday, the column stopped for its noonday meal. While soldiers were erecting a large canopy, so their commander could eat his noonday meal shielded from the sun, Leander, a senior officer, approached Constantine.

"Leander, how far to the Milvian Bridge?" Constantine called out.

"Less than a half day's march," Leander replied. "If we press on, our forward elements can be within sight of the bridge by sunset."

"I want everyone to get a good night's rest. We're likely to hear the clash of swords tomorrow. After the noon meal, end the march halfway to the bridge and make camp."

"Yes, sir."

For many years, Constantine had served in Britain and Northern Europe, where the soil was rocky, the farms were small, and farmers struggled to produce a small harvest. But as he gazed at the large, well-maintained vineyards, farms, and orchards on either side of the Via Flaminia, he was taken aback by their large size and how meticulously they were maintained. Aqueducts bringing water from miles away had made the fertile soil highly productive. By late October, the grape harvest was almost complete, but the orchards were beehives of activity, with slaves harvesting apples and olives.

"This is such a beautiful land," Constantine thought to himself. "One day, I will own one of these grand estates and enjoy the noble life of a farmer."

Constantine glanced up at the sky. Suddenly, he seemed transfixed by what he saw. Leander became concerned and asked, "Sir, is anything wrong?"

"There, above the sun, I see a cross of light with the words 'By this sign, you shall conquer,'" Constantine replied, pointing to a place above the sun. "There, right above the sun, do you see it?"

Leander looked up to where Constantine was pointing. He shielded his eyes with his right hand and squinted but saw nothing except the sun and a few clouds.

"Leander, it's right there, right above the sun."

"I'm sorry, sir, I don't see it. Maybe it's an omen meant only for your eyes."

"Yes, maybe that's it," Constantine replied. The image was so clear, however, that Constantine wondered why Leander couldn't see it.

The image in the hologram moved to the early morning hours of the next day. Constantine was asleep in his large tent. But his was a restless sleep. He continually turned in his temporary bed. Perspiration beaded on his forehead. He began to issue orders in his sleep, but what he said made no sense. The guards stationed at the tent's entrance became concerned over their commander's wellbeing. They woke Constantine's young aide-de-camp, Marcus Sabinus, and reported that a strange spirit had overtaken their leader. Marcus dressed quickly and went to his commander. As he approached, Constantine sat up in bed, with a puzzled look on his face. He wiped perspiration from his brow with the sleeve of his nightshirt.

"Sir, is anything wrong?" Marcus asked. "The guards became concerned about your restlessness and summoned me."

"Nothing's wrong," Constantine replied. "I just had a strange dream. The Christian God, Jesus, appeared to me and said, if the first two letters of his name appeared on the banners our soldiers carry into battle tomorrow, we would prevail. My mother told me about this God. He is nothing like any of our Roman gods. He allowed himself to be crucified to earn forgiveness for our sins. What a strange thing."

"Is there anything you want me to do?"

"Yes, I want the Greek letters Chi-Rho inscribed on our banners before sunrise. You had better start now. You don't have much time."

"Yes, sir," Marcus replied, as he departed the tent to carry out Constantine's order.

The image in the hologram changed to the following day. It showed the two armies clashing. Constantine's legions routed Maxentius's much larger force. Maxentius perished, and most of his army was either destroyed or taken prisoner. Constantine marched into Rome and was declared supreme emperor of the western half of the Roman Empire. The holograph's final image showed Constantine donning a golden crown shaped to look like a laurel wreath.

"During the following year, Constantine and Licinius, another Roman leader, will issue the Edict of Milan, instituting religious toleration in the empire and decriminalizing Christian worship," Dianthe explained. "Thereafter, Constantine will declare himself to be a Christian. He will become a patron of my church and commission the construction of Christian basilicas and churches throughout the empire, including the Church of the Holy Sepulchre, over my Earthly burial site. He will promote Christians to high public office and order that property confiscated from Christians because of their faith be returned to them. From that time forward, until the beginning of the third millennium, Christianity will flourish in the Western World."

"Again, you have chosen well," the Father said.

"I am grateful for the gift of these three faithful servants. They will show many the path to redemption."

"Yes, that will be true. But for each of these individuals, we will be breaking our agreement not to intervene in the material world. Please don't ask for any more of these interventions. There has to be an end to them."

"Yes, Father, I understand."

13.

Several days later, the Father, Dianthe, and Serenious were in their common chambers watching a new play, *When Stars Collide.* The play dramatized the massive rescue effort IAM undertook to save positive life-forms living on planets in the solar systems of two stars that were about to collide.

Dianthe wore an elegant white robe decorated with small tassels hanging from the robe's bottom hem. Her pet tiger cubs, Enou and Gaspin (the names for "love" and "kindness" in an ancient Primary Universe dialect), were fascinated by the way the tassels swayed when the cubs hit them with their paws. The young felines kept striking at the tassels. Unfortunately, their claws tore the robe in several places.

The play was an engrossing portrayal of a seminal event in Primary Universe history, and the performance held Dianthe in rapt attention. It wasn't until the play ended that she noticed the tears in her robe.

"Oh my, look at what you've done to my favorite robe!" she said to the cubs. "Go sit in the corner and think about the need to be more careful."

The cubs trudged off to the nearest corner, looking forlorn. They had rarely been reprimanded, and a reprimand from Dianthe, herself, was especially devastating. Once in the corner, Enou looked back at Dianthe with sad little eyes that begged for forgiveness.

"They're just acting like tiger cubs," the Father said. "I suggest you not wear that robe when you're around them."

Dianthe looked at the Father with a forlorn look that resembled Enou's.

"Yes, Father," she replied. Dianthe summoned the cubs and called them up onto her large overstuffed couch, petting them until they purred with delight.

"Father, earlier we agreed that the prisoners should have a written narrative describing my sacrifice on their behalf and our promise to redeem those who remain loyal to us," Dianthe said.

"Serenious has arranged for such a narrative. It will be a collection of smaller books written by various human authors, an anthology that will become known as the 'Bible,'" the Father replied. "Have you read it?"

"I have."

"What do you think of it?"

"It's a disaster. It must be rewritten."

"A disaster?" the Father said in a surprised voice.

"To start with, it's full of factual errors, errors that will become obvious to humans as they learn more about the material world. It even has me stating falsehoods. In one place in this Bible, I say the mustard seed is the smallest seed. That will not be true. Orchids will have seeds that are smaller than the mustard seed," Dianthe said. "

The Father gave Dianthe a skeptical look.

"Allow me to show you the problems this Bible will cause," Dianthe said, while opening a hologram. The image was of a crowded lecture hall on the campus of Valparaiso University, a small Midwestern university affiliated with the Lutheran Church. The time was 10:13 a.m. on the seventh day of the second month of Earth year 4,543,763,956 (February 7, 1967). A religion class was underway. Joel Franklin, a tall, handsome student with shoulder-length, sandy-blond hair and a shaggy beard, was sitting in the second row of seats. He wore a faded denim jacket that featured a peace symbol on the breast pocket.

Joel was an ardent admirer of Friedrich Nietzsche, the

German philosopher who declared that "God is dead." Like Nietzsche, Joel possessed a genius level IQ. Like Nietzsche, Joel was the son of a Lutheran minister. And like Nietzsche, he was an avowed atheist.

Joel was majoring in both physics and mathematics. He thought of himself as a scientist and a rationalist, convinced that only human reasoning, supplemented by human passion and instincts, would lead to an accurate understanding of human existence. He ridiculed religious belief based exclusively on faith as superstition and delusion, a holdover from ancient times, when men prayed to the sun and built massive stone temples to their gods.

Joel enjoyed a close relationship with his mother, a chemistry professor at the University of Michigan. Joel's father, to whom he hadn't spoken in three years, insisted that Joel attend Valparaiso University, in hopes that life in a religious community would lead him to faith in the one true God. As might have been predicted, that decision had the opposite result: It turned Joel into an apostle for atheism. Joel takes this mission seriously. At every opportunity, he attempts to convince the world, or at least his contemporaries, that religion is spiritual mumbo-jumbo, ignorant superstition dressed up in respectable clothing. Joel took this religion course to spread his atheistic gospel.

On this day, the class was discussing the Bible, its history and its authority. Partway through this discussion, Joel rose from his chair, dramatically raised a Bible is his hand, and said, "How can you claim this book is authoritative, that it's the inspired word of God, when it's full of errors, statements that contradict hard science? Biblical scholars, based on their reading of events and genealogies in this book, claim the earth is about six thousand years old. Radio metric dating says it's around 4.5 billion years old. How can the earth be six thousand years old when botanists have found living trees that are eight and nine thousand years old?"

"Mr. Franklin, I thought we might hear from you on this

subject," Professor Flannan said. "Would you agree that what the Bible calls days might represent whole ages of time?"

"I am not going to let you slip off the hook with that canard. Not only is the six-thousand-year time period fantasy, the order of creation makes no sense. The first chapter of Genesis says that, on the fourth day of creation, God formed the sun, moon, and stars, but on the first three days, he separated light from darkness and created vegetation. Light originates from the sun and other stars, and plants depend on light for energy. You can't have light or growing plants without the sun's rays, and according to Genesis, that didn't happen until the fourth day. Tell me professor, did your god flunk his science class or is he deliberately trying to confuse his followers, to see if they can find him through the haze of misinformation?"

Nervous laughs were heard from other students in the lecture hall.

"Unless this Bible is rewritten, it will do more harm than good," Dianthe said.

Serenious, under whose general direction the Bible had been written, replied, "Dianthe, do you want this Bible to provide a detailed description of how the material universe was created? Should it include the mathematical equations the Father used to determine the compression forces needed to transform energy into matter, the gravitational force needed to form stars, or the force needed to hold electrons and protons in balance within atoms? Should it describe the process by which stars create elements such as carbon, oxygen, and iron? Should it state the seven dimensions of existence or how to create a life-form capable of surviving in a dangerous world? Would humans understand any of that? Would a chapter filled with chemical formulas and mathematical equations present the fundamental truth about the universe's creation more profoundly than the text prepared by human authors? I don't think so. Listen to the professor. He has a good reply to Mr. Franklin's assault on the Bible."

"I don't believe God was trying to confuse us, Mr. Franklin.

.

The Bible contains all the information Christians need to know for redemption—that at some point, mankind turned away from his creator and that, as an act of grace, God offers to redeem all those who are baptized and believe in him. Why he chose to provide that information through the filter of human writing with all its limitations and defects is not revealed to us. But then, much is not revealed to us. We are simply asked to believe as a matter of faith."

Serenious turned toward the Father. "If this anthology contained scientific information unavailable to the material world when it was written, it would suggest that an alien life-form influenced its writing. That would undercut the integrity of this test."

"The problems with this Bible go much deeper than factual and scientific inaccuracies," Dianthe replied. "It is also full of inconsistencies. In one place, it describes my earthly paternal grandfather as Jacob; in another place, he is said to be Heli. In one place, the man who betrayed me is said to have hanged himself. Elsewhere, another cause of death is given. In one place, it says my followers are justified by their faith alone. In another place, it says persons are justified by what they do, not solely by what they believe."

The Father listened but said nothing.

"Also," Dianthe continued. "the first book of this Bible presents IAM as a homicidal maniac, ordering the destruction of whole cities, the slaughter of innocent women and children, all in the name of creating racial purity. The priests of this group, who will identify themselves as the 'chosen people,' will want to eliminate potential threats from survivors of captured cities, so they will order that those survivors be slaughtered. If the priests were to issue these orders on their own authority, there would be opposition. After all, mass killings would violate the very commandments IAM will hand down to these people. To get around that problem, their leaders will say these orders came directly from IAM."

The Father looked concerned but still said nothing.

"Also, this book is filled with false promises. It says those who have faith in IAM can ask and it will be given to them. It promises that the righteous will not go hungry, that the just will be protected from all harm. All of this is fantasy; we never made such extravagant claims. Most of my disciples will be martyred, some crucified. Is that protection from harm? The priests and scribes, who make these false promises, will do so to maintain their followers' loyalty. But when bad things happen to the prisoners—wars, natural disasters, plagues, a holocaust, religious conflicts, genocides—they will feel betrayed by IAM, and rightfully so. While I recognize the irony here—those who deserted us feeling betrayed—I can understand their frustration."

Turning toward Serenious, the Father asked, "Is all this true?"

Squirming in his seat, and looking very uncomfortable, Serenious replied, "Well, you instructed me not to take over the writing myself, but to guide the human authors so they would accurately describe the basic steps toward redemption. And it does that: It states that the traitors disobeyed IAM, that out of grace and a father's love for his children, the Father offers to take back into his kingdom all those who remain loyal to him."

"Yes, this Bible does all those things," Dianthe conceded. "And it is full of these charming little stories meant to be allegories. But many of them have a shocking lack of credibility. They are the products of human minds that will value imagination and romantic appeal over reality. For example, at the beginning of a book called Genesis, there is a story about the prisoners' fall from grace. A male and a female life-form live in a blissful garden, where the female is persuaded by a serpent to convince her male companion to disobey their creator. The woman in this story is intelligent and sophisticated. How realistic is it that she would be taken in by, of all things, a talking snake?"

"Dianthe, it's an allegory written for a patriarchal society."

Serenious said. "It's largely poetry because that will be the writing style of the day. What would you expect?"

Turning to the Father, Serenious said, "The snake is a primitive allusion to Hasatan."

"Ah yes, of course," the Father replied.

"There are more of these fantastic stories that defy common sense," Dianthe said. "There is a story about a disobedient prophet who is thrown into the sea and swallowed by a large fish. He spends three days and three nights in the great fish's belly and then is spat out onto dry land, after which he goes about his way, apparently unharmed by his prolonged stay in the fish's belly, without oxygen and exposed to powerful digestive acids. Now, who would ever believe such a fantastic story? Charming or not, this Bible may cause even those who retain a live seed to stumble in their faith in IAM."

"It is an allegory," Serenious replied. "Again, that was the writing style of the day."

"But this book was supposed to have meaning for those living in subsequent centuries," Dianthe insisted. "By then, the writing style will change and stories like this will not be understood as allegory; they will be rejected as nonsense."

"Not by everyone," Serenious said, as he opened a hologram. "Consider this."

The hologram focused on the old Roman city of Hippo Regius, on the North African Coast of the Mediterranean Sea. The time was midmorning of the ninth day of the sixth month of Earth year 4,543,762,393 (June 9, 404). Dominic, a young priest, was walking over city streets, some built by the Phoenicians two thousand years earlier. Dominic's youthful face wore an earnest expression as he periodically asked bystanders for directions to the residence of Augustine, known throughout the city as the "Bishop of Hippo."

The young priest soon left the city proper and climbed a small hill to the residence that was his destination. It was a warm June day. There was hardly any breeze. Perspiration ran freely under Dominic's black robe, but he hardly noticed the uncomfortable temperature. He had an important mission for someone not yet thirty years of age: He had been sent by his superiors in Rome to get the learned bishop's views on how the first chapter of Genesis should be read—as literal accounts or as allegory.

When Dominic reached the bishop's residence, he turned back toward the Mediterranean. From his high perch, he could see far out over the azure sea. Several miles offshore, a sailing vessel moved slowly in a light breeze. It was a beautiful sight. Caught up in emotion, Dominic knelt, crossed himself, and said a prayer of thanksgiving for creation's beauty.

The front door to the residence opened without Dominic knocking.

"Please come in," the servant said. "The Bishop is anxious to meet you."

Once inside the spacious home, the young priest was surprised by its elegance—finely finished wood tables, chairs padded with the highest quality Egyptian linen, and walls decorated with large, brightly-colored tapestries. The residence had once been the home of Augustine's well-to-do parents. When Augustine inherited the property, he gave it to the church, and then used it as his personal residence.

After being ushered into Augustine's study, the young priest said, "Excellency, I bring you warm greetings from the church fathers in Rome."

"And please convey my warmest regards in return," Augustine replied. The older man was dressed in an unadorned black cassock with a faded red sash around his waist. A plain silver cross hung from his neck. His neatly-trimmed black beard and bushy eyebrows were striped with gray hair, but that was the only indication that the man was almost fifty years old. As Dominic surveyed his host's friendly countenance, he was drawn to Augustine's penetrating stare. For a moment, Dominic feared that the older man would judge him to be intellectually unworthy. But the reassuring tone of Augustine's voice was a welcome salve to Dominic's anxiety, and the young priest was able to relax in the presence of one of the greatest intellects of all time.

Holding up a letter he had received from church authorities in Rome, Augustine said, "Your superiors ask for my understanding of the creation story, as recorded in the first chapter of Genesis?"

"My assignment is to ask for your response to that letter," Dominic replied. "The church's leaders have read your works. They know you are a man not only of faith but of wisdom. They argue among themselves as to the meaning of this chapter, and they hope you can aid them in their quest for understanding."

"The creation story is difficult to comprehend. Why do your superiors think I can be of assistance?"

"Your writings have circulated widely, and your wisdom is obvious to the most casual reader."

Augustine accepted the compliment with a nod.

"Tell me, Excellency, was the world created in six days as the first chapter of Genesis seems to say, or are there deeper meanings to these words?" Dominic asked.

The older man smiled.

"The creation story is an allegory," Augustine replied. "It was not intended to be understood literally. Perhaps when science develops beyond its present lowly state, we will discover that all things in the physical universe were created not in six days but in one instant. Science may one day help us better understand creation. We should keep an open mind about what science tells us, so as not to appear closed-minded or foolish."[3]

"The creation story seems to be in significant detail," Dominic replied. "On the first day, our Heavenly Father created light and separated it from the darkness. On the second day, he created the sky as a barrier between waters above the earth and waters on the earth. On the third day, he separated the seas from the dry land, and on the dry land, he planted vegetation—seed-bearing plants and trees bearing fruit with seed in it. Where is the allegory? Why this level of detail?"

"Look more closely at these words. They are abstractions

lacking sufficient detail to explain empirical events. The first words of Genesis are 'In the beginning, God created heaven and earth?' Does this refer to the beginning of time, the beginning of this universe or something else? What does the phrase 'heaven or earth' refer to? Were these words meant to distinguish the spiritual from the material, the perfect from the incomplete, or something else?[3]

"Verse 3 of the first chapter reads, 'Let there be light and there was light.' To whom was God speaking when he issued this command? And what type of light was this—physical or spiritual?[3]

"In verse 14, God issued a similar command: 'Let there be light from the stars, sun, and moon.' How does the light resulting from these two separate commands relate to each other? And where did the light mentioned in verse 3 go, for we do not see it today? And if God thought this light was good, as verse 3 says, why create the additional light described in verse 14?"[3]

Dominic's mind raced to stay up with Augustine's questions. The bishop paused for a moment and stared at his guest, suggesting that he expected some response from the younger man. But all Dominic could offer was a shrug of the shoulders and a weak, "Excellency, your questions are insightful, but I have no answers."

"Perhaps there is one meaning, perhaps a thousand," Augustine said. "Perhaps our Lord meant for each reader to reach his or her own conclusion as to the meaning of these words. In this way, these verses may be the ultimate allegory: They find their meaning depending upon the faith of the reader."

The hologram closed.

"Unlike the student Joel that we heard from earlier, our servant Augustine is not troubled by the abstract words of Genesis," Serenious said. "And maybe Joel is not really troubled

---

[3]   The quotes and paraphrases of St. Augustine's words on this and the preceding page are based on translations of Augustine's views as set forth in *St. Augustine, The Literal Meaning of Genesis, vol. 1*, Ancient Christian Writers, vol. 41, The Paulist Press (1982). The quotes and paraphrases appear here with the permission of the Paulist Press.

by these words, either. Maybe what troubles Joel is that his seed has died, and he is searching for the meaning of his own existence in science and logic and not finding it."

Serenious and Dianthe looked to the Father to resolve their disagreement.

"All right, give me a moment to read this Bible," the Father said. He read the anthology's sixty-six books in the twinkling of an eye. "This Bible will serve its purpose," he said. "Some who carry a live seed will read these verses literally and understand them to be descriptions of actual events. Others will view them as metaphors or allegories. In either case, those with a live seed will view this book as showing the way to salvation. They will not reject the Bible's fundamental teachings because they do not understand every verse, or they find some verses confusing. On the other hand, those in whom the seed has died will view this book as full of nonsense. That's how Serenious designed it, and that's how it will remain. I congratulate Serenious. This Bible will be an excellent test to determine who carries a live seed."

"But Father ..."

"I'm sorry, Dianthe, but it has to be this way," the Father said. "We must have a rigorous test of the traitors' loyalty before we allow any of them back into our kingdom."

14.

Several days later, Dianthe approached the Father and said, "I spent time last evening examining this new world and found some surprises."

"Oh, what surprised you?" the Father asked.

"I found prisoners whose seeds appeared to have died living kind and generous lives, giving to the poor, making life on earth more pleasant for others, helping those in need, sometimes at grave risk to themselves."

"Yes, there will be such deserters."

"What will happen to them? Are we going to send them back to Hasatan to live in torment? Are we going to ignore their courage, their determination, their efforts to make life on Earth more bearable for their fellow prisoners?"

"Exactly who are you referring to?"

"Consider, for example, prisoner 10,034,078, a male life-form named Werdna, known in the material world as Andrew Lewis."

Dianthe opened a hologram. The image was of a sprawling, forty-room, single-story mansion, located in an exclusive section of La Jolla, California. The house had been featured in a recent edition of *Modern Architecture Magazine,* in an article entitled "An Architectural Wonder Overlooking the Pacific Ocean." On clear days, the view from the house was spectacular, extending far out to the sea lanes where pleasure boats, large cargo ships, and military vessels sailed up and down the California coast. The date was late in Earth year 4,543,764,039 (December 5, 2050).

The image in the hologram switched to Andrew Lewis, who was sitting in his home office at a highly-varnished, ebony desk trimmed with stainless steel. The desk was so large, it had to be constructed inside the room. Several of Andrew's favorite sayings were displayed on the office walls, including "With the right mix of skill and hard work, you can make your own heaven here on earth." Lewis was talking on his cell phone with the service manager for the company that maintained his self-flying helicopter. Lewis was complaining that last evening, he couldn't get his helicopter to fly a direct course to his home. It kept veering west over the Pacific Ocean before landing at the heliport on his property. The service manager explained that the aircraft's navigation system was designed to avoid other aircraft in his area, and that another aircraft was probably headed in his general direction, which is why his helicopter flew such a circuitous route. Lewis listened carefully and seemed satisfied with this explanation.

At the age of sixty-eight, Andrew Lewis was still a striking figure, with a youthful physique, a handsome face, a neatly trimmed beard, and a full head of hair. He wore a black shirt and dark custom-tailored jeans, which provided a stark contrast with his snow-white hair. Andrew resembled his creator in appearance, except that he obviously spent more time grooming than did the Father.

By 2050, Andrew had become the world's richest man, amassing a fortune that exceeded $300 billion. Lewis's biotechnology firm—Le-Alt Enterprises—had identified an enzyme that all cancer cells produced. But what created Lewis's huge fortune was the invention of a small, inexpensive device that could detect the presence of this enzyme in the human bloodstream at a cancer's earliest stages. The use of this device sharply reduced deaths from cancer in most parts of the world, especially third world countries that lacked extensive medical facilities.

When this device came on the market, orders poured into Lewis's firm. Prospective buyers were desperate for the device.

Some offered many times the suggested wholesale price to be put at the head of the distribution list. It took years before demand for the life-saving device could be satisfied on a timely basis.

Andrew was grateful for his good fortune and was willing to share his extraordinary wealth with others. He had already given away $50 billion in grants and gifts to universities, hospitals, public schools, research institutions, and foundations supporting cultural events. He had publicly announced that he planned to give away another $230 billion to worthy causes during the next five years. After that announcement, Lewis received thousands of requests for grants from all over the world.

Andrew's wife, Jenny, knocked on the door and walked into Lewis's office. She was neatly dressed in a white blouse and navy jeans. She had come to discuss the arrangements for a dinner party planned for that evening at their home. Andrew had invited the men and women who helped design the device that could identify the "cancer enzyme" to a dinner party to celebrate the twentieth anniversary of when the device was first offered for sale. Andrew was anxious to see his former associates, and he wanted the event to go smoothly.

At the age of fifty-three, Jenny still retained her school-girl figure. She was partially gray, but she retained a youthful outlook on life that was reflected in her broad smile and playful manner. Looking at the large stack of papers on Andrew's oversized desk, she said, "More requests for philanthropic gifts?"

"Yes, and I'm grateful for every one of them," Andrew said, as he ran his fingers over the pile. "There are so many worthy institutions working hard to improve life on earth. They need resources, and I'm going to give them what they need. At this stage of my life, my biggest fear is that we are not doing enough. We should be doing more, much more, and we should be doing it faster. The world has given us so much. We need to give something back."

Jenny stood behind her husband's chair and wrapped her arms around his neck and shoulders. "I know, and I love you for your kindness and generosity," she said. Looking at the stack of papers on his desk, she added, "I just don't want you to work too hard. Andrew, you're not a young man anymore."

"Oh, rubbish, I'm as strong as an ox."

"No, you're not. And the sooner you realize that you're almost seventy, the better off both of us will be."

Jenny turned toward the door and then turned back again. "I almost forgot why I came to your office," she said. "About this party we're hosting this evening for your old scientist buddies …"

The hologram closed.

"Andrew will meet his goal: During his lifetime, he will give away more than $280 billion, about 95 percent of his fortune," Dianthe said. "He will fund the construction of hospitals specializing in cancer treatments and research dedicated to finding cures for deadly diseases other than cancer. He will financially support the creation of performing art centers and two universities, one with a curriculum designed to attract Muslim students. He will fund organizations attempting to bring about world peace and organizations dedicated to increasing human understanding of the material universe. In his will, he will leave substantial sums of money to his household employees, saying they were like family. How can we send this kind and generous individual back to Hasatan?"

"For most of his life, Andrew will be an unapologetic atheist," the Father said. "His seed likely died eons ago. Consider his own words."

The hologram reopened. It was one Earth year later (December 20, 2051). Andrew, sitting at his desk, was talking on the phone with an old friend. Lewis had recently been diagnosed with Amyotrophic Lateral Sclerosis (ALS), a neurodegenerative disease that destroys neurons in the brain and spinal cord. The friend had called to express his regrets at hearing the sad news. The friend asked Lewis if he had changed his negative views about Christianity. Lewis replied that he had not.

"I wish I could convince myself that there is an afterlife, where we would all enjoy eternal paradise with nurturing angels attending to our every need. It is such a pleasant image. Unfortunately, it doesn't pass the laugh test. Christians believe in a God, who is angry at a world he created and is thus responsible for. This angry creature brings forth a son, in order that the child should plead with him to forgive sinners. But this father is not the forgiving kind. He insists on punishing somebody for the sins of a fallen mankind, so he punishes his own innocent son in the most brutal way possible to erase the sins of the rest of us. Do you seriously believe that? Is any creature who is so cruel to his own son likely to offer paradise to the rest of us? And if it did make such an offer, would you accept it?"

"Did he really say that?" Dianthe asked.

"He did," the Father replied, "and I think he meant every word."

"The problem is that Andrew doesn't understand IAM's attempts to redeem him."

"The problem is that Andrew's seed has died, and he is lashing out at his creator in anger and resentment."

"Still, are we going to lump him together with prisoners whose lives will be full of treachery and violence, prisoners responsible for mass killings and torture, prisoners who will show no generosity or mercy to their fellow human beings? Doesn't he deserve a better fate?"

"Yes, Andrew will provide the material world with many benefits, but the material world will reward him in kind. He will live in luxury for most of his earthly life. His home in La Jolla will have forty rooms with state-of-the-art conveniences. Ten servants will dote on him and Mrs. Lewis night and day. His supersonic jet will take him to Europe or South America in a matter of hours—lunch in Rio de Janeiro, dinner in Paris. His 180-foot yacht will take him up and down the California coast in grand style. World-famous performers will entertain at his parties; his guest lists will include famous celebrities. He will receive constant praise for his gifts; many of the buildings and institutions he will fund will bear his name. How much reward does a generous defector deserve?"

Dianthe tried to think of an appropriate response to that question, but none came immediately to mind.

"Perhaps Andrew Lewis is not the best example I could have chosen," she said.

"Do you have another?" the Father asked.

"I do. Please consider prisoner 41,245,352, the female life-form named Nah, known in the material world as Song Min-a.

A hologram opened. The time was 1:00 a.m. on the twenty-fourth day of the fourth month of Earth year 4,543,764,024 (Tuesday, April 24, 2035). Min-a and her husband, Bin, were sitting at the small kitchen table in their austere quarters at a secret government laboratory in the Democratic People's Republic of Korea (a.k.a. North Korea). The lab, hidden in the mountains about fifty miles south of the Chinese border and southwest of the city of Hyesan, was developing a deadly virus, KXCD, for which only North Korea would have an antidote. The North Korean government planned to place large amounts of the virus at strategically-placed locations around the globe. From these locations, winds would carry the deadly substance to most large and medium-sized cities on earth. KXCD was expected to kill an estimated four billion people, particularly children and the elderly.

Pak Jong-il, who succeeded Kim Jong-un as Supreme Leader in a military coup, had personally ordered that a deadly pathogen be developed. He had contracted an aggressive form of brain cancer and had only a short time to live. In his bitterness and borderline insanity, he had decided that if he had to die, he would take as much of the world's population with him as possible. His military leaders supported this project, thinking there would be no way to identify North Korea as the source of the resulting pandemic and that, after the virus had devastated humanity, North Korea would emerge as one of the world's most powerful nations.

There was one serious problem with KXCD: It had a long incubation period, forty-five days, from when it was first exposed to the natural environment until it became deadly and less vulnerable to attack by an antivirus. This meant that nations under attack would have almost forty-five days to develop an antidote once the airborne virus landed on their soil. Kang Dong Sung, the laboratory's director, had been ordered by his superiors to find a way to reduce this lengthy incubation period, and that is what led him to Min-a and Bin.

While not well known to the outside world, Min-a and Bin were, in fact, world-class microbiologists who specialized in the study of rice plants and the viruses that attacked them. After years of research, Min-a and Bin had identified the genes that controlled the ability of a particular strain of rice plant to resist virus attacks. The couple created various iterations of synthetic genes that they inserted into these plants, in hopes of finding one that would make the plants more virus resistant. After many attempts, they succeeded. Plants with modified genes lived longer and were more productive than plants without the modified genes. As a result of their work, North Korea began to outstrip the rest of the world in rice production per acre, and the regime finally solved its chronic food shortage problem. In other words, Min-a and Bin helped sustain human life in North Korea. Their assigned task at the North Korean lab was to do the opposite: To create a synthetic gene that would reduce KXCD's incubation period, and thus make it more deadly.

Min-a and Bin had agreed to work on the KXCD project—more accurately, they were ordered to do so on pain of death—knowing that they had been given an impossible task. It had taken years to craft a synthetic gene to increase the life span of rice plants, and it would likely take a similar amount of time to shorten KXCD's incubation period if, in fact, that could be accomplished. But laboratory director Kang demanded immediate results, and he could not be reasoned with. He had been ordered to shorten KXCD's incubation period, and that is what he demanded of Min-a and Bin. The couple had no intention of helping kill billions of innocent people. That left only one option: Stall the project for as long as possible, falsely assure Kang that they had succeeded, and then escape from the laboratory.

On the previous day, Min-a and Bin told Kang that they had found a way to shorten KXCD's incubation period to a few days, Kang immediately scheduled a test to verify their claim. It would soon become obvious that the incubation period had not been significantly modified. If Min-a and Bin remained at the laboratory, they would be asked to explain their failure and then punished, perhaps by immediate execution. And so, wide-eyed, with adrenalin surging through their veins, Min-a and Bin sat at their kitchen table early Tuesday morning methodically reviewing their escape checklist in search of anything they might have overlooked.

They knew that as soon as their escape was discovered, North Korea's massive security forces would begin searching for them. Most of those security forces would monitor escape routes to the north, because most North Koreans trying to escape the regime's brutality fled north, attempting to reach the Chinese border. But Min-a and Bin would not be going north. They would proceed east toward the Sea of Japan, where they hoped to rendezvous with an American rescue team on a desolate section of coastline south of the coastal city of Ch'ongjin.

They had carefully planned their escape route. They would avoid well-known roads and pathways. In addition to samples of KXCD, they would each carry dried food and water for four days, the time they estimated it would take to reach the coast and their rendezvous point. At exactly 1:15 a.m. on the twenty-fourth, while the security guards were changing shifts, they left their quarters and walked fifteen yards to a manhole cover that was out of the view of security cameras. Bin raised the cover with a steel bar he had taken from the laboratory. The couple climbed down into a drainage pipe, returned the manhole cover to its original position, and then crawled on their hands and knees to a clearing on the other side of a barbwire fence that held scientists in and the general population out of the compound. Then, they headed east.

For the first time in their lives, they were free. There were no guards, party loyalists, or superiors watching their every move, listening to their every word for evidence of disloyalty to the state. They felt alive in a way they had never experienced before. It was a heady feeling, and it gave them strength for the long journey ahead.

Min-a and Bin had planned well. They travelled at night, when they could not be seen by North Korean satellites. They spotted a few security teams covering passes through the mountains, but their planned route took them on high mountain trails traversed more by bears, deer, and mountain goats than by humans. As planned, they arrived at the rendezvous point on the coast shortly before 1:00 a.m. on the twenty-eighth, almost exactly ninety-six hours after their escape from the laboratory.

From his vantage point behind several large boulders, Bin looked out toward the ocean. Cloud cover had shrouded the beach in darkness, so much so that Bin had difficulty seeing the ocean waves as they ran up on the beach. "This is good," Bin said to himself. "The darkness will provide additional cover."

At precisely 3:00 a.m., Bin used his high-intensity flashlight to send a prearranged signal out to sea—three long flashes followed by two short flashes. Several minutes later, the couple saw two short flashes of light coming from a motorized inflatable rubber boat carrying four Navy Seals toward the sandy beach. The couple waited until the small craft landed behind large rocks at the water's edge. Bin and Min-a looked around for signs of North Korean guards. Not seeing any, they ran toward the Americans.

The couple did not look carefully enough. There were security forces guarding the beach. The North Koreans were equipped with night-vision devices that created images based on body heat. These devices provided rough images of Min-a and Bin, as the couple ran across the sand to what they hoped would be freedom. Min-a and Bin were fifty yards from the water's edge when a hail of gunfire rang out. Bin was hit in his right leg. He fell to the sand with a thud.

Min-a stopped and knelt by her husband.

"Get up!" she screamed over the sound of gun fire. "I'll help you."

She extended her hand to help Bin get to his feet. Bin grasped the hand and tried to get up, but he couldn't. The bullet had shattered the femur in his right leg just above the knee cap. His right leg would not support any weight. He tried to crawl, but he couldn't do that either.

Bin could see the rifle flashes of the approaching North Koreans as they ran to apprehend the fleeing couple.

"Min-a, run!" he screamed. "You must get out! Billions of lives depend on you!"

"What about you?" Min-a replied. "I will not leave you."

Mina-a couldn't decide what to do. She had never considered the possibility that in escaping from North Korea, she would have to leave Bin behind.

"Go! Before you are captured!" Bin shouted. "And tell the Americans that I cannot be taken alive."

From positions behind large boulders at the water's edge, the Americans began firing at the approaching North Koreans, providing cover for Min-a to run the last fifty yards in safety. She ran as fast as she could and dove headfirst behind the boulders.

The launch immediately left the beach and headed back toward a submarine waiting offshore, out of range of small arms. A gunner on the submarine kept the North Koreans pinned down with a large caliber machine gun, allowing the launch and its occupants to escape unharmed.

One of the Seals in the launch—Lee Byung-hun—was Korean by birth.

"Have you been hit?" he yelled to Min-a in Korean, over the noise of the launch heading into the oncoming waves.

"No," she yelled back, "but there is something you must do."

"What?" he asked.

"My husband cannot be taken alive. If the security forces capture him, they'll torture him until he discloses the American contact that helped us escape. Then they'll kill them both."

Looking back at the beach, Lee saw that Bin had raised his upper body to provide a clear target. Lee pointed to Bin and yelled to the team's sharpshooter: "Do it."

The sharpshooter fired a burst of five rounds. Bin's body shook, as all five rounds struck his torso.

Min-a watched her life partner of more than fifteen years fall backwards out of sight.

"I'm very sorry," Lee said.

Min-a did not reply. She tried to remain stoical. Her parents had taught her that life was full of tragedy and that the only way to survive the mental pain was to block unpleasantness from her mind. She had always followed that advice, to honor her parents. As the launch headed toward the submarine, she sat ramrod straight, staring at the passing waves with her head held high. She did her best not to show emotion, and the Navy Seals in the launch marveled at her mental strength. They did not see the single tear that flowed from her left eye, ran slowly down her left cheek, and fell from her face. There are limits to humans' ability to withstand emotional pain, and Min-a had reached hers.

Within hours, Min-a was transported to an American aircraft carrier and flown to Busan, South Korea. While in flight, she provided, by radio, all the information she could about the composition of KXCD and possible antidotes to a hastily assembled group of internationally-renowned biologists. When she arrived in Busan, she gave a sample of the virus to the group. An antidote was soon developed, and its composition shared with all nations. Most nations produced an antivirus and distributed it to their populations.

When the plot to kill billions of people became known, the North Korean regime imploded. There was an internal rebellion led by junior military officers, assisted by a United Nations task force. The Supreme Leader and many of his senior leaders were killed during the insurrection. The laboratory at the secret facility was destroyed, and the country's nuclear weapons were dismantled. North Korea became a United Nations protectorate.

"It is true. Min-a will be a brave woman dedicated to helping others. But she will not be loyal to IAM," the Father said. "Consider this: The image in the hologram changed to Min-a's temporary home in Andong, South Korea. Several months had passed since her escape from the laboratory. Min-a was sitting at her kitchen table, blankly staring at the walls. She was suffering from depression, and Kim Da Hae, a friend and confidant, was trying to console her.

Min-a was wearing an old dress that had frayed in several places. She wore no makeup. She had spent little time grooming herself that morning. Min-a was an attractive woman. Her prominent forehead and small, well-shaped mouth accurately suggested a person who thought more than she spoke. Her dark-brown, deep-set eyes suggested that she was a deep thinker, not given to superficiality. She had a beauty mark on her left cheek. She would have hidden the beauty mark if she could. She was a talented scientist, one of the twenty-first century's preeminent geneticists. By 2035, the North Korean regime had, to its credit, taken steps to eliminate discrimination against women serving in high-level scientific positions. However, centuries-old practices die hard, and the highest levels of North Korea's scientific community remained a male-dominated culture that did not warmly embrace female scientists, especially physically attractive female scientists. To increase her chances of being accepted into this community, Min-a did everything she could to downplay her attractive feminine features.

"Min-a, I know you have experienced a tremendous loss," her friend said. "I know how much Bin cared for you, how much he loved you. How he supported your work. But life goes on, and you must go on."

"I feel so alone without him. He was such a kind and gentle man, always patient with others, including me. He rarely became angry or raised his voice. I think about him all the time. Now that he's gone, I don't know what will happen to me. I fear for the future."

"Maybe you should pray for strength."

Min-a was amused by the thought. She smiled for the first time in months.

"When I was a child," she said, "I believed in fairy tales. My parents believed in the Christian God and encouraged me to believe in him. But when I became an adult, I came to accept the world for what it is, and I stopped believing in fantasies. Maybe there's a god out there somewhere in the universe. Maybe not. But I am a scientist. My god is science. I know how science has saved lives, brought comfort to the suffering, and greater understanding of the world that surrounds us. Science is truth. Christianity is fable. My parents believed promises that the Christian God would protect them and their children from harm. But the Christian God did not protect my little brother from the pain of dying from starvation. The Christian god did not protect my parents from being taken away, never to be heard from again, because they admitted to being Christians. No, I will not pray to the Christian God for strength. My strength will come from within, or it will not come."

The hologram closed.

"Father, Min-a's courage and sacrifice will save billions of humans from a painful death. She will become a professor at Korea Advanced Institute of Science and Technology, one of the world's finest universities. While there, she will receive recognition as a world leader in the field of genetics, and her work will open new frontiers in ways to modify genes and cure disease. Unlike Andrew Lewis, Min-a will never aspire to great wealth, and she will never achieve it. She will, however, devote her life to finding ways to help humanity, and she will die a person of modest means. How can we reject such a brave and caring person?"

"We will not reject her; she will reject us," the Father replied. "She will be raised in the faith but turn away from us when she becomes an adult. Her work as a scientist will persuade her that she can deal with existence on her own terms, that she doesn't need a relationship with her creator. For the rest of her life, she will be praised as a heroine who saved the planet from a pandemic. She will be one of the most recognized and revered scientists of her time. She will receive hundreds of prizes and awards and more than a hundred honorary degrees. She will be given a ticker tape parade in New York City and receive similar honors in England, Germany, Japan, and South Korea. She will receive a Nobel Prize for her work in genetics. A large statue of Min-a and Bin will be erected in Seoul, South Korea. Although she will never become wealthy, she will live a very comfortable human existence. She will be amply rewarded for her bravery and her scientific accomplishments.

Dianthe looked to Serenious for support, but he said, "I'm sorry Dianthe, but I agree with the Father."

Frustrated that her first two choices for leniency had been rejected, the exasperated Dianthe offered a third candidate: "Well, then, consider prisoner 378,021, the male life-form named Edomein, known in the material world as Ed Morgan. Ed will achieve neither great wealth nor fame. He will live most of his adult life in the suburban town of Vienna, Virginia, where he will coach Little League baseball for more than thirty years.

"Ed will teach his players how to play baseball. But more importantly, he will teach them life skills—to be patient with others, to help others succeed, to be a gracious winner, and to learn from their mistakes when they lose. Those lessons will remain with his players throughout their lives. Many of them will become successful baseball players, but many more will become successful citizens and leaders in their communities.

"Ed will play professional baseball. He will make it to the Major Leagues, only to suffer a career-ending injury during his rookie season. But his contribution to others as a Little League coach will far exceed whatever he might have contributed to society as a professional baseball player."

A hologram opened. The time was the third day of the eighth month of Earth year 4,543,764,019 (August 3, 2030). A finely groomed Little League baseball field came into view. The championship game of the Little League's Southeast Regional Tournament was underway. More than five hundred spectators had crowded onto viewing stands to watch the game that would decide whether the Vienna team, coached by Ed Morgan, or a team from Maitland, Florida, would go to the Little League World Series in Williamsport, Pennsylvania.

The Vienna team was ahead 3–1 going into the last half of the last inning. The team from Maitland was at bat. The Vienna pitcher, Lew Evans, was pitching well. He had walked the first batter on a pitch that should have been called a strike, and then struck out the next two batters. Only one more batter stood between the Vienna team and Little League World Series glory. Parents and spectators began discussing the best route to take to Williamsport, when disaster struck.

The fourth batter hit a line drive that struck Lew immediately above his right eye. He fell to the ground, clutching his head as blood ran down his face. Ed and Dr. Terry O'Rourke ran onto the field, followed by Lew's father. A hush came over the crowd.

"We've got to get him to the emergency room," O'Rourke said after a quick examination. "He needs stitches."

With the help of his dad and O'Rourke, Lew stood up. He left the field clutching a towel to his head, while spectators clapped to acknowledge his bravery.

Timmy Worth was the only remaining pitcher on the Vienna team eligible to pitch in this final game. Timmy was an eleven-year-old on a team where every other player was either twelve or thirteen. Timmy was a talented young pitcher, but he was put on the team to give him experience for next year's postseason play. Although he had pitched a few innings against weaker teams in the tournament and had done well, none of the coaches thought Timmy could successfully pitch against the stronger teams. But, with no other option available, Ed called Timmy out to the mound.

Timmy threw twelve warm-up pitches.

"Are you ready, pitcher?" the umpire asked. "You can take more warm-up pitches if you want."

To say Timmy was nervous would be an understatement. His facial expression said he was on the edge of panic.

"I'm ready, sir," he replied, without much conviction in his voice.

"Timmy, just throw strikes and rely on your fielders to catch the ball," Ed yelled from the dugout.

Maitland's best hitter stepped into the batter's box, and the umpire yelled, "Play ball!" Timmy forced a smile, tugged at his cap, and looked at the catcher for a sign. Looking for a sign was a mere formality. Timmy had only one pitch he could consistently throw for a strike, and that was a sixty-five mile-an-hour fastball.

Timmy threw his first pitch. It was about twelve inches outside the strike zone, and the catcher had to lunge to catch the ball. The umpire yelled, "Ball!"

Timmy's second pitch bounced almost six inches in front of the plate. "Ball two!" the Umpire yelled.

"You're okay, Timmy," Ed yelled. "Just relax. Let me see a nice smooth pitching motion."

Timmy's third pitch crossed the center of the plate at about the batter's waist. The batter swung and drove the ball far over the left field fence for a home run to win the game.

Maitland players streamed onto the field screaming with joy. They mobbed their home run hero, as he jumped onto home plate with both feet after rounding the bases. Timmy and the other Vienna players slowly walked off the field and into their dugout. The pain of coming so close to the Little League World Series and then losing was evident on every player's face.

In the dugout, Ed sat down next to Timmy, who could not stop crying.

"Timmy, every great ball player has had at least one day like this, when things went terribly wrong. But the great players put disappointments like this behind them and go on. You'll have more bad days. But you have a lot of talent, and if you can put aside the disappointments, you may someday pitch in the Major Leagues, and people like me will be asking for your autograph. How about if you give me your autograph now, so I won't have to stand in line when you're in the Major Leagues?"

Ed handed Timmy the tournament program and a pencil.

"You really mean it?" Timmy asked.

"Yes, I really do," Ed said. "I hate standing in lines."

Timmy smiled, signed the program, and handed it back to Ed. Timmy seemed relieved, like a load had been lifted from his shoulders. He wiped the tears from his face with a towel, got up, and began stuffing his baseball gear back into his equipment bag.

Timmy's dad, who had observed this conversation from outside the dugout, approached Ed.

"That was awesome," he said. "No wonder you're so good at coaching Little League."

"This type of thing happens at least once a season. I've got a drawer full of autographs at home," he said with a smile. "Maybe one of them will make it to the Major Leagues."

Tim's dad laughed.

The hologram closed.

"Ed Morgan, EM, everyman," Dianthe said. "He will devote his life to helping youngsters master the game of baseball and, more importantly, the game of life. Are we going to send him back to Hasatan, too?"

"Let's have a second look at Coach Morgan," the Father said.

The hologram reopened. It was an early spring practice the following year. Ed and Timmy were sitting next to each other in the dugout, while the rest of the team was warming up. Timmy was scheduled to pitch the second half of a practice game, so he was not warming up with the rest of his team. Normally, Timmy would be thinking about pitching, but on this day, another thought filled his head.

"Mr. Morgan, my mom says you don't believe in God," Timmy said. "That's why you schedule practices on Sunday morning instead of going to church. Is that true? Do you believe in God?"

"Timmy, I believe in God. Mother Nature is my god, and every time I come to this field, I thank her for all the beauty she brings to this world. My church is this field and my prayers are working on this field so guys like you can play their best on it. I may not have the same god as your mom, but that doesn't make me a bad person. I just have a different god. Is that okay with you?" Ed asked.

"That's fine with me," Timmy said while looking at the beautifully manicured field, the freshly cut grass, the carefully raked infield, the straight, white foul lines, and the outfield fence decorated with colorful ads on behalf of local merchants. "I never thought about it like that, Mr. Morgan."

The hologram closed.

"While sitting in that dugout, Timmy will be thinking, I see what Coach Morgan and Mother Nature have given me—a beautiful field on which to play and a coach to help me be a better player. But I'm not sure what the God I learn about in Sunday School gives me," the Father said. "Morgan will plant doubt about IAM in Timmy's mind. He will do the same for many of the boys he coaches. Timmy and others may lose their seed partly because of Morgan's influence. As for rewards, Morgan will be honored each year with a dinner in his honor sponsored by local businessmen. Local newspapers will report his teams' successes and quote him extensively. He will be revered in his community as an outstanding youth leader. Isn't that enough reward for his good work?"

"Father, the point is that these three prisoners will devote themselves to helping others more than many who appear to carry a live seed."

"Yes, that will be so. But perhaps they will do these generous things, not out of love of neighbor, but for love of self—the public adulation they will receive, the power they will feel by putting others in their debt, the self-satisfaction they will experience based on their accomplishments, and in some cases, the wealth they will accumulate. There is only one reason for us to create this universe: To identify prisoners who are loyal to us. We are not trying to identify those who will lead moral lives by earthly standards. What would be the point of that? Earthly standards will be flawed, corrupted by human weakness and wickedness. Earthly standards will often punish the naïve and innocent and reward the brash and assertive."

"Dianthe, your holograms show Andrew, Min-a, and Edward at stages in their earthly lives when they may not be loyal to IAM," Serenious said, joining the discussion. "But when facing human mortality, perhaps one or more will change their minds. All three seem to have a spiritual side that suggests their seeds, while weak, may not be dead."

"That is a kind thought," the Father said. "But given what we know about these three deserters—Werdna, Nha, and Edomein—prior to when they went over to Hasatan, I think it unlikely that any of them will end their human lives as loyal subjects."

"What prior actions are you referring to?" Dianthe asked.

The Father called up a hologram. A large country estate in the Positive Energy Kingdom came into view. A long, tree-lined driveway and a large front courtyard led to an elegant, three-story, white-brick building with fifty-seven rooms. Strictly symmetrical, the structure's architecture was that of the French Baroque Period, featuring prominent dormers in a black, mansard roof. Graceful landscaping and large, sculptured fountains surrounded the building. The house and grounds were magnificent, but a little too showy for most Positive Kingdom tastes.

The home's interior was equally imposing. It featured life-size paintings and sculptures, fine furnishings, and carpeting with intricate designs keyed to Positive Kingdom historical events. The first-floor library was furnished with a large table, high-back chairs, and bookcases that reached to the second-floor ceiling. Twenty life-forms were seated around the table. They had come to the estate that day to discuss treason—deserting the Positive Kingdom and pledging allegiance to Hasatan. There was a sense of excitement, bordering on exhilaration, in the room. The estate belonged to Anryms, an older life-form sitting at the head of the table. Anryms wore a black robe. Wearing black clothing in the Positive Energy Kingdom suggested dissatisfaction with IAM's reign. Anryms wore his black robe proudly, if not defiantly.

Anryms opened the meeting with standard pleasantries but quickly got to the point. To avoid attracting attention from the kingdom's security forces, he spoke in a prearranged code that eliminated any references to leaving the Positive Energy Kingdom, to Hasatan, or to treason.

"I recently spoke with our new friend," Anryms said. "He asked me to convey to each of you a cordial invitation to join him. Suitable living accommodations are being arranged."

"How suitable?" Werdna asked.

"As you can see from my home, I have high standards. I've seen the living accommodations our friend is offering, and they are consistent with what you see around you. You'll be surprised at the luxury that awaits you."

"I'm pleased to hear that. I have done so much to improve the quality of life in the Positive Energy Kingdom. My contributions should be recognized and rewarded, at the very least, with suitable living accommodations."

"They will be if you accept our friend's invitation."

Nah, a female life-form, spoke: "I don't care about living accommodations. Mine are fine. I am on the verge of a scientific breakthrough in how to capture more of the energy created by the natural workings of the universe. If I succeed, all life in the Primary Universe will benefit. But I need additional scientific equipment to complete my work. The Ministry of Science has promised me this equipment for eons, but somehow it never arrives. Before I visit our new friend, I need to know that I'll have a suitable laboratory and the equipment I need to complete my work."

"You'll soon receive a thought-message describing the laboratory that awaits you and a list of its equipment," Anryms replied. "The list is all scientific gibberish to me, but I assume you'll understand it."

Anryms looked around the room until he spotted Edomein. "What are your thoughts, Edomein?"

"What troubles me about IAM's kingdom is the way we are all expected to follow IAM's rules and share IAM's values. There is no room for disagreement or even doubt. I find that stifling. I need the freedom to develop my own philosophy, my own values, my own sense of what constitutes good and evil. We're told we have freedom, but in IAM's kingdom, that means we're free to adhere to IAM's inflexible list of do's and don'ts. I'm tired of rigid rules. I'm not a robot programmed to operate within a fixed moral scheme. I'm a thoughtful being, and I need freedom to think things through on my own."

Nineteen heads nodded in agreement.

"Well said, Edomein," Werdna commented. "We all share your views, because we all labor under the same fiendish form of thought suppression."

Anryms went around the table and asked the others for their views. Everyone agreed with the comments of Werdna, Nah, and Edomein. Akeetom was the only member of the group to voice any reservations about the impending betrayal.

"This is a big step we're about to take," he said. "What if it's a con? What if we're being fed a bunch of lies to convince us to accept this invitation? You know, our new friend doesn't have a stellar reputation for truthfulness and honesty?"

"What could our friend possibly gain from such a con?" Werdna asked. "I can't think of anything, can you? Is he overselling his offer? I'm sure he is. Don't we all exaggerate from time to time? But anything would be better than the frustration I feel here. I'll take my chances with our new friend. I'm tired of being disrespected. I need to be recognized and rewarded for the good I've done."

"I agree," Nah said. "This may seem strange coming from a scientist, but every now and then, you have to take a leap of faith. And this is such a time. When the status quo becomes intolerable, life-forms of courage act. I stand with Anryms, Werdna, and Edomein."

Everyone else in the room, even Akeetom, stood and promised to join what had just become a movement. The excitement at the thought of throwing off IAM's controls was exhilarating. Twenty life-forms became giddy at the prospect of living a new existence, which they imagined would be so much better, so much freer, than their present lives.

"Our friend makes one request: That you share this invitation with your family, friends and associates, anyone you think would like a more fulfilling existence and a deeper understanding of our universe," Anryms said.

"I'd be happy to share this good news with others," Werdna said.

"So, would I," Nah said.

The others promised to do the same.

The hologram closed.

"So that's how the Great Betrayal began. With twenty malcontents on an ego trip whining that they didn't receive all they were due," Serenious said. "And as a result, fifty million positive-energy life-forms now find themselves confined in Hasatan's fiery prison."

"Sadly, these life-forms convinced themselves that their comfort, their work, their knowledge, and their sense of right and wrong were of paramount importance," the Father explained. "Not once during this meeting did any of them express concern about how their actions would affect the well-being of their creator, the being who gave them life, nurtured, and protected them. Nor did they ever mention how their actions would impact those in our kingdom who remained loyal to IAM. These defectors see themselves as the center of the universe. They want to define morality in ways that will make them more comfortable. They reject the idea that they were created to serve IAM and IAM's principles. If they wish to live apart from their creator, so be it. But they cannot follow that path and return to IAM's kingdom."

Dianthe reluctantly agreed, but she still dreaded the thought of sending Werdna, Nah, and Edomein back to Hasatan.

"These three turned away from IAM, yet they accept the idea that they should do good and reject evil," Dianthe said. "In the material world, Werdna will feel compelled to build libraries and universities to help educate others less fortunate than himself, Nah will feel obliged to risk her life to save others from a global pandemic, and Edomein will feel obligated to teach life skills to young baseball players. What explains this compulsion to do 'good' as they see it?"

"When the seed dies," the Father explained, "it leaves behind a residue the deserters will call a 'conscience.' This conscience will tell deserters there is both good and evil in the universe and that they should strive to do good. But when prisoners lose their connection to IAM, they will no longer understand IAM's moral foundation that gives meaning to those terms. Lacking this foundation, they will define those terms on the basis of their own limited understanding of good and evil. Eventually, this self-defined moral code will disintegrate into a primitive form of moral relativism: You do your thing, and I'll do my thing, and so long as we don't hurt each other, we're moral people."

"Traitors whose seeds have died will find this contrived moral code satisfying?" Serenious asked.

"Some will," the Father said, "but many traitors will spend their lives searching for a moral code that gives meaning to human existence that has separated itself from its creator and never find it."

"Will this conscience do anything else?" Serenious asked.

"It will also tell prisoners there are forces in the universe larger and more powerful than themselves that they should acknowledge and worship. In primitive societies, it will lead some to worship sources of great presence—the sun, moon, planets, and stars. It will also cause some to worship things they themselves will create—figures carved from wood or stone, objects molded in gold or silver."

"That's bizarre. Why would anyone worship something they created?"

"Conscience will tell the deserters that they need to worship something. But primitive people will not be alone in worshipping something they created. Many prisoners will create in their own minds gods other than IAM, gods that better fit their own sense of right and wrong, gods that will be more compatible with their own contrived values. These imaginary gods will range from abstract, passive creatures who do nothing but exist, to demanding beings that require constant sacrifices from their followers. Some deserters will worship moral philosophies they invent. In each case, they will worship something they created."

"You're saying some traitors will worship an idea, a philosophy, instead of an active, powerful creator?"

"I know that sounds strange, but it will be so."

"The defectors were created by you. They lived in our kingdom and were exposed to our ideas and values for eons," Dianthe said. "Yet, many of them harbored evil thoughts, ideas that are foreign to our kingdom. What is the origin of these strange ideas?"

"I created these life-forms from positive energy," the Father explained. "But to ensure they would hold together and survive, I had to include in each of them a small amount of negative energy. That negative energy, that dark side, produces evil thoughts. Life-forms need to control their dark side, and most do so. But, unfortunately, some of our subjects did not, and that is what led to their rebellion."

15.

Day 357⁹ ZMC-8624-05-02 was especially beautiful in IAM's capital city. The dual suns shone brightly. The atmospheric plasma had turned a deep blue. A gentle breeze kept the temperature at a comfortable level. It was a perfect day, and Dianthe decided to make the most of it. She transported herself to the Great Mensa Sea and began walking along the beach, taking in the fresh sea air and enjoying the sound of gentle, rolling waves breaking as they approached the sandy shore. She took off her sandals and walked in the surf, occasionally looking back to watch the waves run up the beach and wash her footprints away before retreating back into the sea.

As she watched her footprints disappear, she had a troubling thought. In the Primary Universe, events were predictable. The universe was stable. Suns, planets, and moons moved with mathematical precision in fixed orbits. Yes, life-forms gradually changed over time, but the changes were very slow in coming, and they occurred in a manner that could be foreseen far in advance. Of course, there was one event that was a surprise—the Great Betrayal—but that was the rare exception.

In the material universe, however, change would be the norm, not the exception. Human life-forms would be constantly changing—birth, aging, death—and it would all happen very quickly. Even the environment would be constantly changing. Land masses, floating on a fluid-like substance that humans would call the "asthenosphere," would crash into one another, causing volcanoes and earthquakes that would disrupt life for millions of Earth's inhabitants. Dianthe wondered if the defectors, even those carrying a live seed, would be able to deal with the anxiety brought about by this constant change.

Off in the distance, Dianthe noticed a figure coming toward her. It was a rotund life-form, who nonetheless moved along smartly, pausing only occasionally to look out to sea. When the figure came closer, she recognized that it was Serenious, who had likewise decided to indulge himself with a walk along the beach.

"Serenious," she yelled. Serenious waved and quickened his pace toward Dianthe.

"Out here enjoying the natural phenomena?" he asked.

"Yes, on a beautiful day."

As the two walked along the beach, they mostly engaged in small talk. Then Serenious asked, "Do you think this grand trial the Father has designed will produce the results he's hoping for?"

"Is there any reason to believe it won't?" Dianthe asked.

"Well, this is a very complex project, more complex than anything we have attempted in the past. Once it is set into motion, there will only be minimal control by us. And with Hasatan having free access to this new world, there certainly is reason to be concerned."

"My Father has never failed at anything, and he will not allow this trial to fail."

"I wish I were as confident as you. This project will consume a great deal of energy. And you will be making an enormous sacrifice. Are you not at all worried that it might fail?"

"Well, I do wonder about a few minor things. These prisoners are unpredictable creatures, and they will be functioning in a new and unpredictable world. There will be challenges. But I'm sure the Father has considered all of that."

"Should we, at least, share our concerns with him?"

Dianthe paused before answering. She had never done anything before that might be viewed as questioning the

Father's judgment. She never had reason to do so. The Father's knowledge and wisdom were unsurpassed in the Primary Universe. But Dianthe knew that Serenious was right. This trial was more complex, and it had more potential for disaster than anything IAM had ever attempted before. Finally, she gave in to what her instincts were telling her and said, "Perhaps we should present our concerns to the Father."

That evening, the Father sat at his desk, reviewing the calculations underlying his design of the material world. He was cross-checking his data runs when he heard a gentle knock at the door.

"Come in," he said without taking his eyes off his monitor screen.

The door opened, and Dianthe and Serenious entered.

"Both of you look concerned," the Father said. "Why the unease?"

"I have carefully examined your plans for the new universe," Serenious said. "They clearly show the enormous care and attention to detail that you have brought to this project. I am awed by your dedication to perfection."

The Father interrupted, "Serenious, you didn't come in here to compliment me on my efforts to produce a workable test for the deserters. You have a concern. What is it?"

"The great disparity in the hosts' circumstances concerns me. Some will be beggars, others will have great wealth. Some will be learned and have access to information, art, and music attesting to their creator's magnificence; others will have none of these things. Some will eat well and live in elegant surroundings; others will live at the edge of starvation, their lives full of torment. Some will be sickly and live in pain; others will enjoy good health. Can this be a fair test for all the traitors if they live in such different conditions? Let me show you the problem. Follow me ahead in time to noon on the third day of the sixth month of Earth year 4,543,763,962 (June 3, 1973), to the largest garbage dump serving the ancient city of Pandharpur, in the Indian state of Maharashtra."

Serenious, followed by the Father and Dianthe, appeared at the dump. The three were dressed in the clothing worn by citizens of lower social standing in India.

Ravikiran Sarvasuddi, forty-three years old, was scavenging through recent deliveries to the dump with his bare hands. He wore only a brief loincloth around his waist and sandals that were coming apart. He was dirty. His feet were covered with scabs from stepping on sharp objects. His body had open sores. His ribs were showing. He was on the edge of starvation.

Ravikiran, nicknamed "Ravi" by his father, had once been a successful cobbler. He owned a well-equipped shop, dressed reasonably well, and was loved and respected by family, friends, and customers, almost all of whom were ardent worshippers of the Hindu god Vithoba. In September 1970, Ravi converted to Christianity. Most of those who knew Ravi looked upon his conversion as a betrayal of a sacred trust, and their response was swift and devastating. His customers left him, and he lost his business. He was abandoned by his family, ostracized from his community, and reduced to digging through a trash dump to find enough food to survive.

When Ravi saw the Father, Serenious, and Dianthe standing by the dump, he snarled, "Get away from here. There's no food for you here. Get away."

"Don't be concerned," the Father replied. "We're not here to take your food."

"Good," said Ravi, who continued talking in a semi-deranged rant. "God of Abraham, why am I here...suffering in this miserable life. Look at me. Is there a more miserable creature on this whole earth than me? Grand creator, are you listening? Can you hear me? I hate you. Do you understand?"

"Yes, Ravi, I do understand," the Father said in a kindly voice.

Ravi froze in place. He turned around slowly and glared at the Father with a confused expression on his face. Just then, a large, chauffeur-driven limousine passed by the dump. A man wearing a suit, white shirt, and tie sat in the back seat reading the business section of an English-language newspaper. Ravi pointed to the passenger and continued his rant: "Why am I not him and he not me? Is this fair? Am I being punished for something I did, or is God playing a joke on me? What is the purpose of my life? Great God, why haven't you rescued me from these miserable conditions?"

Ravi continued searching for food until he found a loaf of bread that was several days old. It had been discarded by one of Pandharpur's better restaurants. Except for a small amount of mold that Ravi scraped away, the bread was still edible. He held it up to the sky as if it were a prize of great value. In fact, the loaf was of great value, because it meant Ravi would have enough food to survive for several more days.

At that same time, a young woman, Mahila Andolan, carrying her two-year-old son in a sling next to her bosom, came out from the shadows of a nearby building. She was dressed in a faded, rumpled, blue sari, and she was terrified. As a member of the Dalit caste, an "untouchable," she was required to live in a *kachcha* (a house constructed of natural materials, such as mud, grass, bamboo, thatch, and sticks), away from town. She was not allowed to walk through upper-class neighborhoods, and she was not permitted to wear clean, neat clothing. Doing any of these things would offend Pandharpur's upper classes, and she would be punished for breaking these social norms.

Mahila and her son had not eaten for two days. The boy was screaming from hunger, and she couldn't silence him. Desperate for food, she had walked to the dump in broad daylight, through an upper-class neighborhood and then a commercial section, taking side roads and back alleys whenever she could to avoid being seen. She had run between buildings when traffic was light and hidden in the shadows when she thought she might be noticed.

As she approached the dump, her son saw the bread in Ravi's hands and began to scream. Ravi hid the bread behind his back, but that only made the child scream louder. Ravi knew he could not eat the bread and allow the mother and young boy to go hungry. He approached Mahila, smiled, and handed her the bread. The anger that had marked his appearance a few moments before changed—empathy replaced rage and resentment. Mahila sniffed the bread to be sure it was edible, and then she and her son devoured this precious gift. After she departed, the lonely resident of Pandharpur's largest dump went back to scavenging. He did not notice when the three persons of IAM faded away.

"Now for the contrast," Serenious said. "Follow me ahead in time to 155 Four Seasons Ave. in Manhattan at 12:30 p.m. on the twenty-third day of the seventh month of Earth year 4,543,763,985 (July 23, 1996)."

The three persons of IAM, dressed in business attire, appeared in an alley adjacent to an exclusive French restaurant. They walked around to the front of the building, past a doorman at curbside opening the doors of limousines that had lined up to deposit their passengers. Inside the restaurant, elegant table linens, crystal, fine china, and silverware graced each table. Luncheon entrees started at $100.00.

"Shall we do lunch?" Serenious asked.

"Are you sure we can afford this place?" Dianthe asked jokingly.

The three entered the restaurant. Serenious approached the maître d' who was stationed just inside the front entrance.

"Sir, do you have reservations?" the maître d' asked.

"Yes, they're under the name I. Amson."

The maître d' looked down his list of reservations.

"Yes. Here they are. Please, follow me." The Father, Dianthe, and Serenious were seated at table number 26.

Several moments later, a waiter, Paul Bovier, stopped at their table. "Welcome, I'm Paul, and I'll be serving you this afternoon. I'll be right back with menus."

A harpist at the rear of the restaurant began to play her heavenly instrument, and the melodic sounds of Johann Sebastian Bach's "Jesu, Joy of Man's Desiring" filled the room.

"Listen," Dianthe said. "The harpist is playing Grital's 3rd sonata in harmonic key no. 2. That's one of my favorite Grital pieces."

When Bovier returned with menus, Dianthe asked, "Waiter, who is the composer of the piece the harpist is playing?"

"Johann Sebastian Bach," Paul replied. "The owner of this restaurant loves Bach, so the harpist plays a lot of Bach's music to entertain our guests."

"No," Dianthe insisted, "that piece is ..."

Dianthe's lips kept moving, but no sound came out of her mouth.

The waiter leaned forward, trying to hear what Dianthe was saying, and wondering why he couldn't.

"Yes, that piece is...simply wonderful," the Father said, finishing Dianthe's sentence. "My daughter is so devoted to Bach that at times she becomes, well, speechless."

The waiter looked at the Father and then at Dianthe. He knew something strange, something unnatural, had just occurred in his presence, but he wasn't quite sure what it was. He scratched his head and walked back to the kitchen mumbling to himself.

"Father, that is such a nice addition, bringing Grital's music into this new world," Dianthe said. "And this harpist plays it so well."

"Yes, I thought the defectors would benefit from exposure to Grital's genius," the Father replied.

When Paul entered the kitchen, Henri, the headwaiter, asked, "What's with the mumbles?"

"Take a look at the threesome at table 26," Paul said.

"What about 'em?"

"There is something strange about that group. I don't know what it is, but I definitely sense it."

Henri cracked open the kitchen door slightly to get a better look at table 26.

"Hey, the blonde's a fox," he said. "I bet she's a paid companion."

"Why do you say that?" Paul asked.

"The expensive clothes, beautiful face, clear complexion, slim figure, the perfect blonde 'do' with not a hair out of place. She probably spends five hours a day making herself look that good. Who but a paid companion would have that much time to spend on her appearance?"

"I don't know about that; she looks kind of angelic to me."

"That's the new thing with paid companions—the innocent look. They're all doing it."

"How is it you know so much about paid companions?"

Henri laughed, but didn't answer the question.

"The old guy seems a little eccentric," Henri said. "Probably hasn't combed his hair in ages. But then, we've got several eccentric customers. The stout, middle-aged, black guy...he's probably the old dude's accountant. He's got Deloitte written all over him, from the expensive suit to the button-down white shirt and black and red striped tie. But no, I don't see anything strange about them."

The table across the aisle from the Father, Dianthe, and Serenious was occupied by Solomon Ballenger, the principal in a hedge fund, and Stig Hansen, a salesman for the luxury yacht builder Bruden Marine. Ballenger was in his mid-forties, but he looked older. He was prematurely gray, and overweight, with a pronounced double chin. He wore an elegant $7,000 Savile Row suit—light gray with pinstripes—a white shirt, and a blue striped tie. He had gained weight since the suit was custom fitted, and it no longer accommodated his paunchy body. Hansen was a forty-two-year-old, well-tanned and well-dressed, former professional offshore powerboat racer. His racing career had ended several years earlier when he lost control of a boat going ninety-five knots and somehow miraculously survived the crash.

Ballenger summoned the waiter to his table and, in a stage voice, complained that his veal chop was overdone and that his wine was too warm: "Please remind the sommelier that Chateau La Benadine is supposed to be served no warmer than sixty-two degrees. This wine is at least seventy degrees. Someone left the bottle standing in the hot kitchen. It's awful. I can't drink it. You know, it is a crime to serve fine wine at the wrong temperature."

"I deeply apologize, Mr. Ballenger," the waiter said. "Would you like me to chill this bottle? I could put it in the freezer for a few minutes."

"No. The sudden change in temperature will affect its taste. Besides, that will take too long. Bring out another bottle if you have one at the correct temperature."

"Sir, I can bring another bottle directly from our wine cellar, but I will have to charge you for both bottles. That will add an additional $1,000 to your bill. This wine has become very hard to get."

The conversation between Ballenger and the waiter had carried to surrounding tables. The restaurant suddenly became silent, as the other patrons stared at Ballenger, amazed that he would spend $1,000 for a wine to drink with lunch and wondering if he would double that amount to get his favorite wine at a temperature that pleased him.

Ballenger sensed he was now on stage in a melodrama that could be given the title, "The Vanities of Hedonistic Excesses." By any reasonable standard, spending $1,000 for a wine to drink with lunch is extravagant. Spending twice that amount, even for Ballenger, was over the top. Nevertheless, he did have a reputation as one of the city's most successful hedge-fund managers to uphold, and he had closed a deal that morning that would net him at least $12 million. He certainly could afford another thousand to preserve his status as a big spender.

Two other hedge-fund managers, who knew Ballenger and disliked him for his arrogance and dishonesty, were sitting at a nearby table.

"A hundred says he gets the second bottle," one said to the other.

"You're on," the other man replied.

"Bring another bottle," Ballenger told the waiter.

There were gasps from around the room, and the man who lost the wager said glumly to his colleague, "Is it okay if I write you a check?"

"Very well, Mr. Ballenger, I'll bring another bottle right out," the waiter replied. "And again, I apologize for the inconvenience."

Several minutes later, the waiter brought another veal chop and a second bottle of Chateau La Benadine to Ballenger's table. The waiter opened the bottle with appropriate fanfare and poured a small amount of the rich, red liquid into an elegant, long-stem wine glass for Ballenger to taste. Ballenger said the wine was at the proper temperature, and the waiter filled the glass and then headed back toward the kitchen. As he passed by table 26, the Father asked in a whispered voice, "Is Mr. Ballenger always like that?"

"Unfortunately, yes, but he tips very well," Paul whispered back.

Ballenger's luncheon companion, Stig, opened his brief case and placed a picture of a 160-foot Bruden Yacht before Ballenger. The yacht's white superstructure, framed by beautiful, teak decks, gleamed in the bright sunshine. Scantily clad models luxuriated on the yacht's bow above a polished, stainless-steel anchor that sparkled like a precious gemstone.

"For $20 million, you can have a luxury yacht that will take your breath away," the salesman said in a smooth, seductive voice. "It will take you anywhere you want to go in comfort, luxury, and safety—Bermuda, Nantucket, the Keys, the Virgins. It's just a magnificent yacht. It's state of the art in everything: navigation, communication, sea-worthiness, comfort, styling, power, speed, everything. When it's at the dock at your home in Fort Lauderdale, all your neighbors will know you've made it big, really, really big."

"How much can I get for my present yacht?" Ballenger asked.

"We'll guarantee you $1.5 million."

"$1.5 million? I paid more than $3 million for the thing only three years ago."

"Yes, I know, but the market for previously-owned luxury yachts is a little soft right now."

"Excuse me, Mr. Ballenger," the Father said. "Have you considered giving some of your money away to the poor instead of buying a larger yacht? You seldom use your present yacht, and your tax returns say you haven't made a charitable contribution in nine years."

Ballenger was startled by the interruption. He stared at the Father, wondering if he had ever met this person before. Hansen was clearly annoyed. He turned toward the Father. His eyes flared.

"Did you see that?" Dianthe whispered in the Father's ear. "The yacht salesman is one of Hasatan's angels."

"Yes, I saw it," the Father responded.

"Don't engage this rude intruder into our conversation," Hansen said to Ballenger. "I'll ask security to eject him."

"No, wait," Ballenger said. "This might be interesting. Besides, I'd like to know how he is so familiar with my personal life and my tax returns."

Turning toward the Father, Ballenger said, "You are correct. I haven't made a charitable contribution in years, and I'm wondering how you came by that information."

"Let's just say I had a hunch," the Father replied.

"That's not a satisfactory answer to my question."

"Well, you haven't answered my question either."

"I don't contribute to charity because I pay millions of dollars each year in taxes. My tax dollars provide quite a lot of benefits for the poor. Isn't that enough?"

"The law requires you to pay those taxes. That money is not freely given out of a generous spirit and love for your neighbor."

"Out of a generous spirit and love for my neighbor?" Ballenger repeated in a sarcastic manner.

"Yes," the Father said. "The poor in this city will survive without your millions. If necessary, others will help them. But your spirit may not survive if it has no generosity, no love for others. Your need to help others is greater than the need of others to receive."

"So, several million dollars a year is not enough. Why am I not surprised? With you liberals, there is never enough. Go ahead, call security," Ballenger said to the salesman.

"No need for that," the Father said. "We were just leaving. Enjoy your veal chop, Mr. Ballenger. My guess is that in the next world, you'll find the veal chops overdone for your taste."

Turning toward Hansen, Ballenger asked, "What's that supposed to mean?"

"I have no idea," Hansen replied.

"The woman seemed to recognize you," Ballenger said. "She called you something like 'an angel.' Do you know these people?"

"I don't know who they are or what she's talking about," Hansen replied, as he watched the Father, Dianthe, and Serenious get up from their table and walk toward the restaurant's main entrance. Another small flame shot from his eyes, and the drool common to Hasatan's lesser angels began dripping from his chin. Hansen discretely wiped the drool away with one of the restaurant's fine Irish linen napkins. "I have no idea who they are except the obvious: They're rude intruders into other peoples' business."

On the street outside the restaurant, Serenious said, "Ballenger will have access to all the blessings great wealth can provide: Books explaining IAM's presence, leisure time in which to ponder why he was created, beautiful churches in which to worship, artwork portraying IAM's love for his creation, music attesting to IAM's majesty. The poor scavenger from Pandharpur will have none of these things. All he will see and feel during the rest of his life is misery, debilitating, depressing misery. Will he really have a fair chance to demonstrate his loyalty to IAM? Will he have as much of a chance as Mr. Ballenger?"

"You are overlooking something," the Father replied. "The scavenger will have nothing to distract him from thinking about his creator and the meaning of his existence. He will think about IAM every day. That is a blessing and an opportunity."

"But he will be cursing you," Serenious said.

"Yes, but he will be talking to me, acknowledging that I exist. In fact, after he becomes a Christian, he will never stop talking to me. Ballenger, who will have all the benefits twentieth-century life can provide, will be addicted to material pleasures—cars, boats, and grand houses. He'll think he owns them, but in reality, they will own him. They will dominate his decision-making and be his values. While the scavenger will talk to me every day, Ballenger will never talk to me once during his whole human existence. His creator isn't going to give him a bigger boat, house, or car, so what's the point of talking to his creator?"

"The contrast between Solomon Ballenger and Ravikiran is striking," Dianthe observed. "Ballenger, who has so much, will willingly contribute nothing to the unfortunate, while the poor scavenger, who will have nothing other than what the garbage dump provides, will give a precious loaf of bread to a stranger in need," Dianthe said. "Will all wealthy prisoners be like Mr. Ballenger?

"Many will be like Ballenger. Wealth can be a blessing, but often, it will be a curse, a very seductive curse that will tempt the defectors to reject us and our values," the Father said.

"Are you saying the poor scavenger, who lives a life of almost total deprivation, will have an easier path to salvation than Mr. Ballenger," Serenious said.

"Isn't that what our observations of Ravi and Ballenger suggest?" the Father replied.

16.

The Father turned toward Dianthe: "And do you also have concerns?"

"These hosts will exist in a dangerous world, full of disease, starvation, all kinds of mayhem," Dianthe replied. "They will be fragile creatures. Some will die at a young age, before there is enough evidence to determine their loyalty to IAM. How will we judge them?"

"A fair question," the Father replied. "Here is the answer."

The Father opened a hologram. It showed a young mother, Margaret Bowles, driving her three daughters—five-year-old Linda, nine-year-old Hailey, and twelve-year-old Holly—to a soccer practice in the family's midsize sedan. Holly was sitting in the front passenger's seat; Linda and Hailey were sitting in the back seat. It was 3:52 p.m. on the tenth day of the seventh month of Earth year 4,543,763,986 (July 10, 1997).

"Mom, we need to hurry," Holly said. "I'm going to be late for practice, and Coach Martin doesn't like that. She makes us run laps around the whole field when we're late for practice."

As Margaret's car approached the intersection of Waples Mill Drive and Oakton Road in Fairfax County, Virginia, the traffic light turned red. Margaret brought her car to a stop.

"Mom, Hailey pinched me, and it hurt!" Linda screamed.

"I did not!" Hailey yelled back. "She's making stuff up to get me in trouble."

"She's lying. She pinched me," Linda insisted.

"Girls, please—and Hailey, keep your hands to yourself," Margaret said.

"Why do you always take her side?" Hailey said. "That's not fair."

Margaret turned toward the back seat. "I don't always take Linda's side," she insisted.

The light turned green.

"Mom, the light's green," Holly said impatiently. "We need to go."

Without looking to see if another car was approaching, Margaret drove into the intersection.

A black pick-up truck, driven by Jeff Baker, came racing down Waples Mill Drive from Margaret's left side. Jeff had been drinking to celebrate the completion of a construction job. He thought he could get through the intersection before the yellow light turned red, but he miscalculated. He couldn't stop in time, and his truck struck Margaret's car broadside at fifty miles per hour.

The violent impact pushed Margaret's car sideways about thirty feet, leaving the smell of burning rubber as the tires were pushed in a direction they were not designed to move. The grille of Jeff's truck crashed into the sedan and into Margaret's left side, puncturing vital organs. Margaret died within minutes of impact. The violent collision snapped Linda's young neck, killing her instantly. Jeff, Holly, and Hailey were all seriously injured, but all survived, albeit with disabilities they would carry with them for the rest of their lives.

"It's true," the Father said. "The defector in young Linda's body will not have sufficient time to demonstrate its loyalty to us before Linda's human death. After Linda expires, I will move the defector residing in her body to another human host, where it will remain until there is enough data available to judge its loyalty."

Another image appeared in the hologram. It was the delivery room of a local hospital. The attending physician handed a newborn baby girl to her mother, Lauren Edwards, and said, "Mrs. Edwards, here is your new daughter."

"Oh, isn't she beautiful," Lauren replied.

Have you decided on a name?" the doctor asked.

"Yes, we're going to name her Linda."

The hologram closed.

"An elegant solution, but there is another problem," Dianthe said, as she opened a hologram showing the French Polynesian island of Moorea after human beings had settled the island. A young Polynesian family was eating their main meal of the day—fish and coconut—outside their home, which was constructed of wooden poles and palm fronds. It was a beautiful day. Brisk ocean breezes blew away humidity and lowered body temperatures. A boy of ten and his younger sister, five, were teasing each other. When the teasing got out of hand, the father scolded both children. The teasing stopped, at least for the moment.

"The members of this family will never be baptized," Dianthe said. "They will never hold a Bible in their hands, and even if they did, they couldn't read it. They will never have contact with a Christian missionary or anyone else to teach them the way to salvation. What opportunity will they have to show loyalty to IAM?"

"Not every human life-form will be a host for a deserter," the Father said. "No member of this family will be a host; none of them will have an afterlife. At the end of their human lives, they will simply cease to exist."

17.

"I hate to be a skeptic, but I have another concern," Serenious said.

"Yes, go on," the Father replied.

"Looking ahead, I see that many traitors will profess loyalty to IAM," Serenious said. "They will be baptized and confirmed in Dianthe's church. They will observe church rituals and provide minimal financial support to the church. They will regularly attend worship services and mouth church liturgy, creeds, and prayers, without giving the slightest thought to what they are saying.

"But their loyalty to the church will be, at best, superficial. It will not be a firm dedication. They will worship out of habit, not commitment. Their loyalty to the church will resemble nothing more than the workman's fondness for his union hall, the golfer's attachment to his country club, the sailor's devotion to his yacht club. Without being able to look into the minds of these deserters, how will we be able to distinguish those who are truly loyal to IAM from those whose loyalty is a thin veneer that will disappear whenever seriously challenged?"

"I share Serenious's concern," Dianthe said. "Recall Harold, the passenger who will give up the last seat on the last life boat on the Titanic; Mother Teresa, who will devote her life to helping the sick and dying; Ravikiran Sarvasuddi, whose conversion to Christianity will cost him everything he holds dear in this world; and Juan Vazquez, the Inquisition's victim, whose only crime will be to hope the church will reform itself. Their loyalty will be easy to judge. But many who profess faith in IAM will never have a 'lifeboat moment.' How will we judge them?"

Serenious opened a hologram. The image showed the living room of John Ludendorfs' modest, split-level home at 23 Elm Street in Fort Wayne, Indiana. The time was 3:30 p.m. on the fifth day of the sixth month of Earth year 4,543,763,978 (June 5, 1989). John, who works at the General Motors assembly plant near his home, was sitting in his living room reading the sports page of the *Journal Gazette* newspaper. He had called in sick this day. His back started to bother him when he got out of bed in the morning, and he decided to stay home instead of taking a couple of aspirin and going to work. John doesn't abuse GM's sick-day policy, but he feels entitled to an extra day of rest occasionally, and he chose today as one of those days.

John is forty-seven years old. Thanks to his lifelong participation in various sports, he has maintained the athletic physique he developed as a younger man—a slim waist with broad shoulders and muscular forearms. His sandy-blond hair has begun to turn gray. John has attractive facial features, not what you would call handsome, but attractive in a plain, forthright sort of way. He has always been devoted to his family, hardworking, scrupulously honest, and willing to offer a helping hand to those in need.

John has worked on an assembly line for about twenty years. He started with International Harvester when he was twenty-three years old. That's when he married Alison, who teaches third grade at a nearby elementary school. When the Harvester plant closed in 1983, John did odd jobs, and he and Alison managed to scrape by financially by giving up everything except absolute necessities. When the General Motors plant near his home opened several years later, John applied for a job and was hired. Now that John has a good-paying job, life has become easier for the Ludendorfs. The amenities that disappeared when the Harvester plant closed have returned.

The holograph showed John's oldest son, Michael, coming down the stairs in the family home wearing his pajamas. Michael had worked the midnight to 8:00 a.m. shift at the GM plant the previous night. He had just gotten out of bed. Like his father, Michael is tall, with light brown hair and an athletic build. His handsome face radiates sincerity. He was a star football player in high school and at Indiana University, but now the only thing he tackles is elementary Greek and New Testament studies at Concordia Theological Seminary, also located in Fort Wayne. Michael is studying to become a Lutheran Minister.

John and Alison are delighted with their oldest son. At last year's church banquet, which celebrated Michael's decision to study for the ministry, the Ludendorfs' minister heaped lavish praise on the couple for raising a "good Lutheran boy." For months after the banquet, church members greeted John and Alison with, "You must be so proud."

Michael is now on summer break. GM pays its summer employees well, and Michael will earn enough money this summer to pay tuition and other expenses for the coming academic year. With Michael's academic costs covered, the family will be able to vacation this coming August in Northern Michigan, where John will fish for bass, Alison will join a quilting group and finish several quilts she has been working on, and Michael and his younger siblings will water ski on a nearby lake until their arms and legs feel like they are about to fall off. John has already paid a deposit for the cabin where the family will stay. The kids have looked at the real-estate brochure showing the cabin so many times, the brochure has started to come apart at the folds.

When Michael stuck his head in the living room, John greeted him with, "Good morning."

Michael scratched his head, yawned, looked at his watch, and responded, "Good afternoon."

"How was your first night on the job?" John asked.

"It went fine. The guys on the line are calling me 'Father Mike.' What's his name—Artie Cussero—gave me his mock confession, said he was thinking about strangling the shop steward for cozying up to management too much. He asked for guidance."

"What'd you tell him?"

"I told him to do whatever feels right."

"I bet that got a laugh from everyone."

"Yeah, it did. Tony, the big guy who does doors, said he liked my attitude and bought me a cup of coffee during the break. Said he, too, was thinking about strangling the shop steward. I told him I was only kidding. He laughed and said he was too. It's a good group of guys. I'm going to enjoy this summer. Working on the line is a lot better than pushing a broom, which is what I did last summer. It also pays a lot more, and it certainly is a change from my seminary classes."

"I don't doubt that."

Michael walked across the room and sat down next to his father.

"Dad, can I ask you a serious question?"

"Sure, as long as it isn't: 'Do I still think your mother is beautiful?'"

"I heard that, John," Alison shouted from the kitchen.

John laughed, and Michael suppressed a smile.

"Alright, what do you want to know?"

"Why are you a Lutheran?"

John sat up in his chair, put down the sports page, and stopped smiling.

"I don't know," he responded. "My family has always been Lutheran. My father was a Lutheran. My grandfather was a Lutheran. It goes back as far as anyone can remember."

"Is that it, because grandpa and great-grandpa were Lutherans?"

"I suppose that's partly it."

"I mean, do you buy the whole 'Jesus-as-savior' thing and that we should be doing all we can to bring people to Christ?"

"Sure, I buy it. Haven't I always gone to church on Sunday and insisted that you kids go to Sunday School? I take communion every month. I put ten dollars in the collection plate every Sunday. Your mother works with the Lady's Guild, putting on those nice annual banquets. I work around the church to keep it looking nice. And we're always getting compliments about how nice the church looks. I'm on the church bowling team. What else am I supposed to do?"

Serenious snapped his fingers, causing action in the hologram to pause. "What else am I supposed to do?" he repeated. "What a strange question, when there will be so much suffering in this world, when there will be such a need to reach out to the unchurched."

Serenious snapped his fingers again, and action in the hologram resumed. "Our congregation seems content with itself," Michael said. "The church's finances are stable, and the pews are filled most Sundays. But there isn't a lot of fire to bring new people into our church, so they can hear the word of God."

"What would you have us do?"

"That new church down the street from us—the New Hope Bible Church—they really emphasize evangelism, and they're growing a lot. They even advertise on the radio. If our congregation really bought into the salvation story, wouldn't it be doing more to reach out to the unchurched, you know, to save as many souls as we can?"

John thought about Michael's question for a moment and then replied, "At a church council meeting last year, Doyle Vogt, the evangelism chairman, said maybe we should try advertising on the radio. Pastor Sloan got real angry. Said that isn't who we are. Said the very idea of advertising on the radio—like we were selling cars or something—was out of the question as long as he was pastor of St. Mark's. Said the Holy Spirit would bring people into the church, and we should trust in the Lord."

"Pastor Sloan really said that?" Michael asked. "Professor Schweizer at the seminary says most Lutheran churches claim they emphasize evangelism, but they really don't. Their goal is to reach financial stability—pay the mortgage, utilities, and staff salaries—and once they get there, evangelism takes a back seat to the annual church banquet, church picnics, and who gets to bowl on the church bowling team. Schweizer says we shouldn't expect the Holy Spirit to do our job. And Schweizer is always quoting Mahatma Gandhi, who said: 'You must be the change you hope to see in this world.'"

"Mahatma Gandhi, that doesn't sound like a Lutheran name," John said.

Michael couldn't stop himself from laughing. "No, Dad, Gandhi wasn't a Lutheran, but he did have some good ideas. At least, Professor Schweizer thinks he did."

"Well, when you get your own church, you can run it any way you want, even advertise on the radio if you want. But nothin's gonna change Pastor Sloan's mind. I'd bet the farm on that—if I had a farm. And I kinda agree with Sloan. I mean, if you advertise on the radio, you'd never know what type of person would show up and sit next to you in church on Sunday mornings."

"Dad, please don't say things like that."

"Why?"

"Because it could be dangerous for your soul."

The hologram closed.

"John believes he is loyal to IAM," Serenious said. "He does a modest amount of work for the church. He contributes ten dollars a week to support it, and after all, he is on the church bowling team. But there are reasons to question John's commitment to the faith. He prefers the comfort of a closed community of worshippers and sees little need to reach out to strangers in need of salvation. His faith will never be challenged during his lifetime. If we can't look into John's mind to determine his loyalty, how will we judge him?"

"The problem you describe is inherent in the nature of this trial," the Father explained. "There are only two solutions: We can intervene in this new world millions of times to artificially create situations that will rigorously test each prisoner's loyalty. Or, we can send each traitor through successive hosts until we have enough data to make a judgment. The first option—intervening in this world millions of times—would threaten the integrity of this test. So, the only viable option is the second."

18.

Dianthe was reluctant to ask the Father for another change in his plan for the new universe, but she felt compelled to do so: "Father, near the end of the second Earth millennium and the beginning of the third, after my sacrifice, the last of the defectors will undergo their tests. It will be a scientific age, an age that accepts nothing based solely on blind faith. Defectors being tested in this age will be mesmerized by science's ability to cure disease, produce conveniences that make life easier, and explain the natural workings of the universe. Many defectors will assume that science is the only reliable source of truth and wisdom, that it alone can explain the meaning of human existence.

"Unfortunately, most leaders of my church will never make the intellectual leap to this scientific age. Their minds will remain stuck in earlier times when science will be in its infancy. Church leaders will see science as a threat to religion and will assume that conflicts between science and religion are irreconcilable. They will mistakenly believe that the religious rhetoric that brought people to Christianity in earlier times will do so in the twentieth and twenty-first centuries, even when that rhetoric conflicts with well-established scientific facts. Church leaders will naively assume that young people will remain faithful to IAM because their parents brought them up in the faith.

"But the young people of this new age will have different ideas. They will ask: How do we know there is a God? Where is the evidence? Are we supposed to believe that God exists simply because the Bible says so? Many young people will not find satisfying answers to these questions, and as a result, membership in my church will decline. Seeds of loyalty to IAM that are barely alive, those teetering on the edge of survival, will die because they are not nourished with persuasive evidence and analysis. This new age will desperately need a church leader who speaks the language of science, someone who can present the compelling empirical evidence that a creator exists. We need to provide this new world with such a leader."

"Dianthe, you asked for three individuals to help build a strong foundation for your church—Akim, Saul, and Constantine. I gave you those three to quiet your concerns about Hasatan's ability to influence this trial. I also told you that three was enough, that there had to be an end to these interventions in the material world. You agreed, but now you have changed your mind."

"Father, what if I guided an influential defector without entering the material universe? No appearances by Serenious or me, no voices from above or signs in the sky, just a revelation that this person will think is a product of his own intellect."

"That would be more acceptable," the Father said. "How would you accomplish this?"

Dianthe opened a hologram. The auxiliary dining room in the elegant, five-star Hotel Metropole in Brussels came into view. The time was 8:05 a.m. on the twenty-sixth day of the tenth month of Earth year 4,543,763,916 (October 26, 1927). World-famous theoretical physicist Albert Einstein, wearing a gray suit, vest, white shirt, and dark tie, was seated at a table eating a breakfast of poached eggs over toast. Every so often, Einstein sipped from his coffee cup and read another paragraph from a newspaper article about a sensational murder trial of a Jewish poet that had just ended. The article stated that the poet, who admitted killing a Ukrainian official responsible for a pogrom that had murdered fifteen members of the poet's family, had been acquitted of all charges by a French Court.

A younger man, Georges Henri Joseph Edouard Lemaître, walked by Einstein's table. After spotting the eminent scientist out of the corner of his eye, Lemaître stopped, retraced his steps, and called out in English, "Professor Einstein?"

The older man looked up from his newspaper and replied in English, with a German accent, "*Ya*, I am Albert Einstein."

"*Herr Doktor*, I am Georges Lemaître. I am also a physicist and a great admirer of your work."

Lemaître wore the clothing of a Catholic priest, and it took Einstein several seconds to reconcile what he was seeing—a man in priest's clothing—with the man's introduction of himself as a physicist. Einstein was intrigued by this combination, and he invited Lemaître to join him.

Lemaître seated himself directly across from the esteemed cosmologist.

A waiter soon appeared and took Lemaître's order.

"A priest and a physicist—this is a strange combination, *ya*, linking blind faith in a creator with a scientific approach to understanding the universe," Einstein said. "But I'm sure you've heard that many times before."

"Yes, a few times," Lemaître said with a chuckle.

"Are you attending the Solvay conference?" the older man asked.

"Yes, the dioceses prevailed on the society to invite me as an observer."

"Are you enjoying it? Are you interested in this new quantum theory?"

"I am. This is truly a fascinating conference. There are so many great scientists and Nobel laureates in attendance—Niels Bohr, Marie Curie, Max Planck, and, of course, yourself. I am humbled to be here. Even to sit in the audience is an honor."

Einstein accepted this accolade as a personal compliment and smiled.

"As a priest, I suppose you enjoyed my criticism of Heisenberg's uncertainty principle...That's when I said, 'God does not play dice with the universe.'"

Before the younger man could reply, Einstein added, "But perhaps you enjoyed Niels Bohr's response even more: 'Einstein, stop telling God what to do.'"

Both men laughed.

In a few minutes, a waiter brought the young priest his breakfast—scrambled eggs, sausage, toast and tea.

"Please, eat your breakfast; science can wait," Einstein said playfully before sipping from his coffee cup.

Lemaître hadn't eaten much for dinner the evening before, so he was pleased to accept this invitation.

While watching Lemaître devour breakfast, Einstein took his favorite pipe from his coat pocket. Instead of lighting it, he chewed on the stem, a nervous habit he had acquired years earlier.

"Tell me, what are you working on?" Einstein said.

"The Brussels's Scientific Society just published my paper on the expanding universe. The society publishes a minor journal with a limited circulation. You probably have never heard of it."

Einstein sat up straight in his chair and stared intently at Lemaître.

"Did you say your paper is about the expanding universe?" he asked.

"Yes, exactly."

"But the universe is not expanding. It's static. If it were expanding, it would have become unstable long ago."

"I'm sorry to disagree, but the evidence points me in a different direction."

"What evidence?"

"The light from distant galaxies is showing a reddish color, indicating that those galaxies are moving away from us. These data were collected by the American, Vesto Slipher, using spectroscopy."

"Slipher's data are inconsistent—they show redshifts and blueshifts, indicating that while some galaxies are moving away from us, some are moving towards us. But more importantly,

Slipher made his observations using the telescope at Lowell Observatory. That telescope is a primitive instrument; it's not sufficiently powerful to distinguish the color of light shifts from distant galaxies."

"Slipher thought his observations were clear enough to distinguish red from blue, and most of what he saw were redshifts. The galaxies showing blueshifts might have been exposed to exceptionally strong gravitational forces created by a group of stars located close to one another. Those strong gravitational forces may have reversed the initial direction of the blueshifted galaxies. But you are correct about the telescope Slipher used. It's capacity to view the universe is limited. However, Edwin Hubble has announced that he will try to confirm Slipher's observations. When Hubble looks through the more powerful telescope at Mount Wilson in America, he will confirm that the light from virtually all the distant galaxies is showing redshifts, indicating that all those galaxies are moving away from us, some at speeds approaching the speed of light."

Einstein smiled but did not immediately respond. His instincts told him the auxiliary dining room at the Metropole Hotel was not a suitable forum for a serious discussion about the fundamental structure of the universe. But the implications of Lemaître's theory so fascinated him that he could not resist pursuing the subject.

"If the universe is moving away from its center, then there had to be a starting point, *ya*? Have you theorized about this starting point?"

"In a new paper I'm writing, I call this starting point a 'primeval atom,' or a 'cosmic egg,' that exploded, filling the universe with primitive matter. I may have something to publish in several years."

"You are saying that all the matter presently in the universe was once contained in a single primeval atom?" Einstein asked in a voice that reeked of skepticism.

"Yes, I believe so," Lemaître responded.

Try as he might, Einstein could no longer restrain himself. "*Ich glaube ich spinne!* [I Think I'm going crazy!]," he exclaimed. "How did you ever come up with this nonsense—a primeval atom, an exploding egg?"

Lemaître was taken aback by Einstein's none-too-subtle attack. He paused to collect his thoughts, but before he could speak, the eminent scientist continued: "*Ach,* now I understand. Your superiors in the Catholic Church have instructed you to come up with a new creation story pointing to your God as the creator. But an exploding egg? You will have to do better than that, *mein* priest. The public, or at least the scientific community, will never believe that all the matter in the universe was once contained in a single atom or a tiny egg."

"Professor, I never said my theory was evidence of a creator."

"You don't have to say it. Your theory says it for you. Anyone who hears this theory will see God, standing in his heavens, hurling a lightning bolt at a tiny speck of matter, which then explodes, filling the universe with enough material and the appropriate gravitational forces to create a stable universe. That sounds like it came right out of Genesis, *ya?*"

"I have never spoken to my superiors in the Catholic Church about this theory," Lemaître replied. "They know nothing about it."

"Then, how did you ever conceive of anything so fantastic?"

"Well, I had been thinking about the data showing redshifts for months, and then this theory just came to me one night in a dream," Lemaître answered tentatively, as if he hardly believed that explanation himself.

"*Ach,* it came to you in a dream. Of course, while you were sleeping, your God stuck this theory in your head, so you could lead the flock back to him," Einstein said and then laughed so loudly, it drew the attention of diners at nearby tables.

A slightly embarrassed Einstein whispered, "This theory of yours gets more interesting by the minute."

Lemaître did not reply.

"If the universe was created by such a fantastic explosion, wouldn't echoes of that explosion still be reverberating around the universe?" Einstein asked.

"Yes, and when science develops the proper tools, we will find those reverberations."

Einstein stared at Lemaître as if he were analyzing a physics problem. The younger man seemed to have an answer to all his questions. But Einstein was not persuaded. He knew this theory of an expanding universe was nonsense.

"You must excuse me," he said, looking at his watch. "I need to go to my room before the morning session begins. Please, send me a copy of your paper when it's finished. I will provide my comments. With help from the Catholic Church, you probably will find a journal willing to publish it."

Einstein got up from the table and walked away, mumbling to himself, "A primordial atom, an exploding egg, Jetzt habe ich alles gehort [Now I've heard everything]."

The hologram closed.

"All right, Dianthe," the Father said. "You may have this additional intervention."

"Well done, Dianthe," Serenious said. "Putting a description of how the material universe was, in fact, created into the mind of this young scientist-priest, who will share it with his scientific colleagues, is very clever. Professor Einstein is correct. This theory does point to an active creator—us. As these traitors develop more sophisticated scientific tools, they will discover more and more evidence that the universe was created in one instance by a powerful force. Eventually, this theory of creation may become widely accepted."

The Father joined in: "If you want Lemaître's explanation for creation to be widely accepted, you will need to come up with better names for the universe's earliest phase. 'Primordial atom' and 'exploding egg' seem a little hokey to me."

"I agree," Serenious said.

"Do you have a suggestion?" Dianthe asked.

"Call this first phase of creation the 'Big Bang,'" the Father said. "That has a nice ring to it."

"The Big Bang, I love it!" Dianthe exclaimed. "With your permission, I will cause that term to be widely circulated among scientists and the public. Surely, it will stick in the minds of everyone who hears it."

"As I told you before, many defectors living in the modern era will ignore this term and the empirical evidence that there was a moment of creation," the Father said. "They will have made up their minds that religion is farce, and they will not listen to reason, or consider evidence to the contrary."

"I know, but at least we will have tried," Dianthe said with sadness in her voice.

19.

Following the discussion of the Big Bang, Serenious said, "Excellency, testing all the deserters in Hasatan's control will consume an enormous amount of energy, energy that could be used to improve our kingdom and the quality of life of subjects who have remained loyal to us. The only evidence to justify such a large commitment is the actions of one young deserter in Hasatan's prison. Is this really a prudent step?"

"Serenious, how many subjects who appear to be loyal to us would it take to justify going forward with this test in your view?" Without waiting for Serenious to reply, Dianthe turned to the Father: "If the evidence suggested that there were fifty loyal prisoners in Hasatan's hell, would that be enough to justify this test?"

"Yes, I'm willing to go forward with this test if it appears that Hasatan is holding fifty prisoners who are loyal to us," the Father replied.

"And if the number were five less than fifty, would we call off this trial if there were only forty-five such prisoners?" Dianthe asked.

"I will proceed if there are forty-five," the Father answered.

"And if the number were forty, would your answer be the same?"

"It would."

"For the most powerful being in all of creation, would ten less than forty make a difference? Would you be willing to proceed if there were only thirty such prisoners?"

As the numbers grew smaller, the Father became more

hesitant in his replies. But reluctantly, he agreed that the existence of thirty prisoners who appeared to be loyal to IAM would justify going forward with the test.

In a voice and manner that exuded all her charm, Dianthe said, "My Lord, please do not be angry with me if I speak once more, but what if there were only twenty such prisoners?"

"Are there twenty?" Serenious asked.

"There are," Dianthe replied "The prisoners who will become Mother Teresa, Ravi the beggar, Harold on the Titanic, Juan Vazquez, Saul of Tarsus, Emperor Constantine, Mary the mother of Jesus, Mary Magdalene, Augustine, and eleven loyal disciples."

"Yes, my precious daughter, I will go forward with this test if Hasatan is holding twenty prisoners who appear to be loyal to us," the Father said.

With each question and answer, Serenious became more exasperated.

"Excellency, I have changed my mind about the most powerful force in all existence," he said. "I have always thought it was your will, but now I see it is your daughter's ability to charm her father."

Looking sheepish and in a barely audible voice, the Father replied, "My dear Serenious, our commitment to justice and mercy will not let us ignore the hopes and dreams of twenty loyal prisoners."

"Very well, then," Serenious said. "I suggest we look ahead in time to Judgment Day. That may tell us how many of Hasatan's prisoners are, in fact, loyal."

"Will Judgment Day tell us that?" Dianthe said.

"Judgment Day may not tell us who is loyal, but it should tell us how many are loyal, and that will tell us if this trial is worthwhile."

"You may be right about that!" Dianthe said, while wondering why she hadn't thought of that approach.

Serenious opened a hologram. The time was 3:33 p.m. on

the third day of the eighth month of Earth year 4,543,764,044 (August 3, 2055). A menacing summer sky, filled with dark clouds, looked down on midtown Manhattan, the center of New York City. The horns of driverless cars and trucks scolded jaywalkers attempting to cross streets ahead of changing traffic lights. Pedestrians talked loudly on miniature computer/cell phones strapped to their wrists as they hurried along sidewalks, occasionally dodging flying robots that were delivering packages to merchants.

Suddenly, the sky became clear and the sun became dazzlingly bright. Pedestrians, even those wearing dark glasses, had difficulty finding their way, and many ducked into stores and restaurants when their eyes failed to adjust to the light's intensity. The air became electric with energy. It was an unusual environment—one suggesting something cataclysmic was about to happen. Then, everything—cars, buses, subway trains, pedestrians, pigeons in flight, basketballs in midair on school playgrounds, even the flags in front of the United Nation's Secretariat Building—came to an abrupt stop, as if frozen in time.

Soon, the sky was filled with IAM's angels, creatures of various sexes, sizes, and complexions, all dressed in the Positive Energy Kingdom's gray work uniforms. They began calling defectors out of their human hosts. As the defectors came out, their human bodies fell to the ground, collapsed on park benches, or slumped over automobile steering wheels causing a cacophony of blaring car horns. Within minutes, Manhattan looked like a battlefield littered with corpses. Once freed from their hosts, the prisoners regained their original pure-energy forms, with one exception: They all had the same generic face, making it impossible to identify any individual.

IAM's angels went to cemeteries—New York City Marble Cemetery in Lower Manhattan, Green-Wood Cemetery in Brooklyn, Mount St. Mary Cemetery in Queens, St. Raymond's Cemetery in the Bronx, and others—to summon traitors out of their hosts' graves and cremation urns. Other angels searched the land and waterways in and around New York City for the remains of deceased hosts who had not been interred or cremated in accordance with modern practices. The angels bypassed the remains of life-forms who never were hosts.

Soon, the sky was filled with angels delivering prisoners to Judging Stations, where information showing the prisoners' life histories was transferred into computers from miniature data-storage devices that had been implanted in the prisoners' bodies prior to their human births.

"What information will these devices record?" Serenious asked.

"The prisoners' actions during their human lives—every word spoken, every scream, sigh, or moan uttered, every facial expression formed, every step taken," the Father explained. "These data will tell us if the defectors ever prayed to us. If they thanked us for their blessings and apologized for their failures. If they prayed regularly, or only when they needed our help. If they stood up for IAM before doubters and those who ridiculed the faith, or if they denied us. If they were kind and generous to others, especially those in need, or if they exploited the vulnerable. If they confronted injustice or hid from it out of fear. If they forgave others who were unkind to them, or harbored grudges. These data will tell us if a defector is loyal to IAM."

The prisoners standing before the Judging Stations all had anxious expressions on their faces. Once back in their original energy form, they were aware of their past—their betrayal, confinement under Hasatan, and existence in the material world inside a human host—and their many failures to live a human life of loyalty and love. Some trembled in fear. Others cried out for mercy. Others stood silent, awaiting judgment.

"I assume what these Judging Stations will tell us is whether, over their lifetimes, the traitors' good deeds exceeded their bad deeds," Serenious said.

"None of the prisoners would be able to meet that

standard," the Father said. "The prisoners are consumed with sin, from their original sin—turning away from their creator—to sins committed throughout their human existence: Sins of commission and omission, sins of plotting vengeance on others for real or imagined slights, sins of pride and boasting, sins of... well, too many to mention."

"What, then, will these computers calculate?" Serenious asked.

"They will first evaluate the persuasive power of the evidence. Evidence collected during a host's mature years will be given more weight than evidence collected during youthful exuberance. The computers will then determine which is greater, evidence of loyalty or evidence of disloyalty. Defectors judged to be loyal will be returned to our kingdom; all others will be returned to Hasatan."

"What's the difference between these two calculations? Won't bad deeds always be evidence of disloyalty to IAM, and good deeds evidence of loyalty?"

"Not necessarily. Consider the young priest who murdered Archbishop Arias. He committed his crime out of a desire to protect the diocese from evil. His crime is evidence of his loyalty to IAM. On the other hand, consider the rich man, Andrew Lewis, who generously gave away billions of dollars to deserving causes. His gifts were made not to glorify IAM but to glorify himself. His gifts are actually evidence of his disloyalty."

"Those judged to be loyal to IAM will be burdened with massive amounts of sin. If they reenter the Positive Energy Kingdom with all that sin, it will weaken our kingdom and pose a threat to us."

"To honor Dianthe's sacrifice on the cross, I will forgive the sins of those who have remained loyal to us. When they reenter our kingdom, they will be pure and without sin."

"Made so by an act of grace?"

"Exactly."

The hologram showed two columns of defectors—one

headed to IAM's Kingdom, the other headed to Hasatan's confinement planet.

Those returning to IAM were overcome with joy, praising IAM with song and hosannas. Their faces shone brightly with the rapture of being reunited with their creator. The long nightmare of separation was over. Eternal happiness was upon them.

Those headed back to Hasatan were indescribably despondent. They now realized that an act of supreme love, a sacrifice like no other in all of time, had been made to give them a chance for redemption, a chance to be reunited with their creator, and they had rejected it.

A new image appeared in the hologram. It showed the section of Hasatan's prison where the rebellion's leaders were confined. A male prisoner stood in front of his assigned confinement cell. The door opened slowly. The prisoner stared into the room where he had spent billions of years before being transported to the material universe.

A talented actor, the prisoner had enjoyed great success in the material world, earning more than $30 million per movie. His wealth had enabled him to enjoy unimaginable luxury. He had owned several large residences. The clothes closet in his smallest home was several times larger than this confinement room. He had been adored by movie critics, friends, and fans alike, and that had led to a constant stream of favorable press coverage, tributes from fellow actors, and the adulation of female admirers offering sexual pleasures.

His public persona in the material world had been carefully shaped by highly paid publicists who encouraged him to portray himself as an atheist and to make statements like, "Religion isn't logical; it just doesn't ring true to me." He had no problem assuming the role of an atheist, because he was one. But now, he was back in the ultimate reality, facing the consequences of rejecting his one last hope for redemption.

The command "enter your confinement room" came over

a loud speaker. The prisoner stepped inside the small room and heard the door slam behind him and the lock engage. He looked into the mirrors and saw his inner self. The image was even more depressing than he remembered. He could no longer control his emotions. He let out a primordial scream, a cry so loud that it literally shook the inside of the room. But he was the only person in existence who heard it.

"Father, was that X-Meade?" Dianthe asked.

"I don't know, I hope not," the Father replied.

Another male prisoner stood facing his confinement room, waiting for the command to enter. He had been a successful businessman in the material world, but his success was the result of bluster and dishonesty. He was sullen and angry. He refused to blame himself for his present situation.

"This was not a fair test," he told himself. "It was a set-up job. I never had a real chance to prove my loyalty to IAM. It was another one of IAM's cruel tricks, pretending to help life-forms but instead trapping them in misery. I would rather pledge my loyalty to Hasatan. At least he's honest about his contempt for every life-form except himself."

On command, he entered his confinement room and stared at the mirror that showed his inner self.

"That's not me," he screamed. "It's just another trick to depress me."

In a rage, he picked up the room's only chair and threw it at the mirror in front of him. The mirror didn't break, but the chair broke into a thousand pieces. As a result, this prisoner will have to spend eternity either standing or sitting on the floor.

"You clowns can't even make a chair that will hold together," he said, as the door closed behind him and the lock engaged.

A female prisoner stood in front of her confinement room. In the material world, she had been the wealthy widow of a successful hedge-fund manager. Her name had often appeared on the society pages of local newspapers in articles praising her for her philanthropy. But she had very little interest in the charitable causes to which she contributed. The size of her gifts and the recipients were all chosen by her accountant, tax lawyer, and publicist, with the goal of taking maximum advantage of the tax laws and showering her with favorable media coverage.

All she did was show up at prearranged events in the latest Narciso Rodriguez, custom-tailored dress that had been designed for someone twenty years younger and fifteen pounds slimmer. While the cameras rolled, she gushed the right phrases about helping those in need. When the cameras were off, she reverted to her real self, a demanding, uncaring, and totally self-centered person who once fired an aide for asking to be excused from a publicity event, so she could attend a piano recital by her twelve-year-old daughter.

"There's been a mistake," she said in a loud voice. "Is anyone listening? I've always been loyal to IAM. My life on earth was lived according to his principles. I gave millions of dollars to the poor and needy. The computer that analyzed my data made a mistake. Will someone please listen to me? You're making a horrible mistake."

When she was ordered to enter her confinement room, she screamed, "I'm not moving until someone checks my life's data, so this monstrous error can be corrected."

"Your life history was run on two separate computers and reviewed a third time by a senior official," the computer managing the re-confinement replied. "There is no mistake. At that, a magnetic field propelled her into her confinement room. The door closed behind her, and the lock engaged. She began to sob and repeat to herself: "This is a huge mistake; I am loyal to IAM. I am loyal to IAM's principles." But no one outside her confinement room could hear her lies and self-deceptions.

A male prisoner stood before the gate to the general facility where the non-leaders were held.

"Why am I being returned to Hasatan's control?" he cried out. "I lived a moral life on Earth. I was good to my children, sacrificing economically to put them through college. I was faithful to my wife. I worked hard at my job. I was honest. I never committed any serious crimes. I never even cheated on my income tax. I helped people in need whenever I could. Why am I being sent back to Hasatan?"

"Consider your original sin," the computer replied. "You betrayed your creator, the being who gave you life, who nourished and sustained you, who taught you to love and care for others. Your betrayal and the betrayal of others almost brought IAM's kingdom down. And when he sent his only child into the material world to show you the way to redemption, you rejected him."

"I didn't reject him. I had both my children baptized. Doesn't that show I accepted Jesus?"

"Your parents insisted that your children be baptized. They made all the arrangements. You did nothing except attend the church service at which they were baptized. And that is one of the few times you attended church in your seventy-three years inside your human host."

"So that's it. I didn't go to church enough. But church was so boring; the same tired voices repeating the same old Bible stories and the same old prayers. I couldn't stand going to church; it drove me nuts. My wife and kids hated church too. They complained all week long if I insisted that the family go to church services on Sunday. And besides, Sunday was my only day to sleep late and spend time with my family. I had a difficult job. I needed at least one day a week to relax."

"Sorry if church didn't entertain you, but that wasn't its purpose. Of course, you didn't need to go to church, if, on occasion, you confessed your sins, asked for forgiveness, and thanked your creator for the earthly blessings you enjoyed and for giving you a chance for redemption. Did you ever do that?"

"Well, no."

"Did you ever explain to your wife and children why worship and prayer were important?"

"No, but I wasn't good at explaining stuff like that. And besides, the point is: I lived a moral life."

"Unfortunately, you didn't. You stole minor items from your

employer. You submitted false travel vouchers claiming more money than you were owed. You harbored grudges against your fellow employees who were promoted ahead of you. You lied and blamed subordinates for mistakes you made. You lusted after material goods you could not afford. You lied to your wife about how much money you spent on yourself. You lied to your children about your accomplishments as a young man. You hinted to your secretary that you would raise her salary if she had an affair with you. You ridiculed the Christian faith at cocktail parties. You ..."

"All right, all right. I did all those things, but so did everyone else. No human lived a perfect life."

"True, but those loyal to IAM confessed their sins and asked for forgiveness. And their sins were forgiven. Your sins would have been forgiven, had you asked. But you didn't ask because, under the moral rules you created for yourself, you believed you didn't need forgiveness. How foolish of you."

"I didn't know."

"Nonsense. You were baptized and dedicated to IAM as an infant. You attended Sunday School as a youngster, where you were taught you were a sinful creature in need of salvation. At your confirmation, you were given a Bible, which you never once opened."

"But ..."

"Enough of this! The energy shield is down. Enter the facility."

The prisoner stood still. He gazed in terror at the flames that shot up from the cobblestone courtyard only twenty yards in front of him. A sword of negative energy came down from above and struck him across his back, burning through his clothing and part of his protective outer covering. He screamed and ran through the wall of fire, disappearing into a growing crowd of prisoners.

"Please stop," Dianthe begged. "I can't watch another prisoner being returned to Hasatan. At great cost, we will give these traitors a chance for redemption, and so many will reject it."

"Dianthe, you may find this next image more to your liking," the Father responded.

The image in the hologram was of Judy, a middle-aged, female life-form, standing at the Positive Energy Kingdom's Readmissions Portal. Judy was short in stature, with a dumpy figure. Her dirty-blonde hair was cut short. Her arms showed the needle marks of repeated injections of heroin and other drugs. Her face bore a surly expression that did not radiate empathy or kindness. Her appearance said she had lived a difficult existence, while confined in Hasatan's prison and in the material world as well.

The computer supervising readmissions asked Judy where she would like to reside in the Positive Energy Kingdom. Finally, it asked if she had any questions.

Unlike the other life-forms being readmitted, Judy remained fearful as she stood at the Readmissions Entrance. "Has there been some mistake?" she asked. "Are you sure IAM is willing to take me back?"

"We don't make mistakes here," the computer replied. "The data on your chip was analyzed by two different reviewers. Why do you think there's been a mistake?"

"Well, I didn't exactly lead a wholesome life on earth. I got into drugs when I was a teenager. At first, I stole money from my parents to support my habit. When I couldn't steal any more from them, I turned to prostitution. I never married but had three kids by three different men. I was a terrible mother. All three kids wound up in jail. When I was too old to do tricks, I sold drugs, got caught, and did five years in prison. After I was released, I got back on the needle. I had no way to support myself or my habit, so I started selling again, got caught again, and was sentenced to five-to-ten. That's where I died, in prison, from AIDS I got using a dirty needle."

The computer's response was slightly apologetic: "Hmmm. I understand the reasoning behind your question. I will search your file for the basis for the decision to readmit you."

After a pause, the computer spoke: "While in the material world, you were mindful that there was a creator and that you were violating his will. You were saddened and depressed by your failure to live an upright life. During your last incarceration in prison, after going through withdrawal, you gave hope to other inmates. You showed them compassion and kindness. You listened to their life stories and gave them emotional support. You often prayed to IAM, asking for forgiveness, and you encouraged others to pray. When a depressed young woman came to you and said she was considering suicide, you convinced her that she was loved by her creator and had something to offer the world. The strongest evidence for readmission, however, was the prayer you said before your human death. It showed deep remorse and a willingness to sacrifice for others. Basically, it showed love and loyalty to IAM."

The computer opened a hologram. It showed a hospital room at the Maryland Correctional Institution for Women in Jessup, Maryland. The room was where very ill patients were kept. Judy was alone in the room, lying in bed. She was weeping. She kept mulling over all the lost opportunities in her life, the chances to make something of herself that she had let slip away in her lust for the highs that came from doing drugs. Suddenly, she stopped crying and pushed the blanket back. Using all her remaining strength, she crawled out of bed and knelt on the cold, concrete floor. Shivering in her thin, washed-out nightgown, she said the following prayer:

"Heavenly Father. I got the news last week that I'm gonna die pretty soon. When they brought me in here, the nurse said it was a matter of hours, not days. So, I guess I'd better say my piece before it's over.

"I know I've made a mess of my life—the drugs, the prostitution, the stealing, all the people I've hurt, all the people I've let down. I know I'm going to hell. That's what I deserve, and that's where I'm going. But I'm asking that you not punish my kids. I know they've screwed up, but deep down, they're really not bad. With no father and a tramp for a mother, they never had a chance in life. Put their sins on me. Send me to the lowest place in hell, where the flames are the hottest and the screams are the loudest but have mercy on them. I brought them into this world. I gave them life. The least I can do is pay the price for their screw-ups.

"Thanks for all the chances you gave me to make something of myself, more chances than I deserved. I'm sorry I didn't take advantage of any of them. And sorry I didn't thank you enough for your kindness. I should have, and I didn't. Well, I guess that's all I have to say. I'm begging you: Have mercy on my kids. Amen."

The image changed to 8:00 a.m. the next morning, when a nurse and an orderly unlocked the door and entered the room. Judy was still kneeling, slumped over the bed. The nurse felt Judy's wrist for a pulse. There wasn't any.

"She's gone," the nurse said. "Get a gurney so we can get her out of here."

"She was pretty weak yesterday," the orderly responded. "I didn't think she had enough strength to get out of bed. I wonder what she thought she was doing—trying to escape?"

After noticing that Judy's hands were still folded in prayer, the nurse replied, "Yeah, maybe she was trying to escape, but not in the way you're thinking."

The image switched back to Judy standing at the Readmissions Entrance.

"During your last years and hours, you showed loyalty to IAM," the computer said. "There is no mistake. You are welcome back to IAM's kingdom. Your assigned suite is number 39,043, in the east wing of IAM's palace. You may go there now."

Judy smiled for the first time in thousands of years.

"One last question: How did I get this so wrong?"

"You miscalculated IAM's willingness to forgive the sins of a loyal subject. That's what you got wrong."

Watching the hologram, a teary-eyed Dianthe said, "So it's true, the last will be first, and the first last."

"That will be so," the Father said.

"Let's return to the overall view of Judgment Day. I want to see the number of prisoners going back to Hasatan and the number coming back to us," Dianthe said. The hologram refocused. It showed two columns, both growing.

"Look at the column headed back to us! It has millions of life-forms, almost as many as the column headed back to Hasatan!" Dianthe exclaimed. "My sacrifice on the cross will be well worth its pain. So many will be saved from Hasatan's terror."

The Father and Serenious were also caught up in the surprise of the moment.

"This is amazing," Serenious said. "How could we have so underestimated the number of traitors who remained loyal to us?"

"I don't know," the Father replied. "I have never denied myself knowledge before, so I have no experience in dealing with this type of problem. And by the way, I don't plan on ever denying myself knowledge again. But, thanks to my precious daughter, we will correct a major injustice, and for that, I will always be very grateful."

Dianthe blushed as the Father put his arms around his only child and hugged her.

"When this experiment is complete, will we stop powering the material universe?" Dianthe asked.

"Yes, of course," the Father replied.

"What will happen then?"

"All movement in the material universe will stop. Electrons will no longer rotate around their nuclei, and as a result, atoms will no longer exist. Matter will no longer exist. Gravity, which will hold that universe in stable order, will cease to exist. Observe."

The hologram showed matter starting to disappear, as the energy needed to maintain it was no more. Without hydrogen or helium to burn, stars became dim and then went dark. Without gravity to hold them in place, suns, planets, and moons began spinning out of their orbits. The result was cataclysmic collisions as stars and planets crashed into one another and broke apart, huge sections of their mass drifting off into space before disappearing.

After the last star in the last galaxy went dark, the hologram went dark, just the way it appeared before the creation of the material universe.

20.

Day 357^9 ZMC-8624-03-04 was unique in the annals of the Primary Universe. Extra positive energy, taken from the energy reserves, circulated throughout the kingdom, making the grass greener, the flowers more colorful, the buildings cleaner, and the animals more animated. There were parades, music, laughter, and rejoicing. IAM's subjects sang and danced in the street. IAM had announced that it was to be a special day, a day of celebration, and so it was.

The Father, Dianthe, and Serenious met in their joint chambers.

"One last time, are we agreed on how this test will work?" the Father asked.

Dianthe and Serenious said they were.

"Dianthe, are you still determined to enter this world knowing how your earthly life will end?" the Father asked.

"I am," Dianthe said without hesitation.

"So be it then," the Father replied.

He walked to the doorway leading to the palace balcony, opened the door, stepped out, and faced the crowd that had gathered in the courtyard. When the Father appeared, millions of IAM's loyal subjects let out a cheer that rose like a musical crescendo, echoing off the palace walls and reverberating into space.

The Father raised his arms for silence. When the cheering subsided, he spoke: "This day will live in the memory of this kingdom forever. For what we thought was lost has been found. What we thought was treachery was, in many cases, youthful misunderstanding. What we thought would separate us forever from our loyal children will be no more."

The crowd cheered.

"Today, we begin a long journey," the Father continued, "a journey of reconciliation for those who left our kingdom out of misunderstanding and need forgiveness. It will be a hard journey for all, including IAM. It will require sacrifice, including the ultimate sacrifice made by Princess Dianthe."

A hushed silence came over the crowd, as its members wondered what those words meant for their beloved Dianthe and for their kingdom. The Father continued, "But loyal subjects have cried out to us for forgiveness, and we cannot ignore their pleas. We are a merciful people, and for those willing to live in a covenant of love with IAM, mercy knows no bounds.

"At the end of this journey, many of your brothers and sisters will come home. You have never wavered in your devotion to us. For that, I thank you. But I ask you to take back in love those subjects who did waiver. What IAM is willing to forgive, I ask you to forgive. Princess Dianthe will pay a high price to redeem these subjects. I will honor her sacrifice, and I ask you to honor it with love and forgiveness.

"And now, that journey is about to begin, and Dianthe will take its first step."

As the Father said those words, Dianthe, radiating the beauty of simple purity and wholesomeness, stepped out onto the balcony. The crowd roared again as Dianthe appeared.

Dianthe raised her hands for silence.

"Good people of our kingdom," she began, "the Father is too generous in his praise for me. I accept this task because a great error is about to be corrected, and as a result, this universe, indeed all of existence, will be in greater harmony."

The crowd again roared its approval, and again, Dianthe asked for silence.

As the last echoes of the crowd's applause drifted away, Dianthe ascended from the balcony to a place in the sky above the palace. She stretched out both arms into space and placed her right foot over her left in the position in which she would be crucified. She called out in a firm voice, "It is begun." And immediately, small streamlets of energy began to flow toward IAM's palace.

> "For God so loved the world, that he gave his only
> begotten Son, that whosoever believeth in him
> should not perish but have everlasting life."
> John 3:16, Bible, King James Version

．

About the Author

Mike McCarey and Willi, his wife and chief editor, are lifelong Lutherans. They met at Valparaiso University where they both studied religion among other subjects. They both went to law school and became attorneys.

Mike spent most of his professional career as an Associate Director of the Federal Trade Commission's Bureau of Consumer Protection. His staff drafted the model law on generic substitution that President Jimmy Carter urged the states to adopt to lower prescription drug prices. The U.S. Supreme Court cited an economic analysis prepared by his staff in granting, for the first time in American jurisprudence, limited First Amendment protection to commercial advertising.

Mike served in the U.S. Marine Corps from 1966 to 1969 and spent 19 months in Vietnam where he prosecuted several atrocity cases that received national media attention. Mike's first novel, *An American Atrocity*, is based on that experience. He has appeared on network television news and testified before Congress.

Mike and Willi have two sons, Darren and David, and four grandchildren, Lauren, Matthew, Alison, and Jessica. In 2018, the couple celebrated their 53rd wedding anniversary.

.